SEDUCING MR. HEYWOOD

SEDUCING MR. HEYWOOD
A REGENCY ROMANCE

JO MANNING

Five Star • Waterville, Maine

Five Star First Edition Romance Series.

Published in 2002 in conjunction with Harvey Klinger, Inc.

Cover photo courtesy of Jo Manning.

Set in 11 pt. Plantin by Minnie B. Raven.

Printed in the United States on permanent paper.

Library of Congress Cataloging-in-Publication Data

Manning, Jo, 1940–
    Seducing Mr. Heywood / Jo Manning.
        p. cm.—(Five Star first edition romance series)
    ISBN 0-7862-3400-8 (hc : alk. paper)
    1. Clergy—Fiction. I. Title. II. Series.
PS3613.A355 S44 2002
    813'.6—dc21   2001033367

This book is dedicated to the memory of CB Hayden, beloved friend and professional colleague who left us last year much before his time, much too soon. CB was always supportive of my writing and full of wonderful ideas. He loved my "wicked" character Lady Sophia in *The Reluctant Guardian* and was delighted to know she would be the heroine of my second novel. (She wasn't supposed to be, but she was one of those characters who don't give their creators a moment's peace!) I miss CB and other good friends who died young more than I can express in mere words. Marion Solheim Smith, Toni Thomas Haas, Ron Coplen, Shirley Miller . . . I was blessed to have known them, however briefly.

I want to thank my daughter, wall painting conservator Tracy Manning Winterbotham, for vetting the description of St. Mortrud's Church, and her father-in-law, retired Canon Tony Winterbotham of Portsmouth Cathedral, England, for his help on matters having to do with the Church of England. St. Mortrud and St. Stamia are fictitious saints, but no less interesting, in my opinion. There are many local saints who are unknown to the general populace, and I would not be surprised, one day, to learn there actually is a Saint Mortrud somewhere, and/or a Saint Stamia.

Special thanks go to California public librarian Teri Titus for being so kind as to send me a facsimile copy of *"A Short Account of George Bidder, the Celebrated Mental Calcu-*

lator; with A Variety of the Most Important Questions, Proposed to him at the principal Towns in the Kingdom, and his Surprising Rapid Answers!" I used this fabulous source upon which to base the character of William Rowley, the younger of Lady Sophia's two sons. George Parker Bidder (1806–1878) was a mathematical prodigy of the Regency period. I also used some of the actual mathematical puzzles that were posed to young George. Don't bother to work out the examples—just enjoy them—bearing in mind that the transcription of the questions over the years may have introduced typographical errors. Bidder was the genuine article.

And to my agent, Jenny Bent, for always being there for me, a very special thanks. In addition, I would like to express my appreciation to my editor, Hazel Rumney, for the extraordinary care she has taken with my manuscript.

I hope my modest love story between two most unlikely protagonists suspends your disbelief, and that you enjoy reading it as much as I enjoyed writing it! And bear in mind, as you read, that people are so much more than the sum of their parts. People will always surprise you; that is one of the glorious things about life.

Jo Manning

Men, as well as women, are much oftener led by their hearts than by their understandings. The way to the heart is through the senses; please their eyes and their ears, and the work is half done.
—*Lord Chesterfield, Letters to His Son, 1774*

Rowley Hall, North Riding, Yorkshire, 1811

CHAPTER ONE

Blond, elegant Lady Sophia Rowley, clad in clinging ivory muslin, strode briskly into the drawing room, her cerulean eyes searching for the vicar of St. Mortrud's. Her signature Floris fragrance, Frangipani, perfumed the air in her wake. Where was that gentleman? This vexing interview was not at all to her liking, but George's lawyer had suggested that she and Mr. Charles Heywood should become better acquainted, in keeping with the late baron's wishes, if only for the sake of the boys.

There was a young man sipping a glass of what appeared to be George's best sherry—the bottle was uncorked on the silver tray atop the Elizabethan tulipwood sidetable—a young man gazing fixedly at her portrait over the mantle. Irritation marred Sophia's perfect features. She hated that painting of her as Diana, the virginal Roman goddess of the hunt, which had been completed but a scant year before the death of the artist. What had Romney been thinking? He must have already begun his descent into senility; it was the only explanation. She, the notorious Lady Sophia Rowley, portrayed as a virgin?

But George had loved it, had loved the way the moon and her hair were the same pale, burnished gold, and had given it pride of place at Rowley Hall. Dear, dear, sweet George. Well, now he was gone, and no longer had a say in the interior decoration of his home, so that annoyance could easily be disposed of. Unfortunately, other annoyances would not be as easily dealt with as the Romney portrait her late husband had so admired.

"Sir?" she called. "Have you seen Mr. Heywood?" Who was this stranger, and where was the vicar?

The young man turned, and Sophia was taken aback at his good looks. The gentleman was not much above average height, slender, and possessed of a pleasing, handsome countenance. Perhaps not so much handsome, she thought, as almost beautiful. He had a clear, fresh, young complexion, direct eyes of stormy grey; a short, straight nose; and curling ash-brown hair that tumbled artlessly over a high aristocratic forehead. Not outwardly a very masculine appearing man, not the kind of large, muscular man she usually favored, but attractive, nonetheless. It was a face, she mused, that one would not tire of looking at. He was simply garbed in well-fitting buff inexpressibles and a dark blue coat. His linen was spotlessly white, per Beau Brummell's dictum, and his brown leather boots were polished to a high shine. Yet, he was no dandy. His cravat—always the mark of a dandified gentleman—was simply tied in an unobtrusive fashion.

"Lady Rowley! I am Charles Heywood, at your service." He stepped forward somewhat eagerly to greet her; too eagerly, as he unfortunately caught the toe of his boot on a rucked-up end of Oriental carpet. He pitched forward, spilling the contents of his drink in a great, wide arc that splattered a rich umber stain over Sophia's bosom, seeping into the ivory muslin of her gown. The glass flew, shattering in glittering shards on the polished wood floor not covered by the thick carpet.

Charles Heywood extended his arms to steady himself, even as he lost his footing and landed heavily upon Lady Sophia, knocking her to the floor. An ominous ripping sound was heard and Charles' left hand inadvertently grasped the bodice of Lady Sophia's dress, tearing it below the high waistline. Lady Sophia's bosom, creamy white and wondrously full, was exposed before Charles fell upon her, knocking the breath out of her with a loud "whoosh."

"Beg pardon, my lady," Charles sputtered, even as Sophia's generous curves cushioned and caressed his torso. The lady reared up, pushing the astonished clergyman off her, and against the fireplace hearth. A dull thump registered the meeting of Charles's head with the hard marble surround. His eyes rolled back in his head, and he lay unconscious.

Bromley, the butler, had heard the impact even as he scratched on the door to ask if her ladyship required tea. He saw his mistress lying on her back on the thick, bunched-up rug, her torn dress exposing her bosom, her skirts riding up her limbs. She was breathing hard. He discreetly backed out the door and closed it quietly. Like all well-trained *ton* retainers, he was schooled never to show emotion, and he did not disgrace himself now. Everything he had heard about the baroness—gossip brought back to the Hall by the Rowleys' town servants—seemed as though it might be true. But, the vicar! Bromley rolled his eyes disbelieving what he'd seen with his own two eyes. He had thought much better of that good young man.

9

★ ★ ★ ★ ★

Enraged and breathing hard, Lady Sophia scrambled to her feet, one shaky hand holding the shreds of her dress and her dignity, the other reaching for the bell pull to alert her servants. This fool! This clumsy, stupid oaf! Sophia swore. She'd learned a number of strong barnyard oaths from her first husband before he met his demise in a fall from his horse, and now she muttered her favorites, even as one of the housemaids ran to answer her summons.

"You! Fetch Bewley, now!" The girl looked puzzled. Sophia raised her voice. "The butler, girl, what is the matter with you? Get Bewley and hurry!" The maidservant ran to do her mistress's bidding, even as Bromley reappeared in the hallway.

"Mistress says to fetch ye," the girl stammered, then snickered, "Mr. *Bewley!*"

"None of your cheek, Lizzie, or this house will see the last of you! What has transpired here?" Bromley stepped into the doorway as Lizzie, suitably chastised, lowered her eyes and shuffled away. The butler frowned. The other servants, though they resented it, seemed at the same time to think it a great joke that the mistress did not know their names, but he did not join in the general hilarity. Baron Rowley had known all of his staff by name, their correct names. Lady Rowley, however, was perhaps more typical of her class; Bromley had served an earl in London before joining the baron's staff and knew this to be so.

"My lady?" Bromley inquired, his face free of emotion as he viewed the bizarre tableau of the unconscious vicar lying on the floor of the drawing room.

"Do something!" Lady Sophia's contralto voice rose to a shriek. "He has passed out."

10

Bromley dropped to one knee and attempted to shake the vicar awake. He frowned, rose, and addressed his mistress. "We shall have to send someone for the doctor, my lady," he suggested.

"Do it, then! See to it, Brimley, and get this . . . this . . . man out of my house." She turned in a flounce of skirts, her head held high, her shoulders square.

"Yes, madam," Bromley nodded, a muscle at the side of his mouth twitching in displeasure. Brimley!

Charles Heywood moaned. Bromley knelt beside him. "Sir?" He took the vicar's hands and chafed them in his. "Sir? Are you all right?"

The vicar opened his eyes slowly. Bromley took a glass from the sideboard and poured him another sherry. "Sip this slowly, sir," he suggested, lowering the glass to the vicar's lips.

Between sips, Charles winced. "What happened? My head . . ."

"You appear to have fallen, sir," Bromley ventured.

Charles gazed at the disordered rug and the glistening pieces of broken glass. He winced again. "How . . . ?"

"Do not move, sir," Bromley told him. "I shall send for Mr. Alcott."

In her bedroom, Sophia called for Joan, her abigail, and began to undress, muttering and strewing her clothes all over the floor. Her beautiful new gown was ruined, stained and torn.

Joan was aghast. Her fastidious mistress had been out of sorts these last few months, but never had she seen her so discombobulated. "My lady! What has happened?" she asked.

"Hot water, please, and hurry! I am all over sticky."

11

Sophia discarded her dress, not waiting for the maid's assistance. Her fine, low-cut silk chemise was soaked through from the liqueur.

As Joan moved to do her mistress's bidding, Sophia abruptly put out a hand and stopped her, demanding, "What is wrong with that vicar? Is he deranged?"

Joan seemed perplexed. "The vicar, my lady? Oh, but everyone says he is a lovely man . . ."

Sophia's oath turned the maidservant's ears pink. Joan exited quickly to carry up the water for her mistress's bath.

Lady Rowley peeled off her chemise and took down her hair. Several more epithets warmed the rafters of her dressing room as she stomped about. In the hallway, one of the footmen raised an inquiring eyebrow as the noise level rose. Joan shrugged her shoulders, shook her mop of red curls, and scurried away.

Sharing her news in the kitchen with one of the housemaids, her friend Sarah, Joan was overheard by Mrs. Mathew, the cook, who snorted rudely. "If the madam wore black mourning clothes as she ought, by all that is right and holy, that wine stain would not have ruined her fine new dress, I wager."

"Don't you remember? 'Twas in the baron's will he didn't want her to wear mourning for him," Joan turned on the cook and defended her mistress. "He said she'd worn too much black in her life already."

Mrs. Mathew snorted louder. "She's bad luck, that one! Three husbands dead, and her still a young woman! There's something wrong with her, mark my words. Worse than the Regent's doxy, that Mrs. Fitzherbert! And she's not through yet. She'll kill all and every one of them that's foolish enough to—"

★ ★ ★ ★ ★

Bromley was horrified to catch the end of this unseemly, heated exchange among the female work staff as he appeared in the kitchen carrying the broken pieces of wineglass on a silver tray. "That is enough!" he scolded them, waggling his index finger in disapproval. " 'Tis not up to you to judge your betters! I do not want to hear any more of this loose talk! Mrs. Mathew, you have dinner to prepare. Sarah, there is laundry to sort. Joan, your mistress is waiting! Hurry, now, girl, and make haste. Her ladyship does not like to be kept waiting."

"You won't die, Charles, not yet." Lewis Alcott assured his patient as he checked the large bump, the size of a goose egg, at the back of Charles's skull. Lewis laughed.

"It may be vastly amusing to you, Lewis." Charles Heywood grimaced as his friend touched the grotesque swelling. "But it is hardly cause for such raucous laughter."

"Tell me again how you came to be the object of the beauteous widow's wrath, Charles," Lewis urged, a wicked gleam showing through his wire-rimmed spectacles.

Charles glared at the burly, sandy-haired physician, who looked more like a coachman or a farm laborer than the excellent surgeon he was in truth. "I knew that I would regret detailing those unfortunate circumstances to you! I do hope you have the discretion to keep this embarrassing business to yourself."

Lewis adjusted his eyeglasses. "I never betray a patient's confidences, Charles, you know that." He continued to grin, nonetheless, enjoying the vicar's discomfiture, for all that he was a good friend. Jovial Lewis could not resist teasing, and he especially could not resist teasing the more sober-tempered Charles Heywood.

Charles groaned, running his long fingers through his tousled hair, a nervous habit from childhood that he had never overcome. "How can I ever apologize? Lady Sophia will not want to see my face again."

"Ah, but, Charles," Lewis teased, "it is such a nice, handsome face. Rumor has it that the wicked baroness is partial to handsome faces."

"Most unchristian of you, Lewis, those remarks. Very uncharitable, unworthy in a man of your profession. Lady Sophia is hardly wicked, and as for your allusion to her . . . er . . . habits—" Charles shook his head, unable to go on, then groaned at the discomfort the slight movement caused him. He might not have cracked his skull, as Lewis had assured him, but it certainly felt as though he had.

"At any rate," Lewis continued blithely, "you shall have to face the lovely Lady Sophia again. You are now, per the will of your late mentor, Baron Rowley, the legal guardian to her two sons. You have become part of the family." He squeezed his good friend's shoulder in close, comradely fashion and chuckled, ignoring the murderous glare the vicar sent his way.

I tell you truly and sincerely, that I shall judge of your parts by your speaking gracefully or ungracefully. If you have parts, you will never be at rest till you have brought yourself to a habit of speaking most gracefully, for that is in your power.

—*Lord Chesterfield, Letters to His Son, 1774*

CHAPTER TWO

Lady Sophia's breakfast of eggs and ham lay cold and congealed on the delicate blue tracery of the Wedgwood plate. She took a tentative sip of lukewarm China tea and frowned, pondering her future. Her grim future; she would rusticate forever at Rowley Hall in the wilds of north Yorkshire, which was not at all as she had planned.

The baron's death was not unexpected; he'd been ailing for a long time. The Rowleys were not a long-lived family, and all of his cousins had died years before. No, the surprise had been the defection of her lover, Sir Isaac Rebow. The betting books at White's and Brooks' had been overturned. Overturned as she had been overturned, bested by a slip of a country girl, Isaac's young ward, Mary. He had fallen madly, inappropriately in love and had cast Sophia aside without a moment's hesitation. Isaac and she had been together a very long time. She swallowed. The strong black tea was bitter in her mouth.

She had wanted Isaac Rebow as she had never wanted any of her three husbands. Her father, a dissolute earl addicted

15

to gambling, had traded her youth and beauty three times for money. The first husband spent more time with his horses than he did with his bride, a blessing, for when he was with her, he was a crude and brutal sort; how ironic that one of his cosseted horses had given him the *coup de grace*. He'd died with his boots on, hunting the fox unto eternity.

Her second husband, though not brutish, was phlegmatic and sickly. He had taken it into his head to visit one of his country estates in Scotland during February and had caught cold and died within a fortnight. They'd been married scarcely two months. She'd had little time, with either match, to provide her husband with an heir.

The third time around the Marriage Mart, men were looking askance at her. Though Sophia was more beautiful at eighteen than she had been at fifteen, prospective husbands were not forming a queue to become husband number three. Only dear George, Baron Rowley, had been brave enough to risk the curse. His long-barren wife had recently died, and George was desperate to secure an heir. He was the last of his line, a line that went back to the time of the first King Harry.

A deal was struck: an heir, perhaps two, and Sophia would be free. Wise old George recognized Sophia's robust health and fertility. He settled a yearly sum on her errant father, pronounced that he would be unwelcome in their home, and concluded a generous financial arrangement for Sophia, payable upon production of said heirs to the Rowley name and fortune.

Dear George! He'd understood her so well. After the birth of their sons he was content in Yorkshire, while she dazzled the *ton* in London with her beauty, wealth, and elegance, finding virile young men to amuse her. Though she did not have the number of lovers that the *ton* attributed to

16

her, she found that her wild reputation grew no matter what she did or did not do in fact. Her beauty was a magnet for gossip and lies; much as it drew men, it also drew malicious rumors. Society enjoyed painting her as a frivolous lightskirt.

Scurrilous *on-dits* were out of her control. It was the way of the *beau monde*. Sophia preferred to ignore the rumors than to waste her time denying them. If it amused the *beau monde* to label her promiscuous, no protest from her could alter that fiction.

It was an extremely satisfactory marital arrangement, hers and the baron's. It worried her that George would hear, and perhaps heed, the gossip, but he never chastised her behavior, save to suggest that she should visit the boys more often than was her wont. That she had ignored her sons these last few years—though she visited them regularly when they were toddlers—brought her twinges of guilt and discomfort. She no longer had a husband who insisted on controlling her behavior, much less one who abused her, but she had been remiss in her maternal duties. She had become mired in an endless round of pleasure, a dizzying tune she called, from country house to town, spa, and back again, and she told herself she was content.

Until she met Isaac and suddenly, unexpectedly, wanted something more. For the first time ever in her young life, she wondered what it would be like to be the wife of a man she passionately loved, someone she, herself, had chosen. To be, perhaps, Lady Isaac Rebow. After George died, she'd been so certain it would happen. Everyone had thought so! Until that country chit, all big dark eyes and in the full bloom of youth, had appeared on the scene.

How the *ton* had laughed! It was so very amusing, such rich fodder for *on-dits!* The worldly Lady Sophia trumped by a mere country girl. It had been unbearable. Her world had come tumbling down like the fragile house of cards it was. Isaac had become remote, untouchable. She could not persuade him to come back to her bed. Her practiced charms, her honeyed tongue, had failed her. Sophia could not return now to London after Isaac's public spurning. How could she ever hold her head high again?

She was condemned to spend the rest of her life in north Yorkshire, at Rowley Hall. She had no friends or acquaintances in the immediate area and little knowledge of tiny, rustic Rowley Village. In her heart she harbored the bitter knowledge that London's *on-dits* had traveled north by the fastest stagecoach route, so that, even here at the edge of nowhere, all moor and high country, people smirked and laughed at the rare bumblebroth Lady Sophia Rowley had made of her life. Too many husbands, rumors of many lovers, and no love ever in her life, not really, despite the gossip of those who believed they knew the story of her life and loves. No one knew her; and, most of the time, she had to acknowledge that she barely knew herself.

How could she bear it?

Charles Heywood sat in a comfortable leather wing chair in his cluttered study, his booted feet resting on a worn oak desk, scribbling notes for his Sunday sermon. He was borrowing heavily from a sermon one of his tutors at Cambridge had delivered on the same topic. He was aware of this borrowing, plagiarism by any other standard. At the end of his text, he'd scrawled, guiltily, *"I am a thief!"* He was finding it difficult to think of new sermon topics these days, ever since that humiliating incident with Lady Sophia, the baron's widow. She had been much on his mind of late, to the detriment of his living at St. Mortrud's.

The third son, after three girls, of a land-rich viscount

with holdings in Ulswater and Kendal in the Lake Country, Charles was fated from birth for the church. His elder brother, as heir, managed the family estate; the second son was following a glorious career in the army. His sisters were all suitably and happily married. Every year brought yet another niece or nephew, or both. The Heywoods were a fertile family.

Did he have a clerical calling? No matter; he was bookish and did well at his studies, unlike his two male siblings. It was as good an option for him as any other. He'd had no objection to the church, and the living at Rowley Village was pleasant, the duties hardly onerous. Lord Rowley had been a kindly mentor to Charles, and he had spent more time at the Hall than at the vicarage, playing whist, sipping brandy, and enjoying the use of the excellent library and well-stocked stables. His curate, Mr. Duncan, saw to the efficient running of the little church and was always ready to take vespers, evensong, or matins, when Charles was otherwise occupied at the Hall. It was a most satisfactory arrangement.

Though it was not a requirement of his office, Charles was celibate by choice. Fornication for fornication's sake had never much appealed to him, perhaps because he was a romantic by nature. His present state of agitation was exacerbated by the fact that he had fallen immediately and impossibly in love with the unobtainable Lady Sophia the day he first saw her portrait in the baron's drawing room. She was a goddess, indeed, the woman of his dreams. The artist, famed for his many paintings of Emma Hamilton, had been partial to beautiful faces and perfection of form. He'd emerged from semi-retirement to paint this one last portrait, as a favor to the baron.

George Rowley had chuckled heartily, watching the play of emotions over the young man's expressive face. "Everyone falls in love with Sophia, Charles! You are neither the first, nor will you be the last." The baron had not been offended by Charles's blatant admiration of his lovely wife; indeed, he had seemed inordinately pleased.

Rowley was an amazing old gentleman. He'd been frank with Charles that he and Lady Sophia weren't a love match. George's first wife, Lucy, was the only true love of his life. He was very fond of Sophia, but not in love with her. She had gone her way, as he had gone his. His goal in their marriage was to secure two sons, and she'd fulfilled her part of the bargain in short order. John and William were two fine lads, eleven and ten respectively, now at Eton for their schooling.

Yes, George Rowley had been very frank about how things stood between him and his wife, but not frank enough to enlighten Charles as to the contents of his last will and testament. It had been as much a surprise to Charles as to Lady Sophia that he was named legal guardian to John and William Rowley. With no living male relatives, the baron had had to choose a man to serve as guardian. A woman, even if she was the boys' mother, did not count. Charles understood that; it was simply that he had not been forewarned.

Neither, obviously, had Sophia been forewarned. Charles had to speak to her regarding the boys. And That Other Thing that he owed to old George, that George had refused outright to discuss with him, to the end of his life. He'd gone to Rowley Hall that fateful afternoon to address both issues with Lady Rowley, but the disastrous scene with the lovely Sophia had precluded any discussions.

Now he had to steel himself to see her again. The woman's exquisite blond beauty rendered him almost speechless—he, whose eloquent sermons were always much praised at university and in the pulpit—and how could he begin to apologize for his clumsiness? He had torn her dress; how uncouth, how unutterably crude! How could she stomach the sight of him?

He'd become a dithering oaf in front of the one woman he wanted to please and impress above all others. He was shallow, worthless, a sham of a man. Perhaps the best resolution of his troubles would be to find a nice woman and marry her, as his sisters had been teasing, to marry and leave this blighted spot of Yorkshire for good.

His father had an unentailed parcel of property near Rydal Water that was Charles's for the asking; his favorite sister was eager to introduce him to her young sister-in-law; and there was a neighboring peer's daughter of whom his father was quite fond. Perhaps he, the parson, should allow himself to be led by the nose toward that infamous mouse-trap. And, far better to marry than to burn, according to St. Paul. He was certainly burning now, no doubt about it, if his fevered dreams of a long-limbed, buxom, blond enchantress were any indication. He had glimpsed the moon goddess's breasts through her liquor-soaked chemise, and he would never be the same again.

Real friendship is a slow grower; and never thrives, unless ingrafted upon a stock of known and reciprocal merit.
—**Lord Chesterfield, Letters to His Son, 1774**

CHAPTER THREE

Lady Sophia was restless. Rustication was not all it was made out to be; the infernal quiet of the countryside was driving her mad. It was bad enough during the day, but the nights were worse. How could she sleep when it was so quiet? She was used to the clatter of carriage wheels over cobbled streets, the noises of social activity and occasional fistfights, footpads running through alleyways, the sound of the watch calling the hours. This quiet and boredom was like a kind of death.

She had expected the boredom, that time would pass slowly in her exile, but had not anticipated the tediousness of a constant stream of tiresome visitors, ostensibly her late husband George's friends and neighbors. In truth, they were all gossips and scandalmongers, verifying her lack of mourning costume and coming to ferret out the details of her ill-fated liaison with Sir Isaac.

'Twas a truth she'd not pondered overmuch, but bad news *did* indeed travel fast, per the familiar saying, as fast as the traveling chariots and Royal Mail coaches from London to Leeds.

Yesterday it had been the turn of a Mrs. Ramsbotham and her two simpering, spotty daughters, Drusilla and Annabelle.

22

While the young country girls ogled the light green clocked stockings visible under the vandyked hem of Sophia's high-necked dark green challis walking dress, the mother had rained question after personal question upon her. *How rude!* Sophia had managed to turn the conversation to fashion, raising her skirts so that the girls could have a better look at the unusual stockings that seemed to fascinate them so.

The impulsive gesture had shut Mrs. Ramsbotham's gaping mouth for the nonce, as Sophia chatted merrily about Madame Gruyon's exclusive London dressmaking establishment. It was a place the Ramsbothams would see only in their dreams, never in actuality. The modiste had standards; not just *anyone* could ply her custom at Madame Gruyon's Conduit Street shop.

It was becoming harder and harder to keep herself in check these days. The tale of her impulsively raised skirts would guarantee the Ramsbothams entrée wherever gossip about Sophia Rowley was the main course. Should she be concerned with the unfavorable impression she was continuing to make upon her neighbors and her staff, Sophia wondered? She frequently lost her temper, and the household was learning to keep out of the way, especially when these black humors were upon her.

She knew she should forswear the rough oaths she was lately wont to utter, but found herself unable to restrain her vocal outbursts. Clearly, she was out of control. This was uncouth, unladylike behavior to a fault, more befitting the worst of guttersnipes, and she rued her actions even as she continued to behave badly. Her London reputation was largely false, but this she alone knew. Ruefully, she acknowledged that her irrational behavior could do naught but augment the widely held opinion.

The only member of her staff who managed to retain his

aplomb was the stiff-rumped butler, Bentley or Brownley, or whatever his name was. Nothing, it seemed, fazed that man, not even The Scene in the drawing room over a week ago. As if seeing one's employer upon the floor in a most ungainly manner, her dress torn to shreds, whilst a man sprawled unconscious nearby, was the most normal of events! Yet the butler had quickly taken matters in hand. Sophia did not as a rule think much about the behavior of servants, but she conceded that the butler seemed most admirable, for a servant.

As to that other man . . . she could not stop thinking about the too-handsome Charles Heywood, vicar of St. Mortrud's and friend to her late husband. He had obviously wormed his way into George's great good heart. What else had George given him, besides the guardianship of his two sons? She caught herself. *Their two sons.* Yes, theirs. Hers. *Her two sons.* That other worry was uppermost in her tangled thoughts these days. John and William would be home on school holiday from Eton soon. What was she to do with them? She hardly knew her own boys, having last seen them when they were toddlers.

John and William were scarce a year apart. She had done her duty well by George Rowley; he'd no cause to complain. She remembered how motherhood had taken her by surprise. She'd loved her babies. They'd been so soft of skin, helpless, dependent on her for all their needs. She'd actually nursed John for several months, until her morning sickness with William had interfered. She remembered, out of the hazy blue of long-buried memories, how she'd hated handing her sweet little son over to the wet nurse for his nourishment. Maternal feelings—Yes, she'd once had them; there was no question in her mind about that. And, all of a sudden, with no warning, they seemed to be returning.

But she had been a terrible mother. No one would argue

that point. She had turned her back on her boys after scarcely three years and never questioned her actions. When had she last seen them? Shame suffused her countenance. Among her set, casual motherhood was not uncommon, but surely she had come from better stock? Though her own mother had died young, Sophia remembered her as a loving, caring woman.

What had gone wrong? Why had her life turned out this way? She was at an impasse, a crossroad, or, perhaps more accurately, at the edge of a cliff, below which yawned a wide, ugly chasm that threatened to swallow her up whole.

And now, so slowly as to be barely perceptible to her, the block of ice that had encased Sophia's heart since the eve of her first marriage, the ice that protected her even as it kept her from her own humanity, threatened to melt at its outermost edges. She shivered, as if feeling the cold for the first time in many years. She had not felt so cold when the Thames froze solidly last January as she did now.

What was she to do? What were the choices open to her? The boys had no one now but her . . . her and that decidedly odd vicar. Her boys deserved better, did they not? Why had George left her in this muddle? She was frightened, even if she could not admit it to herself. Indomitable, brazen Sophia Rowley was scared to death.

What was she to do?

Charles had to clear his muzzy head, full of sermons and Sophia. It was hardly the best of combinations; indeed, it was a ludicrous mix. He would go for a walk. A path led from the vicarage and St. Mortrud's to the outskirts of Rowley Hall. He doubted he would run into anyone save a gamekeeper. Certainly not Lady Sophia—that gorgeous hothouse bloom was suited more to London ballrooms than to the robust air of north Yorkshire. Confident that he would be alone and hoping to air his demons, he donned his hat and took his walking stick and a book of Wordsworth's latest poetry. Reciting aloud into nature's silence was a tool he used to conquer his slight tendency to stammer. An hour or two on the wild, hilly moors would do him a world of good.

Why waste a perfectly good walking dress by sitting indoors and giving in to another bout of the dismals? Sophia thought. The day was glorious, bright sun, robin's-egg-blue skies, and sparse, fluffy clouds. She pulled on her sturdy half-boots, a pair left behind from her last sojourn at Rowley Hall, took a Cashmiri shawl for added warmth, if needed, and informed Joan that she was taking a stroll on the grounds. As an afterthought, she grabbed her reticule.

"Do you wish me to accompany you, my lady?" Joan inquired.

"You must be joking." Lady Sophia snorted. "Do you think I will be accosted here, at the very barren edge of nowhere?" With burgeoning impatience, she brushed away the poke bonnet the eager abigail offered her and strode forth. There was a path that led to the village cemetery from the back of the Hall, through a copse of yew trees. Perhaps she would pay George a visit and ask for his help in sorting out her thoughts. She sighed. Ah, how addle-brained she was becoming. As if anyone could help her, much less the mortal remains of her late husband!

Charles walked briskly, inhaling deeply of the fresh, country air, unencumbered by cares. He'd been on a walking tour of Switzerland after Cambridge and had enjoyed it mightily. Perhaps it was time to travel again, he thought. But no, he caught himself up short. There were the boys. George's sons would be home in a few weeks on summer holiday from Eton. They needed a friendly face to greet them when they arrived.

He was inordinately fond of those two; he had tutored them, from time to time, in Latin and Greek. The younger, William, had great mathematical talent; Charles had discovered that the boy could work out huge sums in his head in less time than it took Charles to write them down. Most extraordinary! John was a madcap, a rapscallion, especially in contrast to his younger brother.

It struck him how much they favored their beautiful mother in looks. They were both fair and handsome, with Sophia's unusual blue eyes. The Rowleys, judging from the many ancestral portraits hanging in the Long Gallery at the Hall, were a dark-haired, dark-eyed lot. It was a kindness to call them average in appearance, for there was a conspicuous dearth of beauty in that family. Old George had chosen well when he'd selected Sophia for his bride; she'd given him two fine-looking sons.

And then she had deserted them.

Charles was unable to comprehend the selfish behavior of *ton* females. His family was much less sophisticated, and rarely visited the capitol city of London. His sisters treasured their children and were never willingly separated from them for any length of time. But, according to the village gossip brought to him daily, whether he wanted it or not, by Mrs. Chipcheese, his housekeeper, Lady Sophia had quit Rowley Hall less than two years after William's birth, returning only for brief visits when they were younger. The boys had been raised by George and a series of governesses. For a time, George's elder sister had resided with them and was a surrogate for their mother until her death.

Oh, but how had thoughts of the enticing Lady Sophia once again slipped past his defenses? Here he was, enjoying the day, the walk, and the expansive green miles, and that lady had once more penetrated his consciousness. He made a swift decision; he must endeavor to see her again and discuss the boys and his guardianship of them. He wanted to let her know that he was not about to usurp her position as the boys' mother, and that he'd been as surprised as anyone when the baron's will was read and named him guardian.

The law was clear on that point, a male guardian (preferably a blood relation) was required. Old George had no relatives, so there was no one of blood to contest his last decision. And females, unfortunately, even mothers, had few legal rights in Britain. That disturbed Charles, even as he conceded that Lady Sophia had been a negligent, uncaring mother to her boys these last several years. But what had George meant to convey by naming him, the lowly local vicar? Was there no suitable male relation of Sophia's, someone with closer family ties? Charles wished that there had been a modicum of discussion amongst the three of them before George had written that blasted last will and testament. He could not blame Lady Sophia for resenting him. He seemed a usurper even to himself. Truly, there were a number of things he had to set right with the baron's widow.

Sophia was enjoying her walk immensely. She'd grown up in Kent, a county of manicured natural beauty in the south of England, an area quite different from the wild Yorkshire moors. As a child, though she was a quick and eager student, she'd much preferred the outdoors to the classroom. Her governess, Miss Bane . . . oh, how long it had been since she'd thought of that loving woman, who had been with her since the untimely death of her young mother. Miss Bane had been more than a governess, more than a servant. Miss Bane—

A rush of unpleasant memories crowded Sophia's mental processes. She had been very good at banishing the unpleasant to the deepest recesses of her mind. Miss Bane's memory brought too much pain. She stopped walking, leaned back against a tree, and took several quick breaths. Her father . . . no, that way only more pain lay; she would not surrender to it. She cleared her head of the cobwebs threatening to take up residence there, moved away from the tree, and continued her walk, trying to conjure up more pleasant notions. Or, safest of all, to refrain from thinking at all.

She was also beginning to regret her reaction to The Scene between her and the young vicar. She had overreacted terribly. 'Twas not as if he were the only male who had ever flung himself upon her. She could very well have killed the man, pushing him away so violently! A soft giggle escaped her. He had to be mortified, truly. No wonder he had not returned. She was the one who should smooth over the incident.

She and Mr. Heywood were fated to deal with each other; that was an inescapable fact, and that embarrassing incident had to be set to rest. Her turbulent inner feelings could not be allowed to rule her life. She'd made a terrible mistake with Sir Isaac, allowing feelings and dreams of a different kind of life to fling her into wild, uncontrolled emotion. She'd never done that before and look where it had gotten her! She would be cool, unruffled, the ice goddess everyone thought her to be.

There was a good deal of sorting out to be done. Her life must be put in order. Without order and purpose, she would shrivel and die. She was Lady Sophia Rowley! She

must remember that. Ah, when had life become so compli-
cated? She must take one step at a time, as she was doing
now, on this woodland path. She trod on, striding forward
with new purpose and determination, each well-placed step
reinforcing her new determination.

Charles looked over a slight rise and beheld a rich tap-
estry of wild flowers carpeting the earth. Yellows, pinks,
blues, all the colors of the rainbow jostled for position as he
observed nature's bounty. So short-lived, these flowers
growing in the wild, uncultivated by the hand of man, yet so
lovely, such a feast for the eyes. Nature contented and comforted him, as it did his favorite poets. Finding a rock upon
which to perch, he took out the slim volume of Wordsworth
and began to read aloud his favorite poems, poems that recollected his youth in the Lake District, where the great poet
was born and still resided.

> "I wandered lonely as a cloud
> That floats on high o'er vales and hills,
> When all at once I saw a crowd,
> A host, of golden daffodils;
> Beside the lake, beneath the trees,
> Fluttering and dancing in the breeze . . ."

The bobbing white scuts of a family of rabbits darted out
of Sophia's path through a swathe of newly-emerging
bracken. Above her head, a short-eared owl was hunting
voles for its breakfast, looking huge and fearsome, not unlike a great grey moth as it swooped low over the moorland.
There was more variety in the groupings of trees as Sophia
neared the outskirts of Rowley village: rowans, birches,
larches, dwarf willows, Scots pines. Underneath the wil-

lows, Sophia glimpsed the flickering forms of black grouse, with their red-wattled eyes and lyre-shaped tails.

As a child, Sophia had once witnessed the mating ritual of these creatures. She had gazed open-mouthed as the male birds faced each other and uttered strange bubbling sounds interspersed with loud shrieks. She had been delighted to see the drab brown females strutting between the victorious males (some of whom had battled more than one rival), selecting their mates for the season.

So had Sophia selected her lovers, she reflected; she'd once relished the sight of men bickering for her favors. There'd almost been a duel fought for those favors, in one disturbing instance. A pair of besotted young Corinthians had nearly tasted grass for breakfast because of her. She was not proud of the incident. She'd prevailed upon her male acquaintances to intercede before the hotheads could inflict serious damage upon each other. It had been flattering, at first, when she'd heard of it, but upon sober reflection, she had been appalled. She had hardly known the young men!

Her female friends, coldhearted wretches all, had chided her for being so soft as to show concern over two silly, unimportant young men, but even she, the renowned ice goddess who supposedly expressed no feelings, could not have borne such a horror on her conscience. She was truly taken aback by these women, who cared nothing for the lives of men dueling to the death in hopes of gaining their favors.

She appreciated good-looking young men too much to see them senselessly destroy themselves, she told these women, her gay laughter belying her inner feelings. Slowly, she began to disengage from their company; she had not missed them one whit. The satisfied recollection of jettisoning their unwelcome acquaintance warmed her now, further loosening the icy grip that surrounded her heart.

Sophia smiled, as if glad for perhaps the first time to be removed from the shallow, heartless society of the *beau monde*. She should commune with nature more often, she thought. In London, she had rarely been out and about so early in the day. Late evenings resulted in late risings the next day. She felt suddenly invigorated, the combination of her thoughts and the lovely day perhaps working some magic on her. As she rounded a bend in the path beside a slope of heathery grasses, she heard a sound and stopped, frowning. Someone was declaiming aloud in these woods.

She paused to listen, not quite believing her ears. A man's light, pleasing voice, mellifluous in tone, projected beautifully through the empty stretch of woodland. It was poetry. Sophia concentrated on the words and rhythm. Wordsworth. The romantic poet of the Lake Country. She loved his poems; they were from the heart. Standing in the middle of the path, she closed her eyes, enjoying this unexpected treat.

> "For oft, when on my couch I lie
> In vacant or in pensive mood,
> They flash upon that inward eye
> Which is the bliss of solitude;
> And then my heart with pleasure fills,
> And dances with the daffodils . . ."

Sophia felt her heart lift, straining the bonds of the ice that still held it fast, as she imagined the flash of jonquil-yellow on the green grass of Cumbria, bright patches of blooming flowers dancing beside the hills and deep in the valleys. She had never been to the Lake Country, but the poet's well-formed word-pictures took her there now. She breathed deeply, feeling at peace.

She had to see who was reciting *"I Wandered Lonely as a Cloud"* in her woods. Who was this person so at home with nature and beautiful words? Cautiously, she edged further along the path, keeping to the tall trees on one side. He was not finished; he had begun to recite another poem. It was a very short one and another favorite of hers.

> "My heart leaps up when I behold
> A rainbow in the sky:
> So was it when my life began;
> So is it now I am a man;
> So be it when I shall grow old,
> Or let me die!
> The Child is father of the Man;
> I could wish my days to be
> Bound to each by natural piety . . ."

How lovely! She could listen to that light but sonorous voice forever. It stirred her deeply. Sophia had often sought refuge in books when she was a young girl. Her later life had not centered around London's literary set, but Hatchards bookstore held her standing order for poetical works. It was not something any of her acquaintances knew about Lady Sophia, but poetry filled a need in her life, a need she could not articulate.

She wanted to identify the speaker. Craning her neck and peering ahead, she glimpsed a young man sitting on a rock, walking stick beside him, a slim book in his hands. The vicar! She drew back in surprise, almost stumbling on loose rocks. She should have guessed. Joan had said that his sermons were lovely, that his beautiful voice warmed the heart. The vicar! The last person she wanted to see . . . but, ah, that mesmerizing voice . . . consummate irony! She turned away; he must not see her lurking nearby. She turned, flushing a lackadaisical young roebuck, whose ivory-colored antlers flashed as he suddenly reared in alarm. *"Oh!"* she cried, stumbling and falling backward clumsily on the grass.

What the . . . ! Charles's ears perked up at the sudden cry. He heard a crashing sound in the dense underbrush, and, throwing down his book, raced towards the noise. Was someone hurt? There were no man-traps in these woods—the baron had outlawed these deadly devices from his lands—but a poacher could have set a trap for small game and trapped a person, instead.

There was a woman lying in the middle of the path that led to Rowley Hall, gasping, the breath knocked out of her. *Oh, no, not again!* Lady Sophia, on her delectable bottom, long legs splayed. Charles groaned and raised his eyes heavenward. *Why me, Lord? Why me? Why this, why now?*

This time, however, his conscience was clear; *he* had not brought the lady down. No, he could spy an innocent roe deer, a buck, scarce bigger than a large dog, summer coat of foxy-red a bright blur against dark brown tree bark, making swift tracks through the deeply tangled, almost impenetrable brush as if the very hounds of hell were at his hooves.

Charles could sympathize with the beast. The lady had a unique way of scaring the life out of one. He absentmindedly rubbed the back of his head, no longer bearing a lump, but still sensitive to the touch.

This is absurd! Sophia thought. Charles reached for her hands to pull her to her feet. *Am I forever fated to be horizontal whenever I am in the vicinity of this handsome young man,* she wondered? Then she began to giggle. *Oh,* she thought, *oh, I have been too, too long without a lover!*

"Lady Rowley?" The vicar frowned, wondering at the fit of laughter that emanated from the baron's beautiful widow.

"Yes, Mr. Heywood, I am fine. Thank you for your assistance." She took a handkerchief out of her netted reticule and dabbed at her eyes.

"Are you sure you are all right, my lady?" the gentleman persisted.

Sophia looked into the concerned grey eyes of the vicar of Rowley village. They were almost the same height, so her gaze was on a nearly direct line with his. "I am perfectly all right, sir, but . . . but . . . we must stop meeting like this." Again the giggles erupted, and she brought her handkerchief to her mouth to stifle them.

Charles thought he should introduce Lady Sophia to Lewis Alcott, as they both seemed to enjoy a good laugh at his expense. What was so amusing? He was disconcerted and tongue-tied, not knowing what to say or do.

"Would you like me to accompany you, my lady, to your destination? These woodland paths tend to be rocky; perhaps you would like to take my arm?" he offered.

"Why, yes, of course, sir, thank you. I am on my way to the graveyard, to have a few words with my late husband. George has a great deal of explaining to do, I fear." Lady Sophia put her arm in his, noting the shocked look that crossed his face with amusement.

She peered closely at him. "I am joking, sir! I fell on my *derriere*, not my head." She tapped her temple for emphasis, then waved her hand in the vicinity of her nether parts. Realizing that she must forbear from torturing this young man any further, she continued, "We must discuss this issue of guardianship before the boys come home for their school holiday."

Her eyes twinkled. "But I would like to visit George's grave first, if you will accompany me."

Lady Sophia turned in the direction of the village. "Do not forget your walking stick and poetry book, sir," she said, pointing to the rock, "and do let's be on our way."

Charles was speechless. The lady was in a rare humor. It behooved him to take advantage of it. He wished, however, that she would not gaze directly at him in that manner. Her unusual eyes, a painter's prized cerulean, dazzled him, making him weak-kneed. He squirmed inwardly. He must not fantasize on the lady's unique beauty, including the delightful callipygian charms she'd indicated with that careless wave of her hand towards her lower extremities. That way lay madness.

"Come, sir! No dawdling!" Sophia ordered. "The cemetery, it is! We have a good deal to discuss, you and I . . . and George, of course." She chuckled softly.

Charles could only nod meekly in mute acquiescence, wondering at this new side to the baron's widow. What was next? He prayed for strength and for respite from lascivious thoughts, so unbecoming and unseemly in a vicar.

The life of les Milords Anglais . . . As soon as they rise, which is very late, they breakfast together, to the utter loss of two good morning hours. Then they go by coachfuls to the Palais, the Invalides, and Notre-Dame; from thence to the English coffee-house, where they make up their tavern party for dinner. From dinner, where they drink quick, they adjourn in clusters to the play, where they crowd the stage, drest up in very fine clothes . . . From the play to the tavern again, where they get very drunk, and where they either quarrel among themselves, or sally forth, commit some riot in the streets, and are taken up by the watch . . . They return home, more petulant, but not more informed, than when they left it; and show, as they think, their improvement, by affectedly both speaking and dressing in broken French.

—Lord Chesterfield, Letters to His Son, 1774

CHAPTER FOUR

Thomas Eliot, Earl of Dunhaven, lounged in his favorite chair at Laurence's popular Paris coffeehouse. Robert Winton, Lord Brent, his countryman and latest companion in vice, sprawled opposite him on a leather divan, much the worse for wear after a night spent carousing the seamier streets of the French capitol city. The significant hazards of being English in France during this turbulent time only added spice to their stay; skirting the very real danger was almost an aphrodisiac.

Lord Brent, who seemed to fear nothing, had stopped in Paris on the way back from his Grand Tour of Greece and Italy, spending his father's money freely along the way. Too freely; his vowels were scattered throughout town, and he was dangerously close to falling into River Tick. The jaded nobleman was an ideal companion for the profligate, careless Dunhaven.

"*Enfin, quelquechose pour faire aujourd'hui?* What's on for today? The usual debauched round of amusements? Or have you devised something that will rescue me from this blasted *ennui?*" Brent drawled in execrable French. Dissipation had already shaped strong inroads on his young face.

"Actually, now that you mention it, there is something in the air, something that smells of money." The Earl of Dunhaven removed a badly creased letter from his pocket, passing it under his handsome nose and sniffing volubly. His face broke into a wide grin. "*Voila!* It seems that my son-in-law, George Rowley, that contented cuckold, that wittol, has met his demise. My lovely daughter Sophia is now three times a widow."

Brent came to attention, his sleepy, languid gaze replaced by a narrow-eyed, estimating look. "Sophia Rowley is *your* daughter, Tom?"

Dunhaven nodded. "The same. I have not seen my offspring in a number of years, however." He grimaced, thinking of the long-ago agreement he'd made with Rowley, an agreement not at all to his liking, but one he'd had no choice but to accept. "My son-in-law and I did not get on." He winced at the memory of that acrimonious interview, which had ended with the baron's financing his long stay on the continent.

"Told you to clear out, did he?" Brent inquired, cutting

to the heart of the matter.

Dunhaven's cold blue eyes fixed on his young companion. His lips thinned. "In a word . . . *yes,*" he agreed.

"So, then," Brent stretched his broad, muscular frame, "the lady is left a widow again. A *rich* widow, one hopes?"

"Rowley was a very wealthy man. The family was a tight lot; never spent a shilling. Did not believe in enjoying life. Yes, Sophia should be a *very rich* widow. There are also two boys." Dunhaven tapped the letter from his informant.

"Heirs? That could be a complication."

"Children are a vulnerable lot. Very few survive the illnesses and rigors of childhood. *Quel dommage, mon ami, eh?* Their misfortune. Those who do survive . . . well, sometimes accidents occur, do they not?" Dunhaven's laugh was a harsh, ugly sound.

"You're funning me . . . aren't you?" Even Brent was taken aback by the sharp menace, the veiled threat, in his friend's voice, and the disturbing, malevolent narrowing of his unusual blue eyes.

Dunhaven looked directly into the nobleman's face; the tone of his voice was cold and hard. "That bastard Rowley cheated me out of my due. His sniveling brats ain't going to stand in my way, not by half. I think 'tis time I cut short my lovely sojourn in this fair city." His eyes narrowed. "And you? Do you fancy returning to England? My daughter Sophia is worth the trip, if what I have heard of her amorous adventures these last ten years is even partly true."

"I have heard talk of Sophia Rowley," Brent ventured. "She was all but married to Sir Isaac Rebow, waiting impatiently for her husband to expire, 'twas said among the *ton.*"

Dunhaven snorted. "Well, Rowley has expired, 'tis true, but *ma chere* Sophia's paramour has not come up to snuff. He has married his ward. Sophia is at this moment rusticating in Yorkshire." He guffawed loudly. "She must be dead bored!"

Lord Brent played absently with the dented coffee spoon on the scarred wooden table, tapping it softly. "Is the lady amenable to marrying again?" he asked.

"Her money will draw suitors like flies, as her beauty did when she was a young girl. If she has retained even a modicum of her good looks, the combination should be most appealing."

"Not enough for Sir Isaac, it seems," Brent commented.

"Rebow's ward was wealthy, too, so 'tis said. And, man, why buy a dog if there's a pup available?" Dunhaven slapped his thigh, his eyes twinkling in merriment. "Sophia's thirty years of age and twice a mother; her rival was a young virgin. Where's the choice?"

The younger man was shocked at his companion's crude remarks. He was speaking coarsely of his own flesh and blood, his daughter! Brent shrugged. "One could look at it that way," he drawled, uneasy.

"Only way to look at it! So," Dunhaven's voice took on an oily, cajoling tone. "*Enfin,* what say you? Will you ac-company me to England?"

Brent paused. Things were much of a sameness lately in Paris. He'd been abroad for two years. Time to visit his family, see the pater, arrange for more financing of his plea-sures and perhaps meet the beautiful widow. He had glimpsed her once, at a crush in Mayfair before embarking on his Grand Tour, and had been impressed by her looks. She was a goddess, tall, arrogant, blond and, 'twas said, free with her favors.

And, now, with Baron Rowley's demise, she was a very wealthy goddess. He was not interested in becoming leg-shackled; he was, after all, only past his twenty-fifth birthday, but a little dalliance might be just the thing for his ennui. Yes, Sophia Rowley might cure his lackluster spirits. His pulse quickened at the prospect, even as he acknowledged some misgivings concerning his companion. Burgeoning lust easily won the battle.

"*Oui, mon compere!* I shall have my valet pack my portmanteaux *toute-suite,* within the hour! Ah, England and its many and varied beauties; I look forward to it.

"*Allons!*"

What had occurred in his relationship with Lady Sophia? Charles thought as he walked with her toward the cemetery. He was nonplussed. Only days before, after the disaster at Rowley Hall, he was *persona non grata.* He was certain that the lady never wanted to see him again. Now here he was, walking sedately arm in arm with her to the vicarage, for all the world like people on good, even intimate, terms. It was like night and day, this change in her attitude. He was terrified that it would, at any moment, revert to its former unpleasant state. He must seize the moment to talk about the will, the boys, and That Other Matter.

He cleared his throat. "Er . . . ahem . . . Lady Rowley . . . you must know that I had nothing to do with your husband's will," he began tentatively.

"Oh, of course you did not, Mr. Heywood. I have thought upon the matter a good deal and have come to the conclusion that 'twas as much a surprise to you as to me." She turned her eyes on him, sincerity and friendship in her gaze, her free hand patting his forearm, sending sparks all the way to his shoulder. "I fear I have been overwrought these last several weeks, and I beg pardon if I seemed rude." Her wide, sweet smile could have melted icebergs.

Charles gulped. The lady's mouth was delicious, the lower lip fuller and naturally pouting, the upper curved like cupid's bow. Those gorgeous lips and the close proximity of the lady were nerve-wracking, and nervousness tended to cause him to stammer. "N-n-no need to apologize, my lady! 'Tis I . . . that is, for s-s-s sure, I never meant to replace your influence with your sons. Whatever you desire for them, I will never object in any way. They are *your* children, after all."

Sophia's smile was serene, more beautiful than a Raphael Madonna. "Thank you, Mr. Heywood. I was sure we would arrive at a mutually satisfactory agreement." She beamed at him.

Anything, he would agree to anything. He was putty in her hands, malleable and willing. So long as she continued to regard him with that angelic gaze, so long as those ripe red lips smiled at him. She was perfection in face and form, an angel. No, she was Venus, Aphrodite, Diana—a goddess, by whatever name. Had he died without realizing it and ascended to heaven?

Sophia smiled. It was reassuring to know that she had not lost her effect on men, despite the horrible events of the past few months. She'd noted with pleasure the results of her touch on the vicar. She had been concerned that her once-considerable charms had waned, but dear Mr. Heywood was hers for the taking. It was a heady feeling! Did she, however, want to take him? It was a route she had traveled before, but this was a different game.

Charles Heywood was a handsome man—perhaps a bit younger than she was—and might provide some good bed sport, a pastime Sophia greatly enjoyed. It had been a while since she'd shared a bed with a man. Her first appraisal of any male always gauged his suitability as a lover in a cold, unemotional assessment, and she was rarely wrong. Now she winced inwardly. Sir Isaac had also passed muster at first glance. She had believed that he was the lover of her dreams, after so many forgettable others. Her husbands . . . she winced visibly now at the memory. Her husbands had been duty, no more; one had been unspeakable, a brute. Only George had been kind.

She must not think thoughts that depressed her. She should concentrate on the matter at hand. *Seducing Mr. Heywood.* It might prove to be amusing.

Anything that relieved the great boredom of Yorkshire would be welcome. She cast the vicar a sideways glance. Though she had so far not numbered the clergy among her conquests, there was always a first time. The passion she'd heard in his rich voice as he'd declaimed those poems held promise for other kinds of passion.

Pleased that the issue of who was in control of her children had been settled to her satisfaction, she was now free to pursue other satisfactions. He was a fine-looking man. Charles Heywood, vicar of St. Mortrud's, had no idea what a lucky man he was about to become.

A sweet chestnut tree cast its shade over George Rowley's gravesite. The young tree was a novelty so far north. Its distinctive long leaves and feathery yellow teasels blew gently in the soft breeze. Tight new green grass, velvety in texture, grew upon the slight mound that indicated a newly dug grave. A monumental tombstone stretched wide to mark the resting place of the baron and his first baroness.

Sophia knelt to read the inscription. It was the first time she had ever opened the lychgate and ventured into the small cemetery, the first time she had seen this tombstone; she had not been present at her late husband's funeral service. She looked up at the vicar. "This stone is for both George and his first wife," she stated, surprised.

Charles nodded. He had not known the first Lady Rowley, who had died thirteen years earlier. She was still revered in the countryside and amongst the staff at Rowley Hall. She was said to have been an undemanding, quietly pretty woman, unknown to the members of the *haute monde*. Charles knew she had been George's great love, although sadly barren: Lucy Tipton Rowley, 1750–1798.

George had never spoken much of the first Lady Rowley to her, Sophia mused. Indeed, her portrait was not displayed at the Hall. Where was it, she wondered? Surely, there was one.

"There is an inscription after her name—" Sophia peered at the tiny carving and read the lines aloud: *"A violet by a mossy stone/Half hidden from the eye!/Fair as a star, when only one/Is shining in the sky/She lived unknown, and few could know/When Lucy ceased to be/But she is in her grave, and, oh/The difference to me!"*

"Wordsworth," the vicar commented, his voice grave.

"Yes," Sophia agreed, "for here is the poet's name, and the date of the poem's composition, 1800. George and I were wed in that year . . . when was this inscribed, then, if the lady died in 1798?"

"It must have been after 1800," Charles replied. He squatted to see better, his fingers moving over the deeply incised stone. "Not worn. No more than a few years old. Certainly, then, after your marriage to him, my lady."

"He loved her," she said in a quiet voice, a voice slightly tinged with envy. Even as he married her, he'd loved his first wife.

Charles nodded. "So I have been told. He adored her. I heard that she was his childhood sweetheart. Grew up on an adjoining estate and never left home. The villagers here still speak fondly of her."

Sophia's face muscles felt stiff. Tears stung the back of her eyes, as she pondered such spousal devotion. Something she'd never experienced, not ever. She rose briskly, brushing at the skirts of her walking dress, now stained green by fresh grass, willing back tears. She never cried!

"Well! So George also fancied the poems of Mr. Wordsworth."

"We often read them aloud together in the evenings. He was much comforted by them at the end," Charles added. Rowley had said he enjoyed listening to the vicar's voice, and Charles had been moved by the old fellow's quavering baritone, once-rich, but steadily growing weaker over those last months. He missed him. Should he have spoken so? He wondered, too late, about George's feelings for his late wife. Lady Sophia had seemed taken aback by his remarks and by the deep sentiment of love expressed on the tombstone.

Sophia's eyes flew to Charles's face. "He did not suffer, did he?" There was a sudden urgency in her voice, almost a panic.

Charles's first reaction was to reach out to console her, but he stayed his hand. Though she seemed distraught, it would be inappropriate. "No, my lady, he did not suffer; he passed away peacefully. He had been ailing for a very long time, but he was not in great pain. At least, it never appeared so to any of us. He never asked for laudanum."

"I should have been here, Mr. Heywood, say it! I know that is what everyone thinks. I know it is why everyone hates me!" Sophia's voice rose in bitter self-condemnation. Her arms were stiff at her sides, fists tightly clenched.

Now Charles did reach out, taking her rigid, gloved hands in his larger ones, opening them up, spreading her fingers. "Nay, my lady, nay! Do not think such things! George . . . the baron . . . He never had a harsh word about you. He valued you highly as the mother of his sons. He loved those boys more than any father ever loved his children, I do believe that."

"He did not love *me*, Mr. Heywood. I suspect you know that." Sophia was aware that her display of emotion was unseemly, especially in front of a man she had decided to seduce, but she could not stop herself. She was making a cake of herself, acting the fool, and yet she could not stop.

"Lady Sophia," Charles attempted to console her, "the baron admired you greatly. He often praised you . . ." But his words, meant to reassure her, sounded lame, even to him.

Sophia Rushton Ferguson Rowley, nee Eliot, pursed her lips, speaking slowly. "No one has ever loved me, Mr. Heywood. I fear I am not at all lovable." She laughed, wincing at the hollow sound, hating this maudlin display of self-pity. Hating herself.

The young vicar flinched as if he had been struck, stunned by her self-loathing. "Do not say that, Lady Rowley, it is untrue!"

"La! I am but feeling sorry for myself, Mr. Heywood. Do, pray, excuse me." She hastily withdrew her hands from his and fixed him with a coquettish stare. "Please forget this silly conversation, I beg you. Cemeteries must bring out the worst in me!"

Charles frowned. The lady had let her formidable defenses down, if only for a few moments. The sight of that beautiful verse inscribed on the family tombstone, full of emotion and love, verses from a favorite poet for the baron's much-loved first wife, had upset Sophia, his unloved second wife. Well, he was going to upset her even more, now, he feared, for he had to discuss That Other Matter that Baron Rowley had, up to his last day on earth, refused to discuss with him. He cleared his throat.

And this is law, I will maintain
Unto my dying day, sir
That whatsoer king shall reign
I will be Vicar of Bray, sir!
> *— "The Vicar of Bray"*
> *Anonymous Poem, circa 1734*

CHAPTER FIVE

The moment had come. The Other Matter Charles wanted to discuss was about to be put on the table. The vicar of St. Mortrud's recollected the painful discussion he'd had with his patron, Baron Rowley. Was he deliberately disobeying, disregarding, a dying man's wishes? Yes, he was, he conceded that point, but the baron was wrong, Charles Heywood was sure of that. George Rowley was an exceedingly humble man, for all that he was rich, locally powerful and possessed an old and respected title. As vicar, Charles was overruling his last wish. He had been unable to persuade the baron, but perhaps, he could convince the widow.

Unfortunately, he could see that Lady Sophia had been upset by the discovery of the loving inscription ordered by her late husband for the first Lady Rowley. Women! Created from Adam's rib, wondrous creations indeed, but also man's eternal torment. Charles cleared his throat.

"Lady Sophia," he began, "I do not believe you have been inside St. Mortrud's?"

Sophia's dark golden brows knit together. "No, sir, I do not believe that I have." She was no churchgoer. As a child, she attended the small church not far from the Dunhaven estate, but as an adult, she associated churches with weddings, her weddings. Unpleasant memories. Churches had fallen out of favor with her; she avoided them.

"Well, then, may I escort you inside? You will find this small church most interesting, I think. It is very old and probably was erected on the foundations of an even older Norse place of worship." Charles led the lady under an arch and through the rounded wooden Norman doorway. It was dark and cool inside the church. Motes of dust, caught in the still air, floated in the muted yellow light streaming through the leaded glass windows.

Peaceful, Sophia thought with surprise, *wondrously peaceful.* A very small church, indeed, smaller inside than it appeared from the outside. The stone walls were thick and solid. Sophia took off her gloves and placed the palm of her right hand on the near wall. Cool to the touch, but not clammy. The baptismal font was behind her, a curiously carved basin. It was partially filled with water.

"This appears extremely old," she commented, running her hand around the worn stone rim. She looked up at Charles for more information, strangely interested.

Charles nodded. "From the days of St. Mortrud, according to tradition."

"Who *was* this St. Mortrud? I confess, I have never heard of such a saint. Indeed, I have no idea if this personage was male or female."

"Male. St. Mortrud was an early convert to Christianity. He is thought to have been of Norse ancestry, and possibly the son of a Viking chieftain. He was martyred, killed by a band of marauders pillaging the area. His bones are said to be buried under this baptismal font."

Lady Sophia quickly pulled her hand off and stepped

back from the simple stone font. A shiver ran up her spine. Martyred saint's bones! Relics! This smacked of popery, of the worst practices of Rome.

The vicar noted her quick movements and attempted to reassure her. "My lady, there is no proof that bones are buried there. It is tradition, after all, not fact."

"Why do you not excavate under the font, then," she gestured, "to clear the matter up once and for all?"

Charles smiled, showing excellent white teeth. "These are matters of faith, my lady, and faith is not to be tampered with lightly. It does no harm to believe the mortal remains of a saint are buried here."

"It smacks of popery, Mr. Heywood. I am surprised you condone such superstition. Are you a latter-day Vicar of Bray, sir?"

Charles shook his head, not at all insulted by the lady's reference to the infamous vicar who changed his religious beliefs to suit the times. "The baron, hardly a papist, would never dream of such an act. And in this, I believe he was right." He hesitated. "On other matters, however, I disagreed with him." There, he had created an opening.

Lady Sophia's eyes widened. "What matters were those, Mr. Heywood?"

Charles's voice was firm. "I believe we should establish a suitable memorial for Baron Rowley, my lady, a memorial befitting his status and comparable to the memorials in this place of worship for other members of the Rowley family." He indicated with a sweep of his arm the various sarcophagi and wall monuments that crowded the humble interior of St. Mortrud's.

Sophia's eyes followed his gesture. She walked to the closest object, an intricately carved wall monument. "This is—" She peered at the stone carving.

49

"A memorial to the first baron, Roger, who fell in battle during the invasion of Normandy by King Henry I. His body was buried in France, but his heart was carried home. That, my lady, is called a heart monument. Roger Rowley's heart is contained therein."

Lady Sophia flinched, drawing back in alarm. *Bones! Hearts! Was this a charnel house or a church?* She shuddered delicately.

Charles ignored her reaction of disgust, pointing out the details of the small monument. "Note the intricacy of this carving, my lady, the multiple frames about the carved portrait of Roger Rowley, and the symbolism in each corner, the heraldic elements, the lions, the eagles . . ."

"I'm sure," Sophia muttered. She was vastly uninterested in heraldry!

"And here," Charles continued, pointing to the timber tomb of another baron, a sarcophagus with a recumbent figure clad in armor, his hands together on his chest, pointed upward in an attitude of prayer. "This is a common pose from the early fifteenth century, but entirely carved of wood. It is most unusual." His enthusiasm was clearly not shared by his audience of one, from the bored expression on the lady's face.

Somewhat desperately, Charles walked to a small stained glass window in the chancel, stepping into the area of modest pews set aside for the clergy and choir. "This was commissioned by Henry Rowley, about 1500. Note the imagery, with a portrait of Henry kneeling in prayer and this depiction of Death in the adjacent roundel, aiming an arrow at his breast."

Lady Sophia gulped at the distressing pieces of colored glass, badly mottled by age. Death, a skeleton, wore a malevolent expression on its skull face, clearly pleased at the shot he was taking. Already, she'd had more than enough of these disturbing *mementi mori* and was overcome by a desire for fresh air. The atmosphere had become cloying and unpleasant. "Yes, yes, Mr. Heywood, I am sure this is all very historic, very meaningful, but—"

"My lady, I beg your pardon! I was simply attempting to show you the Rowley legacy inside this modest church. I had hoped that Baron Rowley would consider a suitable memorial to his life. For this," he indicated all the other memorials, "this is a testament to the good lives and brave deeds of his family. This is something for the boys to be proud of; this is their heritage."

Sophia was becoming exasperated. "George was an exceeding modest man, sir, as you well know. I could not imagine him giving much thought—especially as he lay ailing—to a memorial in this church. His primary concerns, I am sure, lay elsewhere."

"Indeed, they did," Charles agreed. "His primary concerns were for his sons, my lady, for their welfare and for yours. I pressed him on this issue, but to no avail; he was unwilling to deal with it. But I petition you, my lady, to agree with me on this. George Rowley deserves a material testament to his life and goodness in St. Mortrud's. It is fitting." He added, "And the people here would expect it."

"Are we to pander to the people of Rowley Village, then?" Lady Sophia's tone was scathing. What she felt about the people of Rowley Village was patently apparent.

"Not pandering, my lady, not at all, but an acknowledgement of how important the baron was to their lives, as well as to his immediate family. John and William need a visual memorial, something tangible, in a continuous line from Roger Rowley to their own time." He pointed to the heart monument and to the imposing timber casket. "It is their heritage."

Sophia was unmoved. "I don't know, Mr. Heywood, if

George did not think it necessary . . ."

"He evidently thought it necessary to inscribe that poem to Lady Lucy some years after her death. He wanted her remembered, my lady. Why any less remembrance for him?"

"You are persistent, sir, I must say." Lady Sophia regarded the vicar with a mixture of amusement and admiration. He was a passionate man, there was no doubt about it, and single-minded, as well.

"I beg you to think upon this, my lady. A simple wall monument; marble, perhaps, nothing ornate, for that would not suit the man he was. Please, do consider this." There, he had stated his case for the memorial. Now it was her decision. If she chose to ignore him, a monument to George would not join the solid testaments ringing the walls of St. Mortrud's, memorializing his valiant ancestors, that long line of Rowleys and the family history. It would be a shame.

"My lady, though your husband never fought in battle for his kings, nor ventured far from his manor, he was no less valiant than these others. He was a kind and generous landlord, a good friend, an excellent husband and father. Surely, attention should be paid to such a man?" Charles pressed his suit with the baron's widow as he had pressed it with the late baron.

"Sir, you thought a great deal of my husband. Your concern is impressive," Sophia commented, moved by his speech.

"I have rarely known his like," Charles replied quietly. "Attention should be paid, my lady. It is simply his due. And . . . and it would mean so much to the boys."

His trump card, the boys. Charles hated to use it, but . . .

Lady Sophia shut her eyes. There it was, that unfamiliar prickling at the back of her eyeballs again. No, not tears!

She never, ever cried. It would not happen now. The vicar's comments were loving and true; George deserved to be remembered. The boys would expect her to show that she cared. And she did care. *She did!* She felt great sorrow, now, more sorrow every day, for that man's death. He had been kind and generous to her. He had removed the greatest threat to her life, her father.

Because of George Rowley, she'd had no more to fear from Thomas Eliot, the despicable Earl of Dunhaven, scourge of her young life. She owed George a great deal. The least she could do was acquiesce to the vicar's request.

Sophia raised her eyes. "You are right, sir. Please proceed with your plans for the memorial. I hope—" she fixed him with a look that could not be gainsaid—"I hope you will keep me informed as to the design of this monument? Perhaps we can collaborate on its construction? I may have some ideas to add."

Charles raised a prayer of thanks heavenwards. *Thank you, God!* Perhaps, in that ethereal sphere, the baron was displeased with him, but this was the right step to take. Charles was sure of it. The memorial that George had refused to consider would be erected after all.

The Earl of Dunhaven was weary. The channel crossing had been turbulent as usual, and the coach from Dover illsprung. His bones ached; he was not getting any younger. That fact galled him. How many years remained to him? He was determined to make the most of them and access to his late son-in-law's wealth would guarantee an extremely comfortable old age.

That witling Brent had suggested they stay at Limmer's Hotel, favored by the sporting crowd. A bad choice! Crowded and dirty, it did not meet the earl's high standards. Only the excellent gin punch raised it to halfway tolerable. They would have to look for other lodgings. Brent's father, a stiff-rumped marquess, had declared that his prodigal son and his friend were not welcome at his Mayfair townhouse. Bad luck; they must consult the newspapers or obtain a reference from someone at Limmer's. They would run out of blunt too fast staying at hotels.

Or, they could hie themselves to Yorkshire. Why not avail themselves of Sophia's hospitality? The use of a bed, nourishment for his belly . . . was that so much to ask? Surely the chit owed him that much—he was her father!

And he was eager to introduce her to his new companion. Brent was easy to manipulate; Dunhaven had no doubt the fellow could be coerced into considering marriage to Sophia. The way Brent was piling up gambling debts, he needed a rich wife, and a husband controlled his wife's fortune. When Sophia's wealth passed directly into Brent's hands, it would be the shortest of trips into the earl's own pockets.

Lewis Alcott leaned back at the vicar's bountiful Sunday afternoon table, stretching his burly arms wide. The vicar's capable housekeeper, Mrs. Chipcheese, saw to it that Charles and his guests ate heartily. The remains of a roast capon shared the table's honors with a half-empty plate of grilled trout, mashed potatoes, a salad of young greens with juicy tomatoes, and a rhubarb pie. Lewis scooped some clotted cream from a blue and white striped pottery bowl to garnish a hearty slice of that pie. Fresh-poured coffee was at his elbow.

It had been a long week, punctuated with lancing Farmer White's boils and seeing the Willett children through a frightening bout of the croup. It had ended with a frantic call from Mrs. Watkins, the midwife, when the Abbott baby, a breech birth, had showed signs of distress shortly after delivery. Thank God all his patients had improved. Lewis had faith in his medical skills, but he also believed in divine intercession.

"Sometimes I envy the quiet, the calm, of your calling, Charles, after such a week as I have had," he remarked. "But then, when I think of your volatile relationship with the beauteous widow at Rowley Hall, I welcome all the putrid fevers and abscessed wounds that come my way." He flicked a crumb of bread in his friend's direction.

"No playing with your food, Lewis! I am surprised your good mother did not teach you better." Charles refused to be baited. He was determined to ignore the doctor's customary teasing. The sermon had been well received that morning. It was one he'd delivered before, but the congregation seemed to enjoy it as much as they had previously. Charles eschewed hellfire-and-damnation lectures, preferring to dwell on goodness and charity and the positive aspects of life. His parishioners left feeling happier than when they arrived, and that always brought them back the next Sunday.

"Ah, that brings up another issue." Lewis would not be quelled; his exuberant nature was too much a part of his personality.

"And that issue is—?" Charles asked.

"Motherhood. Maternal feelings and the instincts thereof. Are you collaborating with Lady Sophia to revive those long-dormant emotions?" Lewis's lips quirked with amusement.

Charles shook his head. "You misjudge that lady, Lewis. You misjudge her badly."

"Oh?" Lewis leaned forward, elbows on the table, all ears.

"She and I have been collaborating to plan the boys' activities this summer. She has been eager to participate and is looking forward to seeing them again."

"No doubt," Lewis commented wryly. "And how does she propose to explain the reason she has been absent from their lives most of this past decade?"

Charles grew sober. "I don't know, Lewis. Frankly—" He sighed. "I would not want to be in her shoes concerning that particular issue. I believe she harbors a great deal of guilt over her abandonment of them. The baron, however, always told John and William that she loved them with all her heart."

Lewis shook his head. "Those little fellows probably never entered her mind, much less her heart, poor boys. Your favorite poet, Mr. Wordsworth, will not write poems extolling Lady Sophia Rowley's maternal nature." He raised his thick, sandy brown eyebrows and wiggled them at Charles, changing the somber subject of a mother's neglect of her children, to a teasing topic closer to his mischievous heart. "So, you would not want to be in that lady's shoes . . . but is there anything else you would want to b—"

Charles stayed him with a look that belied his otherwise benign countenance. "Don't, Lewis! Avoid finishing that sentence if you desire to remain my friend! I warn you, man."

Lewis leaned back again, feigning surprise. "Well, well, well." He chuckled. "I fear that something deep is going on. Rallying to defend the lady's good name, refusing to indulge in a little harmless funning . . . Have you lost your heart to that wicked widow, my dear friend?"

Charles rose from the table and walked to the window that looked out over the graveyard. It was green and quiet. Nothing stirred. "Not wicked, Lewis. That woman, I think,

has been more sinned against than sinning. The baron—"
Charles paused. He could not discuss the confidences
George Rowley had shared with him regarding Sophia.

George had employed a Bow Street Runner to investigate the Eliot family, particularly the earl, Sophia's father.
Sophia had been the victim of her profligate sire for years,
and her first husband had been worse than the refuse running through the middle of a London street. His name was
Rushton, and he had been wealthy and titled, but scum
through and through. Barely sixteen, she'd been sold into
marriage by the Earl of Dunhaven, who'd met his future
son-in-law at a particularly unsavory Covent Garden
brothel, a house that specialized in providing the most depraved pleasures for jaded gentlemen.

The lady had suffered a great deal. If it was difficult for
her to be a loving mother, the reasons were not so arcane.
George hoped that Charles could help Sophia become the
person she might have been were she not handed over to a
brutal husband at such a tender age. George had understood his wife and had felt her pain. He'd asked Charles to
be patient with her, to understand her anger and her selfish-
ness, to aid her in regaining her true path before it was too
late. George thought that Sophia's was a soul worth saving,
and he hoped that after he passed on, his friend the vicar
would try to save his wife's soul. He had urged Charles to
do his best.

But this was not information Charles Heywood would,
or could, share with his best friend, Lewis Alcott. Indeed,
he could never share what he knew about her with the lady
herself.

Not in entire forgetfulness
And not in utter nakedness,
But trailing clouds of glory do we come
From God, who is our home:
Heaven lies about us in our infancy!
*   —William Wordsworth,*
*   "Ode: Intimations of Immortality from*
*   Recollections of Early Childhood," 1804*

CHAPTER SIX

John, the new young Baron Rowley, stepped out of the handsomely appointed carriage emblazoned with the family seal and hesitated. Behind him, his younger brother, the Honourable William Rowley, bumped into his shoulder. "Ouch!" William piped up, "do get on, John!" Horatio, the strapping young footman who'd accompanied them on the journey from Eton, stepped back hurriedly to keep from tripping over John like a third domino.

John turned to his younger brother, mischief gleaming in his eyes. "That is *Baron* Rowley to you, peasant!" he joked, cuffing his sibling good-naturedly in the chest.

William snorted, muttering, "Witling!" under his breath.

A scuffle between the two brothers was averted by the young man who greeted them at the imposing stone steps marking the entrance to Rowley Hall.

"Mr. Heywood!" Both boys ran to their tutor, laughing with pleasure. A familiar face! One beloved face, they knew, was gone forever, and an unfamiliar one was about to make its appearance after a long, long absence, but this was a face they knew and loved. More than a tutor, more than the village parson, Charles was like a young uncle to them.

Charles Heywood accepted the exuberant welcome of his two charges. They threw themselves at him with abandon, John jumping up on him and throwing both arms around his neck, putting the vicar's immaculate neckcloth into immediate disarray. William took hold of his legs and bounced up and down, greatly endangering Charles's stability. The long carriage ride over, they released their pent-up energy with all the enthusiasm of youth. Their school uniforms, already rumpled from the long journey, rumpled further.

Unable to stay on his feet, within seconds Charles was on his back and rolling over the gravel path with the Rowley heirs. Great whoops of laughter could be heard, even into the hallway, where Lady Sophia stood with the butler.

"Bentley, what on earth is going on out there?" Lady Sophia's creamy white brow furrowed in consternation.

Bromley winced. He had more names than a Hindoo god had arms! "The young gentlemen, my lady, have arrived. Mr. Heywood is greeting them."

"Greeting them? Wrestling with them, more like!" Lady Sophia strode forward. She was in a nervous state—indeed, she had not slept most of the previous night—and strove mightily to keep her nerves in check. But long years of practice in dissembling and hiding her innermost feelings stood her in good stead.

"Mr. Heywood!" She called out, standing straight and arrogant in the shadow of the massive oak doorway, a vision in pale lavender sarscenet. Her raised brows seemed to question the rowdy outdoor scene.

"Oops, boys, the game is up! Stand to attention, now, and greet your mother." Charles smoothed down his clothes, but his neckcloth was beyond smoothing. He flushed with embarrassment.

John brushed pieces of sand and gravel from his brother's hair, pulled down his own coat and swept a hand over his knees. They were a sight . . . all three of them. A lump rose in Sophia's throat. She checked her admonishing words as something melted inside her. *Her boys!* These two handsome lads . . . *Hers!* That odd prickling at the back of her eyeballs threatened to erupt in tears. Sophia cleared her throat, trying to ignore the burst of emotion. The boys would not want to see a mother with red, puffy eyes. Oh, but look at them! She viewed them with wonder.

These lovely children had come from her very own body. She unconsciously passed her hands over her flat stomach, twice so full of new life. She had given birth to these boys, labored hard to bring them into this world. How triumphant she had felt then, how thrilled, despite the wrenching pain. For the first time in her young womanhood, she'd had a sense of great accomplishment. The taller had to be John, the new Baron Rowley, and the shorter, William. They were not simply handsome; they were beautiful.

Except for the difference in their heights, John and William could have been twins, so much alike were they. Both were extremely fair-haired; that pale blond shade was an Eliot family trait. She and her young-looking father had often been taken for siblings, with their hair and the unusual blue of their eyes. She winced inwardly as she was prone to do when her father came to mind, praying that the earl's grandchildren were similar to him only in looks.

Dismissing thoughts of her unspeakable sire, Sophia descended the stone steps, one hand on the decorative wrought-iron railing that curved down to the gravel path. She smiled in welcome, though her stomach was knotting and her heart pumping so madly she thought it would jump out of her chest. Could they see how nervous she was, she wondered? Did they note the wild jumping of her heart?

Charles released the breath he had been holding. He had not realized Sophia was close enough to witness the boys' exuberant response when he'd greeted them. He had always encouraged physical contact; they had few friends in the area and their father was too old for boys' play. It had been part of Charles's relationship with them, but, of course, Lady Sophia knew nothing of that. To her, it had probably seemed an inordinately rowdy display.

But she was smiling. What a brilliant smile! No arrogance there, just . . . love. Yes, love, that's what love looked like, Charles knew. And now she held out her arms to her sons. At first, the boys did not seem to know how to proceed. John flashed a quick, sidelong glance at Charles, as if to say, *What now?* Then William ran into his mother's embrace and John followed his lead.

How natural the trio seemed! Charles was pleased, gratified that the baroness was touching her children, embracing them, fussing over them as much as any natural mother. Charles chided himself quickly: she *was* their natural mother. What she was not, was a mother who had ever, to his knowledge, previously concerned herself overmuch with her children.

The vicar was acquainted with a number of mothers in his pastoral visits, and he also remembered the women in his family's circle. Maternal instincts were strong and true, but not all women, he knew, had them. He would have easily put Lady Rowley in the latter class, but for the way she was hugging the boys now, holding them close and exclaiming over their growth, her brilliant eyes shining with love. Maternal instincts . . . he would never have believed it. There might be hope for George's widow yet.

John nuzzled in his mother's arms. The new Baron Rowley was an infant again, breathing her familiar smell, a sweet, sharp fragrance that he had never forgotten. *Mama.* She was here. Finally, she was here, and he was in her arms. He sighed happily. All would be well again. He missed his father terribly, but now his mama had come. He had wondered where she was, all those years, but Papa had said she would return as soon as she could, and he had told him the truth.

She was warm and soft, and beautiful, too. Papa had often reminded him that she looked just like her portrait, but John knew that people sometimes did not look at all like their pictures. His best friend's father had far less hair, a longer nose, and eyes placed nearer each other than they appeared in the miniature Hannibal kept in his desk at school. John had barely recognized Lord Stover from that likeness when he'd visited the school one day. But Mama, if anything, was lovelier than the oil painting over the mantelpiece in the drawing room. She was the loveliest person he had ever seen. She was his mother!

William Rowley, embracing both his older brother and the mother he barely knew, rejoiced in the feel of her warm, sweetly scented body. She felt better than he had imagined. Better, even, than Rudy, the Irish wolfhound pup that his father had given him when he was five years old. Rudy had not lived long. William looked up at his mother and hoped she would live a lot longer than Rudy or his father had lived.

He had been inconsolable when his papa had died. If not for Mr. Heywood, he would still be sad, but Mr. Heywood had told him that Papa was looking down on them from Heaven, and that William must not be sad or his Papa would be sad, too. He caught Sophia's eye. She smiled, bent down, and kissed his brow. His heart swelled in his chest and began to beat very fast.

He hugged her tighter, the silky soft fabric of her dress crushing against his cheek. He would not let her go away, not ever again. He and John and Mr. Heywood would do their best to keep her with them forever. He would be very, very good, so good that no one would ever leave him again.

Sophia felt the beating of her sons' hearts against her abdomen and remembered holding them when they were babes. Their little chests had heaved so when she'd embraced them. She had hated handing them over to their nursemaids. Many times, she'd fallen asleep with one of them in her arms. She could not bear letting them out of her sight in those early days of motherhood. More and more memories of those three years at Rowley Hall were coming back to her. Smells, tactile sensations, emotions. . . .

Why had she ever left them? What madness, what stupidity, had sent her away? This was joy. Why had she abandoned joy for the shallow pretext of her life in London? Sophia had chosen not to dwell on past mistakes, but now she was drenched in regret. It overwhelmed her even as the last remaining fingers of ice that had encased her heart tightly in its frosty grip melted away. She held her sons closer and reveled in their tight, warm, loving embrace, warmth that had set her free.

I will never leave you again, so help me, God, she promised them silently as she bent to kiss their fair heads. Later, she would make them acquainted with Harriett, the always smiling, pleasant young girl she'd engaged to look after them when they were not with Mr. Heywood.

Charles had barely worked out the sum on the blackboard before William called out the answer. The boy's mathematical gift had grown by massive increments over the last few months. The vicar constantly endeavored to be inventive in the problems he presented to William, but no sums he could set seemed a challenge.

"All right, you genius, answer this one, if you dare: from Land's End Cornwall to Farret's Head in Scotland is measured to be 838 miles. Now, and take your time to work this out, at the rate of eight feet a day, how long would it take a snail—a mere snail, mind you—to creep that long distance?"

"Sir, that is not a probable distance for a snail to cover in a day," the literal-minded John objected.

"This is solely for the purposes of the problem," Charles assured him. "We both know that it is im—"

"Five hundred fifty-three thousand and eighty days, sir!" William interrupted them.

Charles and John looked at each other. John started scribbling the numbers on the board and working out the multiplication. Five hundred fifty-three thousand and eighty days. Yes, that was correct.

"How does he do it, sir?" John threw up his hands in exasperation.

"We shall stump him yet, John," the vicar remarked with conviction.

William smirked, crossing his bony arms over his narrow chest.

"All right, sirrah, now pay attention. If a coach wheel is five feet ten inches in circumference, how many times would it revolve in running eight hundred million miles?"

William frowned. In less than a minute, he had scrawled the answer to the problem—which involved changing miles to feet before dividing the numbers—on the blackboard.

"Sir, that is seven hundred twenty-four billion, one hundred fourteen million, two hundred twenty-five thousand, seven hundred and four times, with twenty inches left over."

John, who had barely begun to work out the first part of the problem, threw the piece of chalk he was using to figure the sum up in the air. "Arrrgggh! How does the little beast do it?"

"Wait, John, let me see if he has it worked out properly." Tongue between his teeth, concentrating hard, Charles began the task of working out the long division.

Several minutes later, he had confirmed the ten-year-old's conclusion: "He is correct, it is seven hundred twenty-four billion, one hundred fourteen million, two hundred twenty-five thousand, seven hundred and four, with twenty inches remaining." He, too, threw both the chalk and his hands up, despairing of ever stumping the wondrous boy, this mathematical marvel.

Young William had a remarkable gift; Charles had never seen its like. What the second son of a baron could do with such a gift, however, was food for speculation. At the very least, it was an excellent after-dinner amusement. Wagering on how long it took the lad to come up with an answer would tickle the fancy of the gamesters at the London clubs, Charles had no doubt. As to the future, Cambridge University was noted for excellence in science and mathematics. The great Newton, inventor of the calculus, had been Lucasian professor of mathematics there. And, Charles chuckled gleefully, he could not wait to show Lady Sophia her younger son's gift. She would be amazed!

"Well, he may be able to work impossible sums in his head, this awesome mental calculator," John cuffed his younger brother on the shoulder, and William pretended to be felled by the light blow, "but he can barely spell his own name!"

William flushed. It wasn't true! He could so spell his own name, but other words, as a rule, were not so easy to spell.

"Ah, William, consistency in spelling is for small minds like mine. Your brother is only jesting." Charles knew too many adults whose orthographic skills were at a level not much higher than young William's, if the truth were told, and society cared not a whit. Dr. Johnson's dictionary was over fifty years old and had caused a small revolution in setting down authoritative spellings and spelling rules, but amongst the *ton*, no one paid much attention to such strictures.

"Now, boys, pay attention to me. I am going to read from *The Iliad* today, and we shall translate from the Greek together." Charles's sonorous voice fell into the old Homeric rhythms as he began the tragic tale of the valiant soldier Achilles, the bickerings and whims of the ancient gods (to whom mortals were mere playthings), and the horrors of war. The boys listened in awe, concentrating on the poetic structure, frowning at the pronunciation.

John and William were both aware that proficiency in Greek and Latin was essential in order to pass the entrance examinations of the universities. This was their summer holiday, but Mr. Heywood's tutoring would give them an advantage when the time came to stand for those examinations. Their father had been determined that they attend university, as he had done, and they were determined that their father would be proud of them. They knew that he watched over them from Heaven. Mama and Mr. Heywood had told them so.

William had just performed three mathematical feats involving enormous sums to Sophia's delight. Charles had set him the problems and he had calculated them in his head for less than a minute each. It had taken both Charles and Sophia considerably longer to work them out on paper, Charles noting with interest that Sophia was a faster calculator than he was.

Then John recited his own translation of a passage from *The Iliad*, after first repeating the ancient Greek from memory. The boy had a prodigious memory, and his Greek was improving daily. Sophia's eyes sparkled with maternal pride as the boy recited, acting out the stirring excerpt from the poem. Charles thought she was mouthing the Greek with him and wondered how that could be. Lady Sophia, versed in Homeric Greek? Nay, he must have been mistaken. When would that lady have learned Greek? Ladies learned needlework, how to ride, and dabbled in watercolors; that was the whole of his sisters' education.

Sophia beamed at her boys, her breast swelling with pride. Charles, watching the lady closely, could not help noting it.

She stood and clapped her hands enthusiastically. "Bravo, bravo!" She turned to the vicar, her body swaying seductively toward him. "You have done very well, Mr. Heywood. I am in your debt." Her blue eyes were warm and promised untold payment. Charles caught his breath.

After the boys had gone to bed, Charles and Lady Sophia enjoyed an after-dinner brandy in the drawing room. The cellars at Rowley Hall were excellent; the baron had been a connoisseur of fine wines and spirits. Sophia's eyes glowed warmly as she toasted the vicar.

"To your health, sir." She raised her glass.

"And yours." Charles returned the compliment, smiling.

Sophia sipped the brandy, contemplating the man before

her through the thick mesh of her long eyelashes. She felt a stirring inside that had nothing to do with the infusion of liquor through her system.

Charles caught her appraising look. He took a hurried sip of the brandy and placed his glass upon the side table. That scene in this same drawing room a few short weeks ago returned in all its glory. Lady Sophia's full, creamy white bosom flashed before his eyes. If he tarried any longer, he would disgrace himself with his surging lust. He must leave.

Sophia took note of his sudden nervousness and smiled; she knew how to relax high-strung young men. Putting an arm on his sleeve, she purred like a sleek, satisfied cat. "Mr. Heywood," she whispered, "have you seen the Hall's gardens by moonlight?"

Rowley Hall was famous for its rose gardens. An Elizabethan ancestress, Blanche Snow, had been responsible for creating the fragrant blooms. Indeed, a particularly fragrant white rose, the *Blanca Gloriosa,* had been named for her. That rose was planted all along the far wall of the garden, and it perfumed the soft, warm night air with its presence. Lady Sophia's signature fragrance, almond blossoms, wove in and out of the underlying leitmotif of roses. Charles was intoxicated by the sweet competing odors.

Lady Sophia walked slowly, skirt swaying, to a stone bench set in an ivy-trellised alcove. Her gown was cut low in the back, displaying her white shoulders and long neck. Charles's eyes were fixed at a point between her shoulder blades. As she stopped short, he bumped into her back. "Beg pardon, my lady," he murmured.

"My fault entirely, sir. I stopped suddenly." She turned to face him, her movements sleek and sinuous. Charles's heart lurched in his chest. She looked up at him, the motion feline but unmistakably female, as well. If he had been sitting down, he was sure she would have jumped in his lap for a cuddle, like a favorite kitten. He backed away a step. She walked toward him, closing the gap.

His collar was inordinately tight and he felt drops of perspiration forming at his temples. Lady Sophia took her thumb and ran it over his lower lip, slowly, teasingly. She suddenly pressed down hard and giggled when he jumped. He gulped.

"My, what a soft mouth you have, Mr. Heywood," she cooed.

Charles was mesmerized. Sophia stood on tiptoes and slanted her mouth over his. The pressure of her warm lips forced his to open slightly. Slowly, excruciatingly, the pointed tip of her sweet tongue insinuated itself into his mouth. His arms wrapped around her curvaceous, yielding form and she sighed as his tongue met hers and began to explore her soft, warm mouth.

His hand cradled the back of her head, his fingers kneading the smooth strands of hair, loosening them from the bun at the back of her neck. He caressed the warm nape of her neck, the satiny soft skin between her shoulder blades, and moved on to her ear, fingering a dangling earbob and pulling on it playfully. She moved sensuously against him, backing him against the wooden trellis. Her hands began to explore his chest, his hipbones, his . . .

Charles broke the deep kiss, reaching down to take Sophia's wandering hands. "My lady, I don't think—" He attempted to stay her.

Sophia looked up at him, the moonlight playing over her flushed face, illuminating the loosened strands of pale blond hair on either side of her face. Her lips were swollen, he saw, swollen with the force and passion of his kiss. "Why think at all, Charles?" Sophia asked. Her breath was warm and sweet on his face.

Charles swallowed. Why, indeed, he thought? But he knew why all too very well. "Because, my lady, it behooves us, as sentient human beings, to think, to consider the consequences of our actions."

"I would rather feel than think right now, Charles, I would rather be swept away by what we both are feeling at this moment. I don't—" She shook her head vigorously and more pale yellow strands escaped from the bun at the nape of her neck. She took a short breath. "I do not want either of us to think overmuch."

Charles closed his eyes and prayed for guidance. He still clutched Sophia's soft hands tightly in his. "My lady," he began, "I fear that both of us drank, perhaps, a bit more of your late husband's fine brandy than we should have had. That bit of spirits and the moonlight are not a good combination." He took a deep breath and continued. "I am going to bid you good night now and make my way to the stables, where I will mount my horse and take myself home." He prepared to flee.

Lady Sophia wanted to tell him that she would rather he mounted her than his horse but she refrained from expressing herself so crudely. Two weeks ago she would probably have blurted it out, but she had begun to regain control of her turbulent emotions and disavow coarse language. Two weeks ago, she would probably have boxed his ears, also, but though he deserved a rebuke for this summary dismissal, she would not lose her temper, much as she was tempted.

Charles was thwarting her, nay, rejecting her, and it was painful.

She extricated her hands from his. Though she would not express what she really felt, a demon inside her could not resist a parting salvo. The vicar exasperated and frustrated her; she wanted him. His kiss had awakened desire and more, much more. And she knew he wanted her. How could she not be aware of that?

"Are you a man, Charles Heywood, or a eunuch?" she challenged him boldly, the gauntlet thrown.

Charles flushed. He wanted to defend his raging masculinity, something she would have discovered for herself if her forward explorations of his person had taken her any farther and passed over his trouser flap. Yes, he was a man, a man who responded physically to her touch, to her overwhelmingly desirable presence. She was the epitome of desirable femininity. It was amazing he had even an iota of control left right now.

"I am no eunuch, my lady," he replied, the muscles in his face stiff. "But this is not proper, and you know it. Your children are in the house, your servants are aware that we are out here—"

Lady Sophia Rowley swept him a contemptuous gaze, dismissing him on the spot. "You lobcock," she spat, "you fool."

Swatting him on the shoulder, she strode angrily toward the house. Charles thought her departing back was the most beautiful sight he had ever seen. Her square shoulders, her long legs . . . the feel of her silken skin had been exquisite. He sighed. He *was* a fool, a pious idiot. He had insulted her, making himself out to be her moral superior. He was simply more aware than she of the impropriety of the situation, not only for himself, but for her. It was not a time to give in to their baser instincts.

Though Lady Sophia was an honest woman, she was behaving improperly. What was right for the *beau monde* was not necessarily right for others. If he were more forthright, he would have told her exactly how he felt and why he could not so casually bed her. But he would rather that she saw for herself why it was not proper, why what was *de rigueur* in looser London society was not acceptable here at her late husband's home.

He wanted her, yes, that was the truth of it, for he was a man infatuated with this lady, but he could not take her so casually. Perhaps more than halfway in love with her and in danger of falling further under her spell as he saw her on a daily basis and began to admire her spirit, he still had to reject her advances. She was a remarkable woman, and he no doubt seemed a hypocrite and a fool to her.

Charles could not blame her. Perhaps he *was* a fool and lobcock, as she'd stated he was, but he could not so easily throw over his moral precepts, not even for such a tempting goddess as Sophia Rowley.

How his friend Lewis would laugh at his dilemma!

Men are much more unwilling to have their weaknesses and their imperfections known, than their crimes . . .
—*Lord Chesterfield, Letters to His Son, 1774*

CHAPTER SEVEN

The Earl of Dunhaven stared at the portrait of his daughter Sophia. He and his companion, Lord Brent, had been ushered into the drawing room by the butler who'd poured them drinks per Lady Sophia's instruction. Sophia surveyed her father coldly, as if she wished him at Jericho, her eyes shards of blue ice.

A soft chuckle escaped Dunhaven's lips. It turned into a low laugh, then a deeper one. Finally, he could restrain his guffaws no longer. He threw back his head and laughed so loudly that tears formed in his eyes.

"This . . . is . . . priceless," he exclaimed, barely able to utter the words. "Was this Romney a fool or a prankster, my dear?" He turned to his stiff-backed daughter, standing silent by the side of the mantel. "You, of all women! The virginal huntress! Oh, this is a rare one!"

He took a gulp of his wine. "You, London's foremost Lady Lightskirt, the goddess Diana!"

Eliot's companion, Lord Brent, looked astounded. The coarseness! This was the man's daughter, his flesh and blood. He felt disgusted.

Lady Sophia turned to the open-mouthed butler, noting with no pleasure the breach of his famous iron composure.

"Bromley," she said, for the first time addressing her retainer by his proper name, "please see that these gentlemen are served their dinner. I will take mine in my room."

As she turned to leave, her sire's raw laughter still ricocheting off the papered walls, she whirled suddenly and flung the contents of her sherry glass into Dunhaven's face, freezing the last raucous bray in his throat.

Lord Brent could not believe what had just occurred. He turned to the white-faced butler who seemed ready to faint. Brent put out a hand but the servant had recovered his composure. Lady Sophia, her blond head held high, exited without a backward glance. The drawing room doors yawned behind her as if open-mouthed in wonder.

Sophia rose an hour after dawn the next morning, much to the consternation of her abigail Joan, who noted unhappily that her mistress was rising earlier and earlier these country days. She donned a new riding habit of royal blue and strode briskly to the stables, there to rouse the stable lads and mount her spirited black mare, Jezebel. She rode at a gallop, breaking stride when she came to the upper meadow. There she stopped, surveying the rolling landscape with a brooding look, lost in grim, dark thoughts. Her life was falling apart.

The sudden appearance of her father at Rowley Hall was the final straw in a week that had included Charles Heywood's rebuff in the garden. She had fooled herself into thinking she could easily seduce him. She was losing her powers of attraction. First Isaac, now Charles. No one desired her. No one loved her. She should simply end it all and cease suffering. Who would care if she did away with herself? Her life was pointless.

Hoofbeats alerted her to a horseman drawing near. Lord

Brent, her father's friend, was behind her.

"Lady Rowley," he called, a bit out of breath.

She turned her steed. The atmosphere surrounding her person seemed to drop several degrees, so cold and wintry was the stare she fixed on him.

"My lady, excuse me for intruding on your morning ride. I beg your pardon, but I . . . I wanted to say that I am very sorry for what transpired last night." He fixed a sincere expression on his face, his brown eyes conveying concern. "I have long desired to make your acquaintance, my lady, but in better circumstances than—"

Sophia interrupted his pretty speech; her cutting laugh contained no mirth. "No one knows me, Lord Brent," she replied, her lips compressed. "No one."

She spurred her mare and galloped away, leaving her pursuer in a spray of dust.

"Least of all do I know myself," she murmured, her grim fancy a dark and monstrous creature sitting squarely on her shoulders. Reining in her thoughts and her horse sharply, she narrowly missed a fallen bough in her path. Jezebel did not deserve a broken leg because of her bout of the dismals, Sophia thought, struggling to calm her roiling emotions. She was feeling sorry for herself again and she despised weakness, in herself more than in others.

Soothing Jezebel, patting her smooth, warm black neck, Sophia sat tall in her saddle and cast aside the monster whispering in her ear. It fell to the earth with a loud splat as she laughed and continued her morning ride. It was a beautiful day.

Charles recognized the smug expression on Mrs. Chipcheese's narrow face as she served him breakfast. Obviously, she had news. News she was eager to impart to him. No matter that he had attempted to lecture her gently on the evils of gossip, rumor, and the spreading of unsubstantiated tales, she clucked her tongue and brandished it like a sharp, cutting saber, oblivious to his concerns. He sighed.

"Well, Vicar, some news from the Hall!" she flashed a gap-toothed grin at him.

"Do tell." She would, anyway.

Mrs. Chipcheese placed the sliced cottage loaf on the table alongside the dish of freshly churned sweet butter and the remaining crock of loganberry preserves she'd put up last summer. "Seems as the Widow had a surprise visitor last night. Two visitors, as a matter o' fact." His housekeeper always referred to Lady Rowley as the Widow, purposely disrespectful. Charles's efforts to stem this rude usage were to no effect either.

News indeed traveled fast from the Hall to the vicarage, he acknowledged. It was scarcely seven o'clock. Did the news arrive by sparrow express or on rabbit feet? He almost laughed, thinking of those diminutive creatures garbed as postboys, making their break-of-dawn rounds at Mrs. C.'s doorstep.

"Indeed, Mrs. Chipcheese?" Charles's lips quirked as he reached for the jug of fresh milk and added a good splash to his cup of strong black tea.

The housekeeper nodded her head vigorously, threatening to undo her tightly wound topknot of coarse gray hair. "The Widow's father and a male travelin' companion turned up, just like that," she snapped her fingers with a loud click, "without so much as a by-your-leave, the servants said. Unexpected. No message sent ahead."

"Now, how would they know that? Perhaps Lady Rowley was expecting them. The servants don't know every—" He paused as Mrs. Chipcheese raised her bushy eyebrows. What was he thinking? Of course the servants would know. Servants knew everything. They were the ones who prepared rooms and meals for guests. Visitors meant increased work. Of course, the vails they presented to the staff when they departed could be generous and were appreciated, but Charles rather doubted that the baroness's father was a generous tipper. From what George had told him, that gentleman's pockets were permanently to let.

Neither Lady Sophia nor her sons had mentioned an imminent visit from the Earl of Dunhaven. Charles recollected that Sophia had never spoken her father's name in his hearing; she'd said nothing about him.

And now he was here? Curious. Charles had promised to take the boys fishing today after their Greek lesson. He would soon find out was going on at the Hall. The boys were even bigger gossips than the staff. If he was not out of favor with Lady Sophia after what had occurred or, more truthfully, had not occurred in the garden the other night, he would be dining with the family tonight, as he did each time he visited the Hall to tutor the boys. He looked forward to those informal suppers, just the four of them. Would Sophia's two guests also be at table?

But Mrs. Chipcheese wasn't through with her story. "And Mary Mathew says the Widow's not at all pleased. Tried to send them to Roslyn town, to the Cock and Bull, instead of puttin' them up at the Hall."

Despite himself, Charles asked, "And they refused to go?" This *was* news!

"Mrs. Mathew said they pleaded extreme fatigue from travelin' the past few days, and the Widow was forced to put them up, though she scowled somethin' fierce and Lizzie Turner swears she was tossin' furniture about in her dressin' room later that night! And the butler, Bromley, was out o' sorts, too. Yes, things was at sixes and sevens last night at the Hall! The Widow has a bad temper, she does."

To himself, Charles agreed that his housekeeper was correct in her estimate of the lady's temper. Sophia was indeed a temperamental woman, but since the boys had arrived, it seemed to Charles that she'd been working to gain control of her emotions. The surprise arrival of her father seemed to have shifted her equilibrium badly. It was plain she had not expected him and wanted him and his companion gone.

Charles had to face the fact that he might be another individual Lady Sophia did not want to have in her presence. He would not blame her. Well, it was time for him to mend fences, unless those were irrevocably destroyed. His shins ached with all the mental kicking he'd indulged in these last several days.

Robert Winton, Lord Brent, was beginning to regret returning to England. Even more, he regretted taking up with the Earl of Dunhaven. Tom Eliot was despicable. The man's former good looks were blotted with years of dissipation; he was no longer the fresh-faced, handsome Englishman he had once been. Brent could see the resemblance between him and his lovely daughter, but it was blurred. Dunhaven's dissolute life style had corrupted him in body and mind. The man's coarseness and his crude language were upsetting, suited to brothels, gaming hells, the lowest of venues, but not appropriate in his daughter's home. Brent felt compassion for the woman, a rare emotion for him; her face, when he'd caught up with her that early morning, was bereft.

Dunhaven greeted him in the breakfast room, grunting in approval at the repast set before him. The well-trained

Rowley servants had laid a feast on the grand Elizabethan oak sideboard in the morning room. Eggs, hard-boiled, scrambled, and coddled, deviled kidneys, ham, sausages, muffins and breads . . . there was enough to feed a slew of guests.

"Tom, we have to talk," Brent began, filling his plate with an assortment of foodstuffs. A footman came forward to pour coffee. "Leave us," he instructed the servant.

Dunhaven quirked an eyebrow at his companion. "Hmmn, this sounds serious, man. Dismissing the servants? Who cares what they overhear?" He heaped his plate.

"Evidently, you don't," Brent accused him, remembering the horrified reaction of the Rowley butler, "with your comments last night."

"Bloody hell, Brent! No one keeps me from speaking my mind, least of all the bloody servants!" He sat down heavily at the table. He looked around. "And who's going to pour my coffee, now that you've sent the footman away?"

"For God's sake, pour it yourself, man!" Exasperated at the man's sloth, Brent grabbed the coffeepot and performed the footman's duty. The liquid slopped over the edges of the delicate porcelain cup as he slammed the pot on the table.

"Have a care!" Dunhaven called out. "You'd make a terrible retainer, Brent. God help you if you ever have to work for a living." He laughed.

"What would you know of working for a living, Tom? You've lived off your daughter for years. You're more a pimp than a father."

Dunhaven's face turned an alarming shade of puce. "You go too far, sirrah," he warned, his voice full of menace.

"I could never go as far as you. You were lucky that all

Lady Sophia had in her hands last night was a sherry glass. If she'd had a pistol—"

"Ah, Sophia . . ." the earl chuckled, as if relishing the image of his daughter, Amazon-like, brandishing a weapon. He sipped his hot coffee. "She was never so high-spirited as a child. Used to worry me, it did. Such a bookish little thing she was, always reading. Her governess was teaching her Greek!" He snorted. "What nonsense was that, teaching Greek to a young girl? She was ruining the girl with that bluestocking faradiddle. I couldn't get rid of that hag soon enough, I tell you." The recollection made his eyes glitter.

Brent ignored Dunhaven's tirade. "I don't know how you have the gall to intrude into her life here, Tom. Nor could I understand, last night, how you continued to laugh with the sherry dripping down your neckcloth and coat. It was hardly a laughing matter!"

Dunhaven set his cup down so quickly that coffee splashed out, staining the white linen tablecloth in long brown streaks. "You have no right to meddle in family affairs, sirrah. My daughter is finally an Eliot, spirited, hot-tempered, her father's girl at last. I am proud of what she has become. Do you seriously think she does not want me here?"

"Yes, I do. I think she wants you at Jericho, Tom, the sooner, the better." Brent set aside his plate of food, rising from the table. "Unfortunately, I believe she would have me there also, to my regret."

"Sit down, man! Do not worry overmuch about Sophia's temper. I know her, believe me. She will come around. And when she does, she will see what a handsome young devil you are, what a fine figure of a man." Dunhaven's eyes narrowed. "You are just the kind of man my daughter has always favored. In fact, you remind me a great deal of her first husband, Rushton. A good fellow, he was, died too young. She'll favor you, soon enough! Trust me in this. Sophia is partial to handsome men."

Brent thought about his early morning ride, of his pursuit of Lady Sophia and her coldness toward him. It would take a large miracle for that lady to see him in a favorable light. Dunhaven was caperwitted—or did he really know his daughter better than it appeared? He had, after all, arranged three favorable marriages for her. Taking his seat again and picking up his fork, the younger man reconsidered. Perhaps he should not be so hasty in his judgment of the earl.

"Whatever you do, Tom," he said between mouthfuls of salty Yorkshire ham, "do try, I beg you, to be more diplomatic. The lady is in charge here, and you should respect her status as chatelaine of the manor."

Dunhaven was too busy shoveling eggs and sausages into his mouth to respond. Brent frowned and began to pick away at his breakfast. The food was excellent, but he seemed to have lost his usual hearty appetite.

*Take a Hundred of Asparagus, put the Greatest
part of them with two Lettuces into Three Quarts
of Water–Boil them till they are tender enough to
pulp thro' a Cullender, add the remainder of the
Asparagus, put some Cream and flour to make it
a Sufficient thickness, and add pepper and Salt,
to your taste – The Asparagus you put in last are
to Swim in the Soup.*

*—From a recipe book, Erddig, North Wales,
circa 1765*

(HAPTER EIGHT

Mrs. Mathew was in high alt, directing her kitchen staff
much as a well-organized general directs seasoned troops.
She was Hannibal crossing the Alps, Julius Caesar con-
quering the barbarians, Attila the Hun bringing Europe to
its knees. The mistress had left the dinner menu in her capable hands, as usual, and she was preparing asparagus
soup, trout in red wine, ragout of cucumber, rabbit fric-
assee, potato pudding, and chocolate cream for dessert. She
was displaying her skills for the Earl of Dunhaven, Lord
Brent, and, of course, the vicar. The young lads had already
been served their supper in the nursery.

The Hall's cook and the vicar's housekeeper were bosom
bows and also fierce competitors in the culinary arts. Mrs.
Chipcheese, alas, did not have the resources at the vicarage
that were available to Mrs. Mathew at Rowley Hall. It was a
point Mrs. C. invariably made when Mrs. Mathew boasted

of her elaborate dinners, which was often and at length.

Her broad face flushed with the kitchen's heat and her nervous concern that all must be perfect for Lady Sophia's guests, Mrs. Mathew clapped her pudgy hands, "Lizzie!" She called the maid of all help. "Inform Mr. Bromley that dinner is ready to be served."

As they stood in the drawing room waiting to dine, drinks in hand, Charles did not know what to make of the Earl of Dunhaven. He was a handsome man, with the striking coloring shared by Sophia and her children, the same pale blond hair, those unusual cerulean eyes. There was, however, something not right about him. Even if Charles had not known that the baron had sent a Bow Street Runner to investigate the earl, he would have felt similar twinges of unease. Charles trusted his instincts and his instincts told him that Sophia's father was not a good man. The Bow Street Runner's report had also made that clear.

Though Charles, armed with the knowledge of that report and what he saw with his own eyes, did not want to be uncharitable, Dunhaven was a man lacking nobility and without a modicum of aristocratic bearing. It distressed the vicar to come to such a quick, harsh opinion about another human being, but the man was coarse at the edges; his face bore the ravages of heavy drinking. Charles knew individuals who had succumbed to drink, and their faces were similar in appearance. There was a blurring of features, a looseness that betrayed their vice.

The earl possessed a drink-ravaged face. And something more, something worse. *By the prickling of my thumbs, something wicked this way comes,* Charles murmured to himself. The hairs on the back of his neck stood up; he tried to shake off the distressing feeling. It made him distinctly uncomfortable.

Charles turned his attention to Sophia, who was in good looks. She wore a silk frock in a dazzling shade of peach, a color that complemented her eyes and hair and creamy complexion. Her magnificent chest was set off by the low-cut, clinging design of the gown and an unusually intricate articulated necklace of cut steel. It was comprised of links of shiny, faceted cut metal, riveted onto a setting that supported a dozen larger steel drops.

The shimmering, glowing light from the many candles in the room reflected upon the necklace like many mirrors, mocking the brilliance of diamonds, and drew the eye to Sophia's lovely bosom. Charles unwillingly remembered her naked breasts, full and round, tipped with rosy—Heat flooded his torso and he wished that they could be alone in the drawing room. The space was too crowded, with the earl and his friend—especially the friend, Lord Brent.

Sipping the late baron's fine sherry and willing his treacherous body to cool down, Charles acknowledged that Brent was extremely handsome. He was the type of gentleman Sophia was no doubt used to, large, muscular, good looking and well-dressed. He wore his hair a trifle long, but it was thick and dark, and his brown eyes missed nothing. Right now, those smoldering dark eyes were fixed on Lady Sophia. Charles bristled with annoyance, his hand gripping the stem of the wineglass tightly.

The boys had told him when they were fishing in the brook earlier in the day, that Lord Brent had gone riding with them, and that he was a bruising rider. They admired his stallion, a large grey, and he had let them ride the horse. As they were mad about horses, Brent had swiftly ingratiated himself with them, Charles thought. Had he charmed their mother, as well?

★ ★ ★ ★ ★

"Cook told me that she is poaching the trout you and the boys caught today for our dinner, Mr. Heywood." Lady Sophia intruded into Charles's thoughts. He was quiet this evening, seeming uncomfortable with her father and his friend. Sophia granted that her father would make most decent people uncomfortable, but she wondered what it was about Lord Brent that made the vicar uneasy.

"We . . . uh . . . managed to land a few fat ones, my lady," Charles replied, stammering slightly. Sophia smiled. Although it had exasperated her at first, the vicar's hesitancy and occasional stutter were now endearing, part of his sweet and unique personality. She was cross about the way he had behaved in the rose garden, but that story was still to be continued. Her seduction had suffered a temporary setback only; she was not through with the handsome clergyman. She smiled at him, her eyes half-hooded, and delighted in the flush that covered his cheekbones.

"I vow," she said, her voice a bit husky, "that the boys enjoy Greek as much as they do fishing. John was repeating the speech by Achilles, his argument with King Agamemnon that he had recited for us several nights ago. He was asking if his pronunciation was correct. The piece concerning the slave girl, you remember?"

She spoke in flawless Greek. "How can the generous Argives give you prizes now? I know of no piles of treasure, piled, lying idle, anywhere. Whatever we dragged from towns we plundered, all's been portioned out. But collect it, call it back from the rank and file? That would be the disgrace. So, return the girl to the god, at least for now. We Achaeans will pay you back, three, four times over, if Zeus grants us the gift to raze Troy's massive ramparts to the ground!"

Charles was astonished. She did understand Greek! How on earth?

The earl broke into Charles's thoughts, his tone irritable. "God's blood, Sophia, do you still remember that nonsense from your governess? That bluestocking! Filling your mind with such faradiddle."

Brent interrupted his friend, ignoring the profanity at table. "My lady, you speak as well as my tutor at Jesus College," he remarked. "A Grecian could do no better, I vow."

Dunhaven snorted, then seemed to think better of the situation, stifling his comments into an incoherent mumble.

Charles leaped into the breach. "You shame me, my lady. My own efforts pale beside yours. I congratulate you." The lady never ceased to surprise him. She was so much more than she appeared to the world at large, the shallow world of the *beau monde*.

Lady Sophia peered into her wineglass as if calling up an old memory from its dark ruby depths. "I had a governess named Clarissa Bane, the daughter of a country vicar. Her father taught her Greek and she taught it to me." She raised her eyes. "She left when I was scarce sixteen, Mr. Heywood, and I have always regretted that loss."

Charles registered the pain and grief in Sophia's glance. He had a sharp desire to embrace her, notwithstanding the presence of her father and Brent, a feeling cut short by Bromley's announcement that dinner was served. Moving to offer her his arm, Charles found that Lord Brent was too fast for him. Instead, he found himself walking in to dinner with the earl, who seemed more than a little foxed from his pre-dinner imbibing of spirits.

Dunhaven, the vicar noted, had an odd look on his face. Was he annoyed, or was it something more? It was a furtive, guilty look. Did the man now think he'd been foolish to denigrate his daughter's education, seeing that Brent admired her facility with Greek? Charles suspected something else was afoot. Dunhaven's remark about the governess had been telling, but what exactly did it say? There was an inference there . . . perhaps his imagination was playing tricks on him, but he felt ill at ease.

The trout was served from two cunningly designed porcelain tureens, their covers realistically painted fish that appeared ready to leap off the table in a showy arc. The handles resembled twisted green seaweed resting on the long, fish-shaped bowls, which were in turn set on round platters decorated with painted scallop shells and sea grasses. Brent remarked on the fine pottery.

"It is from a dinner service commissioned by George's mother from the Derby pottery, my lord. She had an eye for lovely dinnerware; we have many examples of Bow, Derby, Chelsea, and Spode at Rowley Hall, enough to serve a houseful of guests."

"Your late husband was not much of a party-giver, if I recollect, Sophia," Dunhaven commented.

Sophia toyed with her fork. "No, that is true. George preferred a more solitary life."

"He was not an antisocial man," Charles hastened to defend his deceased patron. "But, as he aged, it was a strain on him to entertain large groups. He did have many visitors, nonetheless, who dropped in to inquire after his health and well-being."

"I gather you were rather thick with the old boy," Dunhaven remarked.

Charles recalled the last time he'd sat at dinner with the baron. It seemed so long ago, though it was only a few months. "We became friends, yes," he replied.

"I'm glad you were here for him, Mr. Heywood." Sophia's voice was barely above a whisper. She took a quick sip from her wineglass.

Her father frowned; talk of the late Baron Rowley was not his favorite subject of conversation.

The boys had told Charles, when they were fishing, that their mother and grandfather did not seem to be on the best of terms. They'd learned from a footmen that there had been an argument in the drawing room the night before. Bless those lads! Charles chuckled to himself. Like their father, they were on easy terms with the servants. There was nothing the staff would not do for the boys, including supplying the latest gossip.

Sophia was wary. She had noted the change that seemed to come over her father. He was making an effort to be pleasant, attempting to stifle his own unpleasant comments, making small talk, even paying her a charming compliment or two, and he'd not drunk any more wine. His behavior was as transparent as the clear crystal glasses on her table; he was up to something.

She sighed. She wanted to be rid of him and his friend, but she could not forcibly evict them from her home. If he would not voluntarily go to the Cock and Bull in Roslyn, she could not make him do so. He was her father and the boys' grandfather. Much as she disliked doing so, much as his presence made her uncomfortable, she felt she must endure his visit as graciously as possible. There were no warm father-daughter feelings between them, and she sensed he had little interest in his only grandchildren, but the rest of the world did not need to know those details.

The earl's vicious taunts on the evening he arrived had driven her to throw sherry in his face, but now, if she could take that impulsive action back, she would. Regrets were useless, however; uncontrolled emotion was ever her downfall.

"Wine, Father?" Sophia asked, motioning the footman to pour for her guests. "As St. Paul says, *'Take a little wine, for thy stomach's sake'*." She slanted a glance at Charles and winked. He almost spilled his wine in surprise at the Biblical quotation and the irreverent wink of her eye.

"No, child, thank you. Perhaps later." Dunhaven smiled somewhat absently. He had up-ended his wineglasses on the tablecloth.

Sophia's blood froze. Tom Eliot, continuing to refuse wine? He was surely up to no good.

In the kitchen, downstairs, the servants were gossiping as they sorted, stacked, and prepared dirty dishes for washing. Events upstairs had given them food for thought. It was evident that there was bad blood between the mistress and her father. For the first time, sympathy was swinging in favor of Lady Sophia; the Earl of Dunhaven was a bad lot. Lizzie had complained that he'd pinched her bottom, and another of the maids said he'd pushed her up against a door and attempted to fondle her.

Such behavior was unheard of at Rowley Hall. The old master, Lord Rowley, did not stand for such nonsense. Guests who trifled with his servants were summarily given their hats and asked to leave, unlike the case in other great houses in the county. The baron had brooked no trifling with his servants and they adored him for it.

Even Bromley—the servants whispered, recollecting the butler's pallor the previous night. One of the eavesdropping footmen said the mistress had thrown a glass of wine in her father's face! Bromley, he said, had near fainted. There was trouble brewing upstairs that was for certain.

Sophia and her guests were consuming the last bit of chocolate cream, the finishing touch to an exquisite meal. "Bromley, my compliments to Mrs. Mathew," Sophia declared.

The butler blinked. Not only had Lady Rowley called him by his correct name, but she'd remembered the name of her cook, also. Recovering his usual aplomb, he nodded solemnly. "Very good, my lady, I shall carry your compliments to Mrs. Mathew."

Lady Sophia had more to say. "And the rest of the servants, also. The service at Rowley Hall is exemplary. I have been to many country homes, and I know whereof I speak. My compliments to the entire staff, and to you for your good training of them."

For once, Bromley was speechless.

Charles stifled a grin. He had been working with John and William to devise ways of letting their mother know that the servants liked to be complimented. Lord Rowley believed that those of every station in life delighted in being appreciated, and that they preferred to be addressed by their name. Evidently the lads had succeeded. Lady Sophia, he knew, wanted very much to be in her boys' good graces, even if that meant learning the names of Rowley Hall's many retainers. Satisfied servants made for a happy, efficiently run household; it had been so in his own home.

Now the next step was to rally the servants in support of Sophia. Her absence during the baron's last illness and failure to arrive for his funeral did not sit well with them. Nor did the fact that she had been an absentee mother to her sons, the Rowley heirs. She had a good deal to atone for, if she chose to do so.

Sophia rose smiling from the table, the folds of her silk

gown gracefully fluttering. Her smile, Charles thought, intensified the light in any room. The candles seemed to glow brighter, as if encouraged to do their best. He harked back to *The Iliad*, and Queen Helen, whose lovely face had launched a thousand ships. She could have been no more beautiful than this latter-day goddess.

Once more, he wished they were alone. There was much he wanted to say to her, much to explain. His heart was full, nearly bursting in his chest.

"Shall we take a stroll in the rose garden?" Sophia asked. "The moon is large and bright, the evening warm. The blossoms will be in full scent."

Brent spoke for all of them, leaping to the fore, Charles noted with annoyance.

"My lady, the roses will pale in comparison to your beauty," he declared, offering her his arm before the vicar could do so.

Charles fumed inwardly. The rose garden! That was *their* special place, was it not? Or was he merely a besotted fool? He had no claim on her or her prized flowers, but still it rankled. How could she?

Brent led her out. Charles remained behind with Dunhaven, who offered him snuff from an elaborately painted china box. Charles declined; he did not enjoy the vile substance that made him sneeze violently and set his brain abuzz. As he politely refused, however, his head swiveled back for a closer look. That box! Charles had never seen such lewdness depicted on delicately molded porcelain.

"Josiah Spode's factory makes more than tea and dinner services for genteel ladies to collect and display, Vicar," Dunhaven smirked. "This is a prime piece, don't you think?" He twirled the box in his hand, making certain

91

Charles saw every bit of the clever, hand-painted design.

Despite his revulsion at the scene depicted, Charles was fascinated. He'd not thought such coupling was possible between a man and a woman; they must be boneless to achieve such feats of contortion. He cleared his throat. "I hope, sir, you keep that out of sight of ladies," he admonished the earl.

Dunhaven quirked a fine blond eyebrow. "Some women, Mr. Heywood, relish such rarities as this. You would be surprised, sir."

"No doubt." Charles's lips thinned in disapproval. The earl laughed coarsely.

"Well, then, shall we join my lovely daughter in the garden? Or shall we—" Dunhaven fashioned a lewd gesture, making his left thumb and index finger into a circle and inserting his right index finger inside. In-out, went the quick motion, crude and obvious. "Or shall we give Brent a bit more time?" he snickered.

Charles's heart missed a beat, even as his bile rose at Dunhaven's coarseness. Sophia was in the garden with Brent, who was no doubt a practiced womanizer! Brent, no fool, no lobcock, but a man who would know precisely what to do with a warm, willing woman in a moonlit garden. He rushed for the French doors leading outside.

Behind him, he heard the earl's cackling, derisive laughter. It rang harshly in his ears.

. . . I saw her upon nearer view,
A Spirit, yet a Woman too! . . .
A perfect Woman, nobly planned,
To warm, to comfort, and command;
And yet a Spirit still, and bright
With something of angelic light . . .
—William Wordsworth,
"She Was a Phantom of Delight," 1807

CHAPTER NINE

The moon and the night were communing, or so it seemed to Charles when he rushed into the garden and saw Sophia's pale hair brushing against Brent's dark head. They were closer than close, it seemed, touching intimately. Charles felt a murderous rage; the lewd scene on Dunhaven's snuff box burst into his brain, mocking him. He approached the pair, hands itching to wrest them apart. Their heads bent over a prolific stem of *Blanca Gloriosa,* they were chatting amiably.

Charles drew in his breath sharply, clearing his head. Simply smelling snuff had set his brain buzzing with vile thoughts unworthy of the vicar of St. Mortrud's Church. He was ashamed of himself.

Lady Sophia looked up at his approach, her smile sweet and welcoming. "I was showing Lord Brent our unusual rose, Mr. Heywood. He would like to take a cutting home for his father, who is an amateur horticulturist."

Charles restrained the impulse to snort. Gammon! He'd bet a monkey, not that he was a betting man, that Brent's

93

father didn't know a rosebush from a field daisy. The man was attempting to install himself in Lady Sophia's good graces, even admiring her blasted roses. "Indeed?" he replied, forcing his face muscles into what was more grimace than genuine smile.

Sophia frowned. The usually mild-mannered vicar was decidedly out of sorts; she immediately recognized the difference from his habitual demeanor. They had been interacting daily for several weeks now, and she felt she knew his humors. He had none, really; he was astonishingly even-tempered.

A thought leapt into her mind, a lovely, welcome thought! *Mr. Heywood is jealous! Of Lord Brent!* So, all was not entirely lost, then. Jealousy was a volatile emotion, as she well knew. A memory of the woman who'd won her last lover flashed across her mind, and she winced. Oh, yes, she knew jealousy. It was monstrous and it was powerful. Sophia would wager that it was an emotion Charles Heywood had never really experienced. She would take full advantage of that knowledge.

Sophia put one arm through Brent's and offered the other to the vicar. She was in her element, now, a man on each side. She smiled; it was almost like being back in London. She had missed the open admiration of handsome young men such as these. Slanting a glance first at Mr. Heywood and then at Lord Brent, she compared them. Brent was a charming devil, saturnine and wearing his masculinity easily and well, but Charles had a quality she had rarely encountered. She realized more each day that he was a good, moral man. She swung her gaze toward him again. And why did his looks attract her more, now, than those of the virile male on her other arm?

Sophia frowned. What was there about Charles Heywood that touched a side of her she'd never known to exist? He warmed her heart and melted her insides. She swore she could feel herself melting, like chocolate left outside in the sun. What was it about the man? She vowed to find out.

Edging her body closer to the vicar's, she noted the clean, fresh smell of his person and the particular shape of his mouth. She adored that short upper lip and remembered pressing her lips against his and nipping at that sweetness. Her body grew warmer and suddenly she wanted Brent gone.

"Lord Brent," she purred seductively, "I forgot my wrap. Would you be so kind as to fetch it for me? The air is cooler than I thought."

Looking displeased to be singled out for fetch-and-carry, Brent nonetheless bowed and hastened to do the lady's bidding. Sophia turned to Charles.

"Well, Mr. Heywood, alone together at last . . . and in the rose garden." She placed her hands on his chest and looked into his grey eyes. "Was there anything you wanted to say to me, now that we are alone again?"

Charles was not used to feminine wiles. Although he had sisters, he had never been in the petticoat line. What, did she want him to kiss her, with Brent about to tear back at any minute with that blasted wrap? If not, why had she sent the man on a foolish errand? The air was warm; balmy, in fact. Sophia was a practiced seductress; he well knew it. But she was playing with fire.

"My lady, Lord Brent will return at any moment."

"Lord Brent must first find my abigail, and she will then have to go to my dressing room to find a wrap. It may take her awhile to find a suitable one." She opened her eyes wide. "Joan has been with me a very long time, but sometimes . . . sometimes she has trouble finding things."

"You are incorrigible." Charles was impressed with her stratagem. He quickly surmised that this "finding a wrap" ploy was one that she had used many times in the past, with Joan as abettor and collaborator. Women and their tricks!

Sophia pretended to brush lint from his waistcoat, looking up at him through a warm golden veil of curling eyelashes. "I am single-minded, sir, and I know what I want. If you continue to reject me, I shall have no choice but to pay more attention to Lord Brent." She reached up to touch his mouth. His lips burned as her long fingertips played over them.

"My lady," he breathed deeply, "what is it that you want from me?"

Sophia looked into his eyes and told him.

Even the best abigails could be bribed, however, and Brent was no fool. He returned to the garden in time to interrupt a moment of burgeoning passion. The vicar's hands were cupped about the lady's face and they appeared to be drinking deeply, hungrily from each other's mouths. Brent was taken aback. The vicar and Dunhaven's notorious daughter? He tiptoed backwards to the French doors and made some noise, whereupon the couple flew apart, Sophia smoothing back her upswept hair and Heywood pulling down his waistcoat. Brent sauntered over to them, pretending he'd seen nothing untoward.

There was more than one way to skin a cat, he mused, or to attract the amorous attentions of a woman who was clearly no better than she should be.

Behind the French doors, the Earl of Dunhaven chuckled as he viewed the charming scenario. It appeared that his protégé would require his interference if he were to make it to Sophia's bed. Clearly, Brent had what appeared to be serious competition in achieving that goal. It behooved the earl to remove the vicar of St. Mortrud's as a rival to Brent for his daughter's affections.

Lady Sophia thought she had never in her life been so happy. She had told the vicar exactly what she wanted from him, in succinct if bold terms, and he had cupped her face in his hands and kissed her thoroughly. It was not the shy kiss of that previous episode in the garden, but a man's kiss, deep, aggressive, and . . . She was warm all over, thinking of it. He *was* a passionate man; she'd known it all along. And that surprising kiss had signified a wordless acceptance, one that overwhelmed her senses. She'd melted in his arms, her bones liquefying. When had that last happened?

She was exhausted and exhilarated. She would have lovely dreams, all night . . .

Joan approached her mistress hesitantly. "My lady, about that wrap . . ."

Sophia barely heard her. "What? Oh, the wrap . . . I do hope Brent made it worth your while to find it quickly, Joan. I am too tired to discuss it now, my girl, but I do believe some matters must be clarified, don't you?" Sophia's eyes, half-teasing, half-serious, turned to her maidservant.

Joan's skin turned the color of her flaming hair. "Ma'am, I . . . I thought you fancied the gentleman. He is very handsome," she added.

Sophia was overcome with a sudden fit of laughter, a rush so strong that she felt her eyes beginning to water. *Lud!* What a mistake! Yes, there were several things she and Joan had to discuss, clearly. Yes, Brent *was* the type of man Sophia had always favored, 'twas true, but Joan had gotten her signals crossed. She was a faithful servant, after all, just uninformed of the present situation.

"But, Joan, I do not fancy the man. I do not fancy him at

all!" Sophia hoped that was clear enough. She began to take off her jewelry and put it in the ornate carved walnut box on top of her dresser.

There was a scratching at the door. Sophia raised her eyebrows. *Who?* "Answer that, Joan. Perhaps it is Harriett, and one of my boys is unwell." Sophia's exuberance dissipated like a bladder quickly deflated as Joan ran to do her bidding.

Lord Brent slipped a large, booted foot into the room as Joan opened the door. He held Sophia's pink and green paisley wrap in his large hands. "May I speak to your mistress?" he asked the maid.

Joan frowned. "My lady is abed, sir," she lied. Brent was determined, however, maneuvering his foot further into the breach. Joan would not let him in; she made a grab for the shawl, but Brent held it out of her reach. A stalwart farm girl with six older brothers, she leapt for the fabric and secured one corner. Brent was put slightly off-balance, but recovered, lunging forward to pull it back.

Sophia had had enough of this bizarre dance; she was too tired to enjoy their lively *pas de deux*. Marching to the door, she ordered, "Sir! Unhand my wrap, if you please."

"Lady Sophia! I wonder if I might have a word."

"Wonder no more, Lord Brent; the answer is *no*. Good evening, sir." She pulled the shawl from his hands in one swift, graceful motion, pushing him back into the hallway. Now he did lose his balance, possibly from the pull of gravity on his jaw when it fell open in disbelief. As the door slammed shut and Sophia turned the key in the lock, she and Joan heard a loud crash as the nobleman fell backward against the hard wooden floor.

Sophia leaned against the shut door and began to giggle. Joan joined her in mirth as they walked backward to the bed and collapsed, overcome by the fit of hilarity. Brent's face!

The man was not used to rebuffs, that was for certain.

Downstairs in the drawing room, Brent was disgusted. "How could you be so wrong?" he challenged Dunhaven. His rump hurt; he had landed heavily.

The earl was consuming the wine he had not drunk at dinner and was now on his third bottle of George Rowley's best claret. "What are you talking about, boy?" His words were slurred, his eyes slightly unfocused.

Brent sat down, too hard, on the drawing room sofa, wincing in pain as the wood responded with a creak of protest. "Your daughter is not interested in dallying with me, sir!"

Dunhaven snorted rudely. "My daughter is renowned for lifting her skirts merely at the sight of a handsome face. The fault must lie in you, my lad. Perhaps your technique needs improvement." He laughed at his own insulting joke.

The younger man leaned forward, fixing the earl with a direct glare. "And perhaps your daughter is not the doxy you make her out to be."

The older man's drink-clouded eyes snapped into focus. "What are you talking about?"

"It is a distinct possibility, my lord," Brent responded, his tone sarcastic, "that your daughter and this vicar may be truly in love."

Dunhaven choked, spilling the contents of his claret glass over his trousers. Recovering, he blurted, "You are out of your head, man! That girl is only interested in two things: men and money. As for the priest," he scoffed, "that wet-behind-the-ears cleric is hardly a man. More a monk! And a poor, down-at-the-heels monk, at that. There's no money there! Sophia would have no interest whatsoever in such a specimen."

"Well, sir, I was certainly fooled, then. That was a lover's kiss I interrupted in the rose garden after the lady sent me away searching for her blasted shawl. It was neatly done, in truth. No, my lord, that man is no eunuch . . . and I would say he has your daughter's heart," Brent swore.

Glaring, Dunhaven poured himself another glass of claret. The servants could wipe up the spill on the carpet. "Listen to me, Robert Winton, my Lord Brent," he spat out each word, "my daughter has no heart." He stood and jabbed his index finger at the left side of Brent's chest. "She has no heart, sir! I saw to that."

Brent pushed away the jabbing digit. Dunhaven was foxed, and wrong, so terribly wrong. His daughter and the vicar were lovers. It was plain to anyone with two eyes in his skull. He had no chance with the lady, whatever her scheming father thought. Yet Brent's hope persisted. Could it be that he was falling a little in love with the notorious lady, himself? She was certainly beautiful and intriguing.

The vicar of St. Mortrud's was unburdening himself to his best friend, after receiving the physician's promise that he would not say a word or quirk an eyebrow, until Charles had finished. "Lewis, I count on your discretion, man. Unfortunately, there is no one I can confess to but you."

"You are placing impossible restrictions on me. I am but a mortal man, neither cleric nor confessor," Lewis protested. They were walking on the outskirts of Rowley Village; it was a beautiful early summer's day.

"Nonetheless, Lewis," Charles faced the larger man down (no easy task), "I rely on you to hear me out and perhaps provide me some guidance. This is the most important matter in my life."

"What have you done?" Lewis sat down heavily on a

boulder at the side of the footpath.

"Nothing." Charles ran a hand through his hair, betraying his nervousness with that habit. "That is, nothing much, nothing much yet . . ."

"You are confusing me," Lewis warned, pushing the spectacles up on his slightly hooked nose.

The vicar sighed, plucking a large handful of rye grass and chewing the stems thoughtfully. "Lewis, I may have made the biggest mistake of my life."

"I doubt it," Alcott interrupted. "Please dispense with this Cheltenham farce, I pray you."

Charles winced. "I assure you, this is serious. Pray listen."

Lewis was not convinced. "Go on, then; I am listening." He assumed an intent pose on the rock, hand on chin, elbow on knee.

"I rebuffed Lady Sophia's amorous advances." He looked at his friend, whose expression betrayed no surprise. He waited.

"She kissed me." Charles slanted a glance at Lewis again, but the surgeon's expression had not changed. "And I, uh, I kissed her back." He paused.

"And?" Lewis inquired.

"*And,* Lewis, *and?* I am a simple, poor country vicar and she is a worldly, sophisticated woman, the wealthiest in the county!" Charles flung out his arm, narrowly missing Lewis's leonine head.

"Calm yourself, Charles, I beg you," Lewis suggested, leaning back on his elbows and assuming a languid pose on the outcropping of rock. "I fail to see your problem. We have already discussed the possibility of the beauteous widow falling for your handsome face." Lewis's eyes seemed to twinkle merrily, or was it a trick of the early morning light?

Charles looked at him suspiciously. "Lewis, are you taking me seriously?"

Lewis rose from the boulder and dusted his hands on his breeches. "Charles, Charles, you are a man, and the lady is a woman. What is the problem?"

Charles turned his back on his friend. "I rebuffed her the first time, Lewis, but there was a second."

"And?" Lewis repeated his question.

"And, indeed." Charles swallowed. "The second time, I did not spurn her, Lewis, and I fear I gave the lady the wrong idea."

"What idea, Charles?" Lewis asked.

"I . . . I asked her what she wanted from me, and—"

He ran his hand through his locks again. He must look as though he'd been dragged through a hedge backwards, he thought. "And she told me."

"I can't bear the suspense," Lewis commented, his tone sarcastic.

"I find it difficult to repeat her exact words, Lewis, and I beg that you forget them the instant I utter them, or I will feel terrible, nay, worse than that, immoral! The gist of what she said is that . . . that she desires my body and wishes to bed me." He flung the handful of wet, chewed grass to one side of the footpath and took Lewis's former position on the boulder, hanging his head in shame.

"Am I supposed to commiserate with you?" Lewis asked. "Because, if that is what you expect, be forewarned that I will not. I know few men who would hesitate to accept the beautiful Lady Rowley's advances, myself amongst them!"

"Lewis," Charles's voice was muffled from the vicinity of his chest, "you know I do not believe in casual fornication. I cannot do it, man! The notion troubles me. I have not been with a woman—in that way—for a long time."

"But you want to," Lewis remarked. "You want to, don't you, old friend?"

Charles rose from the stone outcropping and paced, rounding the rock twice. "Yes, yes, I do, so help me, God." He looked heavenward as if expecting divine intervention. None came.

Lewis brought him back to earth. "What did you tell the lady, then?"

"I had no chance to say anything. We kissed, and—"

"No more *ands,* Charles, I beg you!" Lewis pleaded.

Charles stopped pacing and looked directly at his friend. "Lord Brent came upon us, with milady's wrap, and thus ended the conversation . . . and the kiss."

"You did not say *nay,* then, to the lady's bold suggestion?"

Charles shook his head. "I did not have the chance to say *nay* or *yea,* Lewis."

Lewis pursed his lips. "Well, well, well. What a pretty kettle of fish we have here."

"Does silence give consent?" Charles wondered.

"You kissed Lady Sophia after, or before, she made you this proposition? More important, did you initiate the kiss?"

A flush wiped across Charles's face. "After," he whispered, adding, "and I think I initiated the kiss." The last part of his answer sounded strangled to Lewis's ears; he could barely hear his response.

"Then, I would say you consented, my dear fellow, consented wholeheartedly. Yes, you certainly did!" It was to Lewis Alcott's everlasting credit that he did not laugh or otherwise gloat at the vicar's predicament, and for that Charles was grateful. He was in a rare old coil, one that might be impossible to escape.

The surgeon's big hand clapped his shoulder in sympathy. "You poor sod, you," Lewis murmured.

"What shall I do?" Charles pleaded.

Lewis shook his head. "Remember that Catullus, one of your favorite poets, said that it was difficult to lay aside a confirmed passion, Charles. Those Romans were serious folk." Here his lips did twitch as he added, "And the lady is no less serious than our good Catullus, it seems to me."

You are doomed, my friend, was what Lewis did not say aloud, but what his face confirmed in silence.

CHAPTER TEN

The dinner party invitation was from the Ramsbothams. Lady Sophia was sipping tea in the morning room when the young footman Fred (she thought that was his name), brought her the unexpected note. She and her guests were invited for an evening three days hence. It would be a small, intimate gathering, she read, and they would very much like the pleasure of her company. A Ramsbotham footman was waiting in the hall for her reply.

Sophia pressed the letter against her bosom and closed her eyes, recalling the woman who'd paid her that morning visit, the one with the two daughters. Sophia remembered being less than cordial to them. In truth, she had been rude. She thought quickly, her mind astir. Did this mean that the country gentry were accepting her, or did they want to see her . . . and mock? To laugh at her from behind their hands?

She pressed her lips together. What to do?

There was a scratching at the door. Bromley, no doubt, indicating that the Ramsbothams' footman was awaiting her answer. "Yes, Bromley, a moment, please," she called out.

Charles Heywood entered the morning room, looking as fresh as a new-minted coin, his ash brown hair shining, his step buoyant. She smiled, her heart thumping as if she were sixteen again, not thirty years of age, remembering that extraordinary, passionate kiss in the garden, that precursor, mayhap, of a more wonderful union to come. Charles!

"Beg pardon, my lady," he began.

"You are not disturbing me, sir. What can I do for you this morning?" *Or afternoon, evening, or break of dawn, my dear?* she thought, her eyes brightening at the romantic prospect. Since that devastating kiss in the garden, the vicar had been much on her mind. She blushed now at the boldness of her proposition to him, but he had asked her what she wanted from him, had he not? She had responded honestly to that question. Still, her boldness, perhaps more suited to sophisticated London than to rustic north Yorkshire, to *ton* bucks, not country vicars, now embarrassed her. It was not easy, this developing relationship with Charles Heywood. He was not like the other men she had known and so casually and easily seduced. She wondered, too, at times, who was seducing whom?

She brought her wandering thoughts back to the matter at hand. "Do sit down."

Charles complied, smiling. "I was visiting one of the families in our district, my lady, and they asked if you would respond favorably to an invitation some nights hence. I took the liberty of saying you might, and that you had houseguests. I am also invited. The Ramsbothams are a pleasant family with two lively girls and a young babe. You may know Mrs. Ramsbotham?"

"She paid me a visit some time ago," Sophia replied, nodding.

"Ah, yes, she mentioned that coming to see you was one of her very first ventures out of the house since the birth of her youngest child, a healthy boy I will be honored to christen in a month's time."

"Indeed?" She was surprised. Mrs. Ramsbotham had not mentioned a new baby. Upon further recollection, Sophia realized that she had done most of the talking, dominating the discourse. How rude! Her face grew hot.

She fanned herself with the letter. "I was just about to send a note of acceptance with her footman, who waits in the hall." She quickly stopped fanning herself and attempted to smooth the crumpled missive on the breakfast table. It remained adamantly wrinkled.

Sophia put out a hand. "Will you not stay a while, sir? I can ring for more tea—"

"I promised to take the boys fishing after their Latin lesson. We are reading Virgil's *Aeneid*," he explained.

"Ah, Queen Dido's most tragic love story. Well, then, perhaps you can stay for luncheon?" She did not want him to go, ever. "Or . . . here's a thought, Mr. Heywood. Mayhap I can accompany you and the boys on your fishing expedition?"

"My lady, that would be an honor—"

She smiled. "Hardly that, sir, hardly that, but some pleasant exercise for me in good company. I fished as a child in Kent."

"We were to practice the Latin conjugations as we fished, but if that would bore you—"

"Latin verbs! It has been so long since Miss Bane drilled them into my poor head! Perhaps I shall remember some of them, the easier ones." She fixed her eyes on his. "You are in good looks, today, Mr. Heywood. Is it the prospect of conjugating verbs and casting lures with my sons that is the cause of this?" she teased.

Charles blushed, replying gallantly, "My lady, it is simply the pleasure of your company."

Sophia was brought back quickly to the task at hand. *The pleasure of her company* . . . she must reply to that invitation and hasten to her rooms to dress for fishing. What attire, she wondered, does a lady don for fishing? Joan, that clever girl, would know. And later, they would discuss appropriate dinner party garb for rustic north Yorkshire.

"Give me a few moments, sir, to dash off a reply to the Ramsbothams and to change into clothes more suitable for fishing."

"Amo, amas, amat," Sophia declaimed in a clear voice. "I love, you love, he loves—" She was wearing a pair of close-fitting doeskin trousers that left little to the imagination, and it was all Charles Heywood could do to keep his mind on Latin verbs and the trout jumping in the stream in frantic pursuit of cut-up pieces of earthworm. *Trousers!* So far, he was succeeding admirably in keeping his head clear of unwelcome thoughts, but it was hard work indeed to fish while ignoring the lady's long limbs and Venus-like callipygian charms. Memories of taking his elder brothers' dares and jumping into icy Lake Windemere in January helped him through the ordeal of having to witness the delectable Sophia in trousers.

He was endeavoring to put aside his long, serious discussion with Lewis. He'd reached the conclusion that he must never again be alone with Sophia, for the sake of his sanity and his principles. It was the only answer. He'd been safe in the morning room, with the two footmen outside and Bromley lurking nearby, but occasions for kisses and for bedding must be avoided, if he was to remain true to those principles.

Ah, temptation! He had never prayed so fervently in his life. God had probably grown weary of the feeble moans and groans of his disturbed priest, Charles Heywood! If a thunderbolt streaked and burned him to a crisp, he would well deserve it; the Almighty must be sick of his servant, Charles, whose burnings and yearnings had already singed his own skin, if not his soul.

He'd excused himself from luncheon at Rowley Hall following their fishing excursion when John reminded him that they were to visit the Rowley tenant farmers that afternoon. The cook had packed a portable lunch, one they could munch on horseback. Sophia had been visibly disappointed.

"Is this important, Mr. Heywood? Can it not be rescheduled?" she'd wondered.

John had piped up, "Papa always had our steward Mr. Woods take us around to the farms, Mama, but we wanted Mr. Heywood to accompany us this time. He knows the people so much better, and we—" John turned to William, who nodded in somber agreement, "we want to know them better, as well. They are responsible for the success of our agricultural program, after all."

Sophia looked stunned at his speech, so adult, so . . . baronial. Charles Heywood smiled at the look on her face, a look that seemed to be made up of equal amounts of pride and amazement. "My lady, the boys have the makings of fine landlords. The baron would be proud of them." He tousled their blond locks, teasing them. William almost lost his precarious balance on the slippery rocks, but Charles caught him under the arms. "Oops! Mustn't join the fishes! We might hook you, my plump young man, by mistake."

"Charles! I have one!" John cried out, forgetting to address the vicar politely.

William saved him from his gaffe. "He means Mr. Heywood, sir," he assured him. "He is just excited." William saw the size of the trout John had on the end of his line as it leapt out of the water. "Brilliant! John, don't lose him! Mama, do you see it?" The youngster began to jump up and down.

Sophia's eyes widened as John, with Charles's help and none from the excitedly bouncing William, landed the large fish. She stepped carefully from stone to stone to help him lift it into the creel, as excited as her sons.

"The Irish have a saying, Mr. Heywood," she called out over the rushing water. "They say *'it's not a trout until it is landed!'* "

"An excellent saying, my lady," Charles agreed. The trout was a sleek fellow, deep in the flank and muscled across the shoulders, its belly a buttery yellow below its brown back. They were so intent on the shining brown fish, its reddish-orange spangles glistening in the sunlight, that they momentarily forgot William, who promptly slid off a mossy stone and into the stream.

"Help!" he shouted.

Charles moved quickly, handing his fishing pole to Sophia and bounding over the rocks to aid the boy. "Got you!" Charles laughed, hauling him out of the drink. William was drenched but no worse for it.

"Nodcock!" John jeered at his younger brother.

Sophia fixed him with a chastising maternal glare. "John!"

"Oh." John's voice became small. "I'm sorry, Mama. Sorry, Wills!" He turned his face to his mother, suitably chastised.

"That's better, darling," she whispered, giving him a hug.

William was instantly jealous. "*I* am the one Mama should be hugging, Mr. Heywood," he complained to Charles. "*I* was the one who was almost drowned."

Charles raised an eyebrow. "Hardly, William," he laughed, "but your mama, I am sure, has enough hugs for everyone."

Sophia heard him. "For everyone, William!" she called out, laughing with Charles.

Charles acknowledged that the astute brothers were correct in their description of the late Baron Rowley's steward, Herbert Woods, who was competent enough, but had few social graces. He dealt fairly with the farmers, but he was not a naturally friendly person. As the local vicar, Charles had a much different and better relationship with these people. He visited them often, saw them at church services, and consoled them in their grief. He'd lost track of how many babies he'd christened and how many marriages he'd performed—sometimes in that order. He understood rural folk, having been brought up by a father whose open, generous attitude toward his tenants was much like George Rowley's.

They were visiting the Browns, Bart and Jenny, and their lively little four-year-old daughter, Chloe. The boys were taken with the elfin charmer, Charles noted. She was, in fact, quite beautiful, though the Browns were plain in looks. If Chloe lived up to the promise of her beauty, she'd rival diamonds of the first water among the *ton*.

She peeked from behind her mother's wool skirts, one twinkling green eye fixed on John Rowley. "Who is that pretty boy, Mama?" she piped in a crisp, high voice.

Jenny Brown blushed at her tiny daughter's bold remark. "Here now, Chloe, show your respect. That's the new Baron Rowley, he is."

John squatted on his haunches so that he was eye to eye with the bold little miss. "Do I have the honor of addressing Miss Chloe Brown?" he asked in a loud voice.

The child appeared from behind her mother. "You do, sir." She smiled prettily, adding, "And I think I will marry you."

John started laughing. "You think so, do you, lassie?" he teased.

The Browns were horrified at such cheek. "Chloe!" Bart Brown seemed on the verge of chastising his presumptuous offspring, but John stayed them with an upraised, lordly hand. "No, please allow her to have her say. Young women have a right to express their opinions."

"And if John doesn't want to marry you, Miss Brown, *I* would be delighted," William bowed, tongue firmly in cheek, taking advantage of an occasion to tease his older brother.

Chloe frowned, considering the offer. "That is all well and good, kind sir," she replied, "but I would like to be a baroness, I think, like the pretty yellow-haired lady."

It was all Charles could do to keep from laughing. He saw from the corner of his eye that the Browns were now enjoying themselves, their lips quirking. She was a little imp, this Chloe Brown, with her eyes green as grass and her curly hair black as ink, a self-assured little beauty. Would that spirit be gone, Charles wondered, sobering, with the harsh realities of farm work as she grew older?

John, his arms akimbo, was facing down his brother. "She asked me first, William, and don't you forget it!"

William raised his chin in a stubborn challenge. "Hah! We shall see, sir!"

"It is 'my lord baron,' you looby," John corrected him.

The two boys collapsed in laughter. John's baronial airs and lordly mien evaporated in boyish glee.

"Well, thank you for the lemonade," said the vicar. It was time to end this visit. "We shall let you get back to work, now, shall we, lads?" He was ushering them out the farmhouse door.

"Wait!" Chloe called, her tone rather imperious for such a little thing.

"Yes, Miss Brown?" Charles responded.

And in front of them all, Chloe Brown dropped into a perfect curtsey. She dipped, then rose slowly, her pudgy little arms carefully fanning her linsey-woolsey skirt as she flashed

112

them a brilliant smile that showed a charming dimple deep in each round cheek. She dropped her eyelids. "It was a pleasure to meet you, my lord." Opening her sparkling eyes wide, she glanced at William. "*And* my lord's brother."

The little minx! Charles thought. She could give Lady Sophia—"*the pretty yellow-haired lady,*"—lessons in elfin enchantment.

The choice was between the white net with the figured-leaf design and the daring red silk with chenille embroidery at the hem, sleeves, and bosom. White gowns were always appropriate, at any time or place; the popular ladies' magazine, *La Belle Assemblee*, had stated so, but Sophia had never favored white. She'd worn it during her first season when she was paraded about the Marriage Mart by her father, but seldom since then. As a blonde, white was never her color. The red, however . . .

The deep red of the silk net gown set off her pale coloring well, adding luster to the cerulean depths of her eyes. She knew what suited her and dressed for maximum effect, always. But was the red too daring for a dull dinner party in Yorkshire, even with its relatively high-cut bosom?

Or would they, her neighbors in this godforsaken bit of England, expect it of her? To be daring, to live up to her notorious reputation? Would she disappoint them by leaving off the red gown? (And how disappointed they would be if they found out she was not nearly so notorious as the worst of the gossip would have it!)

"What do you think, Joan?" she asked her abigail.

Joan seemed flattered to be consulted. She furrowed her brow in concentration. "My lady, you are beautiful in any gown you wear . . . but the red, my lady, it is *you*."

I? Sophia thought. *It is I? And who am I now? The noto-*

rious London lady? *The baron's relict, his widow? The mother of two boys? Who am I, indeed?* she wondered, fingering the lovely though machine-made net and caressing the thick, colorful chenille appliqué of leaves and roses.

I am what I decide to be, she mused. *From this day forward, I am the sum of all I was, and am, and shall be. Not exactly a phoenix rising from its ashes, newborn,* she smiled wryly, *but perhaps reborn. Yes, reborn. My past will not drag me in the mire; it is over, it is done. A true part of me, but not the very best part. No,* she promised herself, *the best is yet to come.*

"The red, then; the red silk it is. Thank you for helping me decide." She pressed the girl's hand warmly. Joan seemed surprised, but pleased, as she bobbed her head in acknowledgement.

Sophia sat down gracefully at her dressing table, her hands smoothing back the pale blond tendrils at her temples. "Now, what shall we do with my hair? A Psyche knot, a coronet, or the usual twist at the nape of my neck?"

Mr. Harold Ramsbotham was a tall, slim gentleman with a merry gleam in his friendly eyes. He'd greeted Lady Sophia and Lord Brent warmly. The earl, pleading the headache, had remained at the Hall. Mrs. Ramsbotham, Katherine, was prettier than Sophia remembered. She was petite, dark-haired, and charming. Sophia's first impression, from the visit Mrs. Ramsbotham and her daughters had paid to her, had been false; she had not truly seen the woman. There were blinders on her eyes on that first occasion; Katherine Ramsbotham could be a friend. With a start, she realized she had never had a female friend, not a true one; she had never cared to have one. *My life has truly changed,* she thought, *for me to consider the possibility of another woman as a friend.*

"And where are your charming daughters this evening, Mrs. Ramsbotham?" Sophia queried the young matron.

"It's Katherine, please, Lady Sophia," Katherine replied, clasping Sophia's hands in hers. "The girls are in the nursery with my son. It is almost as if he were their baby, not their brother!"

"I'm certain that he is a darling baby, Katherine," Sophia was careful to say the woman's name. "And please call me Sophia. Formality is out of place in the country, amongst neighbors."

Katherine flushed slightly. "It is kind of you to say so, my . . . Sophia," she hastily corrected herself.

"I should like to see this sweet boy of yours, Katherine," Sophia heard herself saying. "Mr. Heywood tells me he will be christened soon."

"I would be . . . I would be honored, my . . . Sophia." A flush darkened the proud mother's cheeks. "Please, do come upstairs. The girls will be thrilled to see you again. They so loved hearing about the new London fashions." Katherine ran her eyes enviously over Sophia's red silk gown. "And they will adore your gown! It is so beautiful, and you look so well in it."

Sophia accepted the gracious compliment, and incredulously heard herself saying, "They must come to visit me again. We shall go through my wardrobe and play at dressing up. Do you think they would like that?"

Katherine stammered, "That would be extraordinarily kind of you!"

Sophia smiled. She liked this woman. "Not kind at all. We are neighbors, and we should endeavor to know each other better." She patted Katherine's hand as they arrived at the nursery door to greet the delighted young faces of Drusilla and Annabelle. Faces, Sophia noted, that were not at all spotty. Why had she ever thought so?

★ ★ ★ ★ ★

The meal was uneventful. The Ramsbothams set a good table, but Sophia began to appreciate the culinary artistry of Mrs. Mathew even more, in comparison. She was seated between the vicar and Lord Brent and was enjoying herself thoroughly. She purposely ignored both men throughout dinner, flirting outrageously with the gentleman seated across from her, an elderly knight whose property adjoined that of the Ramsbothams.

Sophia found Sir Peregrine Bartlett delightful and full of charm, while enjoying the inability of either Brent or Mr. Heywood to insert many words into the animated conversation. What made it more difficult was that she and Sir Peregrine conversed fluently in French, a language Charles barely knew and one that Brent only thought he knew; that gentleman's French was execrable! Neither man could join in their lively conversation, and the frustrated looks on their faces were priceless. Was she terribly rude? Ah, but she was having such fun!

Charles surveyed the remarkable lady over the rim of his wineglass. Greek, Latin, and now French! Lady Sophia's old governess had to have been a remarkable teacher—and Sophia an outstanding pupil—for the woman to be so well versed in languages ancient and modern. The gossips and rumormongers did not give her enough credit, that was certain, and Charles was beginning to realize it more and more. Someday he must ask her about that amazing woman, the governess who had mysteriously disappeared on the eve of Sophia's first marriage.

When I was eighteen I took a wife,
I loved her dearly as I love my life,
And to maintain her both fine and gay,
I went a-robbing,
I went a-robbing on the King's highway,
I never robb'd any poor man yet,
And I was never in a tradesman's debt,
But I robb'd the lords and the ladies gay,
And carried home the gold,
And carried home the gold to my love straight-
way . . .
　　　　　—"The Robber," English folk song

CHAPTER ELEVEN

The Earl of Dunhaven was not ill. He had feigned the head-ache to create an opportunity to visit the Cock and Bull in Roslyn Town, to scour the environs of that isolated inn for whatever scum, highwaymen, or robbers might be skulking about. A long-brewing plan was about to be hatched; he was determined to do away with Sophia's children, the heirs to the Rowley fortune. With his grandsons removed, every bit of old George's wealth would immediately be Sophia's. From there, he would maneuver his daughter into a liaison with his easily manipulated protégé, Brent, and all the money would then flow directly into the earl's coffers.

Dunhaven had scoffed at the nonsense the younger man had spewed several nights before, claiming that Sophia and the vicar of St. Mortrud's had a *tendre* for each other.

Tendre, indeed! The parson was after her wealth; it was as simple as that. The earl knew that the priest was like any other man as regarded the widow's fortune. Worse! Country parsons' pockets were perpetually to let.

A casual word to the landlord, greased with a few coppers, brought two rough-looking specimens of rural manhood to the table. The landlord had asked no questions; noblemen's foibles were none of his business. Safer that way. The earl appraised the men.

"I require some assistance," he began, clarifying his needs to the scruffy duo, "for which I will pay well." The earl found it distasteful to be in the same room with these ruffians, who reeked of the stableyard. He did not ask them to sit but rather kept them standing, attending carefully to his every low-pitched word.

The older of the two, a scarred man whose wild hair called out for the services of a barber, nodded. "A bit o' highway robbery, milord?"

"Exactly . . . and a bit more," Dunhaven answered, miming the cocking and firing of a pistol.

The younger fellow shuffled his feet, clearly uneasy, but the older man silenced any objections with a quelling glare. "Yes, milord, we gets ye."

Dunhaven nodded. "Be sure that you do. I do not want this matter botched." He threw a small leather bag at the ruffian, who caught it adroitly. "Make sure your firearms are primed and ready." The earl rose to leave. "I will leave word with the landlord when I'll return to give you further instructions. You will earn twice what is in there—" he indicated the money sack, "when this deed is brought to a satisfactory conclusion."

"Ye can trust us, milord," the older man averred.

"Why, sir," Dunhaven smiled, his lips curled in menace,

"it is not a matter of trust, is it, now? If you are not here, I will hunt you both down and shoot you myself." He brushed the dust from his trousers, a sneer fixed on his face.

Though his facial expression did not reveal his feelings, he was elated. The rough pair would not disappoint him; he had dealt with their kind before. Hired assassins were all greedy, and cowards, to boot. The deed was good as done. He resisted an urge to rub his gloved hands in glee as he quit the tavern.

Lord Brent was determined to have a few private words with Lady Sophia. She'd ignored him in the carriage ride to the Ramsbothams, preferring to chat with her maid instead. That, and the earlier undignified scene outside her boudoir had given him the strong impression that she was uninterested in him. Or, was it simply her particular brand of teasing? The lady was a puzzle. Brent did not enjoy puzzles; he was a straightforward man.

"My lady," he greeted Sophia in the morning room, where she was drinking a cup of tea. The remains of her breakfast, a hearty one, from all appearances, sat on the table in front of her.

Lady Sophia regarded him rather coolly, he thought, as she raised her eyes. Undaunted, he plunged ahead. "May I sit down?"

She gave a regal nod of her head and continued to sip her tea.

"I fear that we may have started off on the wrong foot, my lady," Brent began, hesitant.

"Really, sir? And what foot is that, pray tell?" she drawled.

Brent was momentarily taken aback. " 'Tis but a figure of speech, my lady—"

Lady Sophia placed her teacup very carefully on its saucer and pushed it away. She sat forward, elbows on table, hands under her chin, and looked him up and down. "I am not interested in figures of speech this morning, my lord. I have many duties I must perform before the day is done. If you have anything to say that you believe I should hear, pray continue. But please do not go on at length."

"Is my presence so unwelcome, Lady Rowley?" he asked, his lips stiff.

Sophia rolled her eyes upward, toward the decorated plaster ceiling, and sighed. "Your presence, sir, is tolerated, but you and my father were not invited guests. I do not believe I am under any obligation to entertain you or your figures of speech."

How rude she was, Brent thought. She had the right of it, though. The Earl of Dunhaven was *persona non grata* to his daughter, and he, riding on the earl's coat tails, must be equally so. "My lady, I regret this intrusion upon your privacy more than you could possibly imagine."

She raised a dark blond eyebrow, an imperious gesture so like her father's that it nearly discomposed him.

"As I have said before, I wish we had met in happier circumstances—"

"What leads you to think, sir, that I would have found that hypothetical meeting with you more pleasurable than this one has been?"

"My lady," he raced ahead, recklessly, "I cannot believe you find me unattractive."

Sophia sat for a moment as if stunned, then she threw her head back and laughed, long and hard.

Brent was humiliated. "My lady—"

She was gasping for breath; there were tears in her eyes.

"Shush, my lord, shush," she admonished him. "This is . . . too . . . much!"

Brent's eyes narrowed. The lady was more than rude. A number of phrases he could employ to better describe her behavior ran through his mind, but he resisted the impulse to articulate them. He was a gentleman, after all. He stood, preparing to leave.

"Sit down, sir, sit down!" she ordered him.

Surprised at her commanding tone, he acquiesced. Though not used to taking a woman's orders, it was a possibility he could learn to like it if the woman ordering him about were Lady Sophia.

She leaned forward, moving the plates before her to one side, and fixed him with a direct look. "Sir, my father has put you up to this, has he not? He has dangled me in front of you as a lascivious woman who must have a man, a desperate woman who cannot live without a lover, a pitiful widow only too eager to grant a virile companion access to her late husband's fortune. That is so, is it not?"

Brent felt his face flame. "My lady, I find you very attractive—"

Sophia dismissed his comments with a wave of her hand. "Pshaw, Brent, everyone finds me attractive . . . and rich! You know nothing of me, nothing of who I am."

Brent swallowed. "That is true, my lady, I know nothing of you, save your reputation—"

Sophia's eyes hardened into blue stone and she regarded him with a flat glare. "My reputation always precedes me, sir, but it is not an accurate representation of my true self."

"You are more than I expected, to be sure. Your father did lead me to believe that you would not be averse to my attentions."

"He was incorrect, sir," Sophia interrupted him.

Brent leaned back in his chair. He regarded Sophia with a speculative look, his hands dropping to his lap. "So, you are in love with the vicar, then."

Sophia stared. He had rendered her speechless. *I am right,* Brent thought. *Alas, the vicar has captured her heart. Ah, well, bad luck.* It was truly time to depart, then, to leave Rowley Hall, with or without the Earl of Dunhaven. Brent had had enough of that crude fellow. He hoped that Sophia could deal with her father before he did her some harm; he was suddenly concerned for her well-being.

"Well, my lady, it has been a pleasure meeting you. I will depart before nightfall." He rose, sketched a bow and turned to leave her.

"Brent—" she stopped him with her next words. "Do not go . . . yet."

She had been rude, and the young nobleman did not deserve it. Her father had put him up to his suit. The earl was negotiating her fourth marriage. *Bloody hell!* Not if she had anything to say about it, and she did. She was no longer a frightened fifteen-year-old virgin, nor the hardened sixteen-year-old bride. She had lost the protection of her third husband, George Rowley, who, she realized too late, had been a saint. He alone had saved her from her father, who was back in her life only because George was now absent from it. He thought he could bully her into another marriage, a marriage in which he stood to gain financially, as he had from all those before this.

No, not this time!

But she should not take out her anger on this young man, who did not know her history and surely could not truly know her father or what he was capable of doing.

It was time that he knew the truth about Tom Eliot, the Earl of Dunhaven.

"My Lord Brent," Sophia began, "I apologize if I have

seemed rude. I was never so as a child—my governess saw to it that I had fine, polite manners—but I was early put into the company of men who were coarse and wicked, when I was still a young girl, and it has sadly affected me."

Closing her eyes (Lord, she was weary!), she continued. "My father met my first husband, a vile cur named Rushton, in a brothel. He lost great sums to him playing Hazard and other games of chance. He married me off to that brute to discharge his debts, and for a large settlement. My Lord Rushton was fond of deflowering virgins, you see, and I was the kind of pure innocent he favored."

Sophia opened her eyes; Brent looked pale. He was a kind man, she realized; but he had fallen into bad company. She would not burden him with recounting the brutality of her wedding night, when Rushton had repeatedly raped her. She had fought him each time and had borne the bruises for weeks. The new Lady Rushton never went to balls, routs, the theatre, or dinner parties, as her purpling bruises would have caused comment. When Rushton had tired of her, she was no longer the young girl from Kent who thought the world a lovely place. In the place of that girl was a creature hardened by abuse, beaten, wary of men. It was a wonder she'd survived.

"My lady, please," Brent interrupted her, "do not pain yourself any further by speaking of these things. I suspected—" Brent bit his lower lip. "I suspected you had been used badly by your father."

"My father uses badly anyone who gives him a chance to do so. He has no loyalties, no heart, caring only for himself and his pleasures." *And he tried to make me in his image,* Sophia realized with a jolt. She had become his creature, a heartless jade.

"I am beginning to put my life together, sir, the rest of my life. Rusticating in Yorkshire, though I was loath to believe it at first, has made me see what my life has been and how it must change, if I am to survive."

Brent's concern seemed evident in his sympathetic brown eyes. "I admire your bravery, my lady. Truly, I do. I wish you well." He held out his hands to his hostess. "But do be careful. I fear your father plans some mischief. I worry for you, and for your boys. If I can be of any assistance—"

Sophia pushed back her chair and stood facing him. "What do you mean, sir? What has that villain told you?" Her heart beating a loud staccato in her chest, she grasped Brent's hands and held them tight.

The door to the morning room opened to admit the Earl of Dunhaven, who looked pleased. He smiled broadly at them, rubbing his hands in delight. "Do not let me interrupt you." He turned to the sideboard and began to help himself to breakfast, humming a popular bawdy air.

Sophia couldn't breathe. She released Brent's hands and left the room, hurrying toward the nursery. *The boys! If he* . . . she gathered her skirts and ran up the winding staircase, stifling a sob with her fist.

But the boys were in fine fettle, she realized when she stood at the nursery's open door. They were safe, safe with the vicar. John, the undignified new Baron Rowley, was pounding the scrubbed old deal table, exhorting Charles Heywood to pose his younger brother a mathematical problem he could not readily answer.

Charles's right index finger was at his temple, his left arm across his chest. He wore a look of mock solemnity on his face. "Ah, yes, Master William, let us cast our thoughts to a box, sir, a box I have, alas, recently lost."

Sophia saw that William's face was alert, his eyes fixed on his tutor.

"Now, this box, the one I have recently lost, this inlaid wooden box was a gift from my father, brought from India by a traveler; it was a box that I treasured, a teak box inlaid with ivory."

"Do go on, sir!" John urged him.

Charles stayed him with a gesture. "There were a number of guineas and crown pieces in this lost box, but the only recollection I have of their number is that the crowns were seven times the number of the guineas, and that the number of shillings of the whole was one thousand, six hundred and twenty-four. So, young William, my question is: how many guineas and crowns did I lose?"

William shut his eyes in concentration. John set a large stopwatch he held in his hands. All eyes were on William.

"I have the answer, sir," his little boy's voice chirped. "It is twenty-nine guineas and two hundred and three crowns."

John clicked the watch. "A minute!" he called out.

Charles looked down at the paper on which he had previously figured the answer to the problem. "He's correct."

"Well, that settles it, Mr. Heywood, sir," John called out, "we must take him to the fair next week. We can bill him as the Midget Mental Calculator! He can amaze all the country folk for miles around."

"Boys, I hardly think that your mother would be in favor of having her son on display for the amusement of country folk—" Charles began.

Sophia stepped quietly into the classroom, laughing. "You are right, sir, she would not."

"Mama!" The boys jumped from their places and ran to embrace their mother. Engulfed in their enthusiastic expressions of love, she felt a lump in her throat, then remembered Lord Brent's warning and shivered. If anything happened to her sons now, after they had become so dear to her . . . She turned her mind to more pleasant thoughts.

"But this fair sounds as though it would make a charming family outing, Mr. Heywood." She beamed at the boys, her arms tight around their shoulders.

A family outing. Charles was elated at her use of the phrase and her evident intention to include him the excursion. Was he now part of the family in his role as guardian to the boys as Lewis had once teased? He very much wanted to be part of it, but in another manner entirely. He adored the boys, and their mother, also . . . yes, he adored her. From his initial impression of her as a fierce and belligerent beauty, he had progressed to seeing her as a kind and loving mother to the boys and a friend to him. Since that intimate moment in the rose garden, he'd known the lady desired more from him; well, so did he, from her. 'Twas time, he thought, to sort it all out. He would gird his loins and ask the lady to marry him. She might very well laugh in his face, but if he did not make the attempt . . . Was it unreasonable of him to expect her to consider his proposal? She had said a number of times that she had no wish to wed again.

A line from one of Shakespeare's plays flashed into his brain. "To say the truth," a character had stated, "reason and love keep little company nowadays." Words as true now, in the second decade of the nineteenth century, as they ever were in the days of Elizabeth, the Virgin Queen.

Its I hev' been to Weyhill Fair,
An' Oh what sights did I see there,
To hear my tale 'ud make you stare . . .
   —William Cobbett,
      The Weyhill Fair, 19th century poem

CHAPTER TWELVE

The fresh-faced footman, Fred, had brought in another letter. It lay on the chased silver tray, white and plump, embossed with a red wax seal. Lady Sophia picked it up with no little curiosity. Her second missive in as many weeks! She recollected, with no regret, the masses of invitations she was wont to receive in London as she was a favorite, a leading hostess and partygoer, among the *ton*. So many . . . and so forgettable. Had she ever truly enjoyed those crowded, noisy events? She picked up the letter and broke the seal.

It was from someone she did not know. She pursed her lips, considering the request. She would have to speak to Charles; perhaps he knew these people. But Tuesday was not one of the days he came to Rowley Hall for the boys' lessons; she would have to send for him.

Fred was awaiting milady's pleasure. He was a tall boy; footmen were hired for their height. Sophia frowned. There was a bruise on his jaw. Were her servants engaging in amateur fisticuffs? Ah, well, men will be men, she thought, and the pugilists Mendoza and Cribb were heroes, both to the common men and the men of the *ton*. She refrained from commenting on it.

"Fred, would you please walk to the vicarage and ask Mr. Heywood to come here this morning if his schedule allows it? I need to confer with him."

The boys were in the stables discussing the upcoming fair with Lord Brent when the vicar arrived on horseback. Charles frowned. When were these London visitors going to leave? Brent was becoming an annoyance, too much in the company of the boys and Lady Sophia for his peace of mind. *I am jealous,* he thought. *Envy is one of the seven deadly sins . . . as is Lust . . .*

John rushed to greet Charles as he dismounted. A stable boy came to take the reins. "Mr. Heywood, sir! Lord Brent has been telling us of the Nottingham fairs, where he saw geese being driven to market in the springtime. Did you know, sir, that the drovers often encased the feet of the geese in little cloth shoes?"

The big man sauntered over, at ease with his body and his good looks, Charles could not help noting, as he enlarged upon his story. "Lads, I saw great gaggles of geese, thousands strong, being driven by gooseherds and bonneted young goose-girls with crooks. They were weeks on the road, these creatures, on their way to becoming some family's holiday dinner, having been plucked of their feathers at least twice, their down at least five times."

Brent turned and squatted beside the boys, who had taken seats on a large bale of hay, entranced by the bizarre story. "I did myself see the cunning cloth shoes, once or twice, but more often the geese were fitted for their long journey, some 80 to 100 miles, by being driven first through a shallow pond of tar and then into a patch of sand, to harden their feet. This procedure was repeated at intervals throughout the drive, and that, too, was an odd sight."

Throwing back his head, Brent recited in a deep baritone voice, "Who eats goose on Michaelmas Day, shan't money lack his debts to pay. At Christmas a capon, at Michaelmas a goose, and something else at New Year's Eve for fear the lease fly loose!"

"Bravo!" John applauded the oft-quoted proverb.

Brent grinned, ruffling young John's hair. Charles grimaced, again acknowledging his jealousy of Brent as a possible rival for Sophia's affections and those of her sons. Why was he so proprietary? It was unseemly. He was not their father . . . yet . . . though he desired to be. Years of proximity to the boys had nurtured his love for them. And now Sophia was added to the emotional mix.

"Mr. Heywood," William asked, "why are you here today, sir? It is Tuesday."

"Your mama has asked to see me, William. I am here in response to her message," he replied, noting that Lord Brent's ears seemed to perk up at the mention of the lady.

William nodded. "Will you come riding with us, sir? Lord Brent is taking us to the high moors this morning."

"I don't know if I can, William. I have no idea what your mother wants to discuss with me; I may be closeted with her a while." The boy's mouth turned down in disappointment.

Charles turned to Brent. The gentleman did not seem pleased he was going to see Lady Sophia. Or was it his imagination? " 'Tis rocky terrain there, sir, with many rabbit holes difficult to see. It warrants careful riding."

Brent nodded. "Thank you, sir, I am aware of that. I've ridden up that way. Do not fear. I will be careful with the lads." He patted William's head. "I will take care of them as if they were my own sons." Brent smiled.

Not while I live will they be your sons, sirrah, Charles thought, shaken by the sudden ferocity of his feelings.

★ ★ ★ ★ ★

Sophia pointed to the open letter on the table. "Who *are* these people, Mr. Heywood?" she asked the vicar.

Charles picked up the letter and scanned its message. The boys were invited to the home of an Eton classmate from the Lake District. Charles smiled. "I know the Mainwaring family, my lady. Their manor lies not far from my father's, near Bowness Bay on Lake Windemere."

"Good people, then?" Sophia queried with an anxious look.

"Excellent. They have been close friends of my family for years. In fact, their daughter and my sister Beth are bosom bows." Charles stopped himself. The Mainwaring daughter, Charlotte Anne, was one of the young women his sisters were forever teasing him about. Sweetly pretty and devout, Charlotte Anne would make an ideal vicar's wife, they said.

"Sir?" Sophia's voice brought him back to the present. He cleared his throat.

"So, then," she continued, "it would be safe to send the boys for a visit?"

Charles was puzzled at her choice of words. "*Safe?* Of course they would be safe. Why do you ask?"

Sophia laughed. "Did I say *'safe'?* La, sir, I meant to say . . . would they enjoy themselves?"

"Shall we ask them if they would like to go?" Such visits among country families were common, and could last several weeks. The boys would miss the fair, but there would probably be a fair or two in Cumbria, in the Lake District, to make up for it.

"Yes, of course. Let us do so. Where are they now, do you know?" Sophia seemed anxious, Charles thought. Something was worrying her.

"Are you all right?" he asked.

Sophia's blue eyes flew to meet his. "Charles—" He was

130

conscious of her intimate use of his name. She laid a slim hand on his arm. "Charles, I worry so about them. If anything were to happen to either of them, I could not bear it. I could not."

"Sophia—" They were alone, a dangerous situation, and addressing each other by their first names. He swallowed. "My lady, nothing will happen to them. I swear to you, I will not allow it." And he would not, he knew, if he had the power to protect them; he would give his own life for them.

Lady Sophia's reconciliation with her two sons was a miracle. She loved them with a fierce maternal passion, and they adored her. George had wisely kept Sophia alive for her boys, despite her physical absence.

Her hand brushed his cheek. "You are so good to me, Charles. I do not know what I would do without you, truly. You—" She stood on the tips of her toes and brushed her lips against his. Charles trembled.

"Sophia—" he whispered, cupping her face with his hands. "Sophia—"

She was in his arms, holding him tight, and weeping openly. The tears seemed to stun her as much as they did him. They welled up from somewhere deep and hidden inside her, as if a large block of ice had melted suddenly and overflowed its boundaries like a river in flood. Charles held her while she cried. It seemed to him that she was crying not only for her boys, but for herself, for George, for everything that had ever happened to her. The notorious Lady Sophia Rowley . . . who would have thought it? He held her closely as she drenched his new brocaded waistcoat with her tears.

Charles stayed for luncheon, sitting at the table in his damp waistcoat. When the boys returned from their ride with Lord Brent, they were enthusiastic about the invitation from Hal and Thaddeus Mainwaring until they remembered the upcoming fair.

"We were so looking forward to the fair, Mama," William pouted.

John elbowed his brother. "Looby! There will be others!"

Sophia frowned, and John straightened up. "Sorry, Mama," he whispered. She continued to frown. He turned to his little brother. "Sorry, William."

"That is better," she replied, hugging her sons. "There will be other fairs, Mr. Heywood assures me, and probably some in the Lake District. His family is from there, as you know, and the Mainwarings are great friends of the Heywoods. Perhaps you will have the opportunity to visit his family home." But she was leaving the choice of whether or not to accept the invitation to them. "If you do *not* want to go, however, that is fine, also."

"Hal and Thaddeus are great guns, Mama," John assured her.

William agreed. "We like them. It would be fun to visit. We have never been to Cumbria."

"You make the decision. Whatever you say, that is fine with me." She looked at Charles. "Of course, you will miss your lessons with Mr. Heywood."

John considered this. "We could make up for them when we return, Mama." He looked at the vicar for confirmation. "And Mr. Heywood says we are ahead of ourselves, anyway."

Charles nodded. "The boys have been very diligent, my lady. The visit will not affect their studies."

"Well, then," Sophia said with a smile, "it is settled. I will send Joan to help Harriet sort out your clothes for the visit, and I will reply to this invitation forthwith." The boys clapped their hands in glee.

132

★ ★ ★ ★ ★

The Earl of Dunhaven hung back, taking in the scene between his daughter and his grandsons. Perfect! As soon as he found out when the boys would be leaving for Cumbria, he would contact those rogues in Roslyn Town. Sophia would be putty in his hands with her sons disposed of. He would comfort her on her great loss even as he made plans to relieve her of George's fortune. He grinned inwardly, pleased with himself.

Sophia was instructing Joan in laying out the boys' wardrobe for their visit. As she ticked off the necessary garments, she noted that her abigail was subdued, unlike her usual vivacious self. Sophia frowned. "What is the matter, Joan?"

Joan blinked. "Naught, my lady," she replied quickly.

Sophia sat down on her bed, her blue eyes fixed on her longtime servant's flustered face. "Nonsense! I have known you for many years. What is troubling you?"

"My lady, I do not want to burden you with the staff's problems and concerns."

Sophia sighed. It was much easier when she had not concerned herself with her servants, when she had not bothered to know them as people. Sophia had been shamed by the boys' admonitions to use her retainers' correct names and resolved to mend her ways.

During her childhood in Kent, she had known all the house servants by name; they were her friends. But time and circumstance had changed her for the worse. Her father, who had been absent from home during the greater part of her formative years, considered servants less than human. Unknowingly, she had become like him. John and William had opened her eyes, but now she found herself perhaps too involved with her servants and their lives. The footman Fred's bruise the other day had concerned her, though she'd said nothing. And today she was concerned for Joan. Something was amiss.

"You are burdening me with your downcast looks, Joan. Come, let me hear what is concerning you, girl."

Joan blushed. "It is Sarah, my lady—"

Sophia nodded. Sarah, a pretty little brown haired girl with large blue eyes, was one of the housemaids. Joan had mentioned once that Fred was sweet on her.

"Mr. Bromley had to fetch the surgeon, Mr. Alcott—"

Sophia rose, clearly upset. She took Joan by the shoulders. "What happened?"

"She said she fell, my lady, that she fell and broke her wrist. The doctor set it, and gave her laudanum for the pain."

Terrible thoughts began to form in Sophia's brain. "And—"

Joan's eyes filled with tears. "She did not fall, my lady! She was thrown to the floor by . . . oh, my lady, I don't want to say—"

"How did Fred come by his bruise, Joan? The truth, now!" Sophia shook the girl's shoulders.

Joan wiped her eyes. "He put himself between Sarah and . . . oh, my lady!"

Sophia's voice was firm. "Joan!"

"Your father, my lady, the earl, he—"

Sophia's face fell. *The bloody bastard!* She remembered all the pretty young maidservants in Kent who had left under cover of night. She had stopped learning the names of her servants because of the rapid turnover. After her mother's death, they had come and gone so quickly. Then Miss Bane, too, had disappeared . . . Sophia winced at the memory.

"Thank you, Joan. That will be all. Leave me now, please."

"My lady, I did not mean to upset you—"

Sophia patted her shoulder. "No, Joan, I am grateful for your candor. I am sure none of the other servants would have spoken. They would keep their own counsel, as servants are wont to do. Thank you for telling me."

Sophia turned and went to the window. She looked out onto the rolling lawns and hugged herself tight. The nightmare was beginning again; her father was abusing her servants. She would not allow it! She had been powerless once, but no longer. She needed to speak with Charles, but he had left. Brent . . . she would speak with Brent. Something had to be done about her father.

She began to calm down. The boys would depart on the morrow. She would deal with it then, with the boys gone. She did not want them to be present when she confronted the earl. He had to go, and she would make it clear that this time, it was forever. Brent would back her up. They had become friends, surprisingly so, after clearing the air between them. They would never be lovers. And Charles . . . Thank God for Charles! He was her rock, her strength, always there for her. What would she do without him?

Sophia recalled her breakdown in his arms. She had wept all over his chest, drenching him. She could not remember when she had last cried. No, that was not true; she did recall the last occasion when she'd permitted herself the luxury of weeping.

It was when her mama had died. Lady Miranda Eliot had been young and beautiful. Sophia remembered the laughing dark-haired woman who'd played with her, sang lullabies and songs to her, brushed and plaited her long blond hair, held tea parties and pick-nicks with Sophia and her dolls in the long summer afternoons. Lady Eliot had fallen into the artificial lake behind the manor house, the servants said, lost her footing on the slippery shore at night and drowned.

Oddly, she had been alone, so there'd been no one to save her or to call for help. Odder still, no one had missed her until the next morning. Her funeral was a sad, hurried affair. Miss Bane had taken charge of Sophia, held and comforted her as she'd cried out her heart. The Earl of Dunhaven had been conspicuous by his absence. He had left at dawn, before his wife's body was found, before she was missed and the search was begun. He'd been hell-bent for London and its pleasures.

How warm this woodland wild recess!
Where quiet sounds from hidden rills
Float here and there, like things astray,
And high o'erhead the skylark shrills . . .
— *"Recollections of Love,"*
Samuel Taylor Coleridge, 1807

CHAPTER THIRTEEN

With much fussing and kissing from their mother, John and William and their baggage were on their way to the Mainwarings'. John Coachman was accompanied by footmen Fred and Horatio, one sitting beside him on the box, the other on horseback, riding alongside. Sophia had found a brace of pistols among the baron's personal effects, had them cleaned and readied for use, and had given one to each footman.

Sophia waved as they departed, hiding her sniffles in a lace-trimmed handkerchief. Her heart thudded in her breast. She turned to Lord Brent, who'd seen the boys off with her.

"I'm worried, my lord," she whispered. "I fear my father may be up to some mischief. He has been too quiet of late, keeping his vile remarks and humors to himself. It is not like him at all. I know the signs too well." She wrung the damp handkerchief in her hands nervously.

Brent nodded, but reassured her. "You have taken adequate precautions, my lady. Your father could not be so stupid as to attempt mischief with the protection afforded by two armed footmen. Never fear." He patted her arm.

"Fred told me that my father went out the evening he pleaded illness, when we were at the Ramsbothams' for dinner—"

Brent's brow furrowed. "I was not aware of that. Did Fred have any idea where the earl went?"

"No, he did not know where my father had gone." Sophia continued to worry the fragile piece of cloth in her hands. "I have now given instruction to the staff to keep an eye on the earl, and to follow him if he leaves Rowley Hall on horseback."

Brent pursed his lips. "Do you want me to question him, my lady?"

She shook her head. "No, I do not want him to know we are suspicious of him."

The nobleman laughed. "I've not yet made it clear that I am not interested in his plots, my lady." He stroked his chin. "But I believe he would be foolish to apprise me of any plans to injure your sons. Your father is far more clever than that."

"We shall keep our eyes on him, you can be assured, my lord. My servants are not fond of him. They shall report his movements to me." Sophia tucked the wrinkled wisp of cloth into her sleeve, taking Lord Brent's arm as they went into the manor house.

The Earl of Dunhaven chortled in glee from behind the draperies in the library. He was in a good position to watch the boys' departure from home, and to note that his protégé and his daughter had formed the seeing-off committee. From all appearances, they were getting on well. As soon as the lads were done away with, Sophia would turn to Brent for support. Marriage bells would follow after an appropriate period of mourning.

The earl had conducted the rest of his business with the highwaymen last night under cover of darkness when the household was asleep. He'd passed on the details of the boys' departure and the route the Rowley carriage would be taking to Cumbria. Parts of that road were desolate, ideal for an armed ambush. Soon, soon, he would have good news from that disreputable pair of ruffians.

He felt like dancing a jig.

A parishioner had made him late after Matins, but Charles caught up to the Rowley's crested carriage a few hundred yards from the Hall. Breathless, he wished the boys a good journey and gave them letters to take to his family. Among them was a letter to the Mainwarings, explaining that the boys were under his tutelage but had worked so hard this summer that they were entitled to freedom from Greek, Latin, mathematics, geography, and all else that smacked of school, while on the visit.

Charles hoped the boys would take advantage of the area where he had grown up, that they would sail the lakes, fish the streams, hike the trails, and otherwise enjoy themselves as he had. The Mainwarings, he knew, would see to it, but the lads had asked him to put all this in writing. They cheered as he explained the contents of his missive and sent them on their way to the easternmost reaches of England's north.

"And you will go to the fair and tell us all about it, will you not, Mr. Heywood?" William queried.

"Never fear, my lad, your mother and I will make note of it in our journals and describe all to you in detail." He laughed.

John elbowed his younger brother. "Looby! As if Mr.

Heywood and Mama do not have better things to do than laugh at a Punch and Judy show, or gape at a bearded lady!"

William elbowed his brother in return. "He said they would go!"

"*Boys!*" Charles chastised the duo. "Do you think your mother sent you off in this coach to maul each other all the way to Cumbria?"

John and William looked at each other, shamefaced. "No, sir," they chorused in unison.

"Well, then, see that you both behave," Charles warned them, smiling.

"Please don't tell Mama that John elbowed me, sir," William begged.

"We shall endeavor to behave as gentlemen do, sir," John assured the vicar, his tone assuming a baronial inflection. "Do tell her she has naught to fear."

As Charles rode away, he heard what sounded like "*Looby!*" but continued to ride on, chuckling to himself. Despite Sophia's efforts to train them, her boys were high-spirited, and there was nothing wrong with that.

"My lady, the doctor is here," Bromley announced shortly after the carriage disappeared from sight.

Sophia's thoughts immediately turned to her sons. "Has there been an accident? Has the carriage overturned?"

"No, my lady!" Bromley was alarmed at the thought. "No, nothing to do with the young masters."

"Has my . . . is it one of the servants?" Was her father again assaulting her staff?

Lewis Alcott walked into the drawing room. "I am sorry, my lady, it's urgent that I see you. It's about your servants—"

"Has my father—" she began.

The doctor looked puzzled. "Your father? No, I have come to ask if you could spare some of your staff. There is an outbreak of putrid sore throat and I require assistance with my patients. If you could spare one or two—"

Putrid sore throat! It was highly contagious, Sophia knew, and she was immediately glad her boys had left the vicinity, but others were suffering. "What would you like me to do, Mr. Alcott? I am at your disposal, sir."

"My lady, you need not be involved personally. If Lizzie or any of the footmen or stable lads could be spared, that would be a great help. I am going to the Ramsbothams next, to see if they have staff to lend me."

"Sir, Lord Brent and I are able-bodied, as well. We will gather what we need and accompany you." Sophia rose in a trice, determined to be of use.

Lewis blinked. The sun streaming through the windows glinting off his round spectacles. "Well, my lady, if you insist . . ."

Sophia nodded. "I do, sir."

"Well, then, if you would go to the Browns' farm with Lizzie, that would be of immediate help. They are all ill with fever and their cows need milking for a start."

The Browns? John and William had told her stories about a small child named Chloe Brown, a sweet charmer who had captivated both of them in one meeting. "Not little Chloe?" Sophia asked.

Lewis nodded. "Her parents are recovering but still need rest. The child, though . . . well, it does not look good. She hovers between this life and the next. This dread sickness attacks the very young and the very old and many succumb."

"I am on my way, sir." John and William would not forgive her if she stood by and allowed this child to . . . well, she must hope for the best. She and her mother had seen to sick servants and tenant farmers, and what she did not remember, Lizzie would. The girl's mother was the local midwife and herbalist. They should make an effective pair.

"Bromley," she turned to the butler, who had been privy to her conversation with the doctor, "do get Lizzie for me, please, and as many of the male staff as we can spare. There is an emergency, and Rowley Hall must do all it can to assist." She strode briskly from the drawing room. They heard her call to her abigail for a change of dress.

Lewis and Bromley looked at each other, and the doctor spoke first. "Is this the same lady who arrived too late for her husband's funeral, Bromley, and incurred the wrath of the entire countryside? Is this the same London lady whose notorious reputation preceded her . . . or a changeling who has been put into her place?"

Bromley's lips thinned. "Lady Rowley is a fine mistress, sir, and we are lucky indeed that she lives at Rowley Hall. I will hear nothing ill of her." He glared at the surgeon, spun on his heel and walked away, leaving Lewis wide-eyed in disbelief.

"Stand and deliver!"

The chilling words rang out over the quiet country road as two masked highwaymen, pistols in hand, drove the crested carriage over the far shoulder. The Rowley heirs had been scarcely two days on the road, headed in the general direction of Kendal and from there to Lake Windermere, when they were accosted.

John was seated on the box between Horatio and the coachman. William was sleeping in the carriage, and Fred was on horseback alongside. Horatio feinted right, to shield

John, as the coachman swerved to keep from overturning; Fred moved his horse forward quickly and took out his pistol, surprising the smaller of the attackers, who dropped his own gun to the ground.

The larger of the two highwaymen turned and raised his weapon toward Fred just as Horatio fired, blowing the pistol from his hand. Meanwhile, the other man leaped from his horse and moved to recover his gun. Fred, confused by the rapid progression of events, was uncertainly turning his pistol toward first one of the highwaymen and then the other.

Pulling himself together, the bigger man swore, groping for another loaded pistol from the wide leather belt about his waist. He fired with his left hand, and Fred fell from the horse. William, from inside the carriage, now began to shout.

"John! What is happening?" he screamed, his small face pale at the window of the coach.

John leaped recklessly from the box toward the bigger of the two highwaymen. He knocked him down, causing his mount to rear. The ruffian swore, cuffing the boy hard on the side of his head. John whimpered, then lay very still on the rocky ground. William continued to scream as the coachman struggled to contain the frightened horses. Horatio was still attempting to reload his pistol as the smaller highwayman fired, grazing his upper arm. The footman dropped his gun.

Flinging open the carriage door, one of the villains grabbed William by the nape of his neck, ignoring the boy's violent kicking. The other man picked up John with one hand and the reins of Fred's horse with the other. He flung the boy across the horse's back and sped off, heading back toward Yorkshire, closely followed by his companion. The other man was struggling with the burden of the kicking and cursing William.

Fred and Horatio, both bleeding from their wounds, stared after them helplessly as, despite the driver's efforts, the coach wavered, then overturned, wheels spinning in a mangle of screaming horses, hooves and limbs flailing the air.

High overhead, the shrill cry of a skylark pierced the early morning air, cutting the abrupt silence.

Chloe would not die, not if Sophia could possibly prevent it. *Such a sweet, pretty child,* she thought. Chloe's harsh breathing was the only sound in the modest bedroom of the farm cottage. Sophia mopped the fevered little brow, tenderly smoothing the wet curls of dark hair.

"Chloe, my dearest," she crooned, "Chloe—"

The door opened quietly and Lizzie peered into the dwindling twilight. "My lady, how is she?" she inquired.

Sophia looked up, and Lizzie seemed taken aback at the sight of her mistress. After two sleepless nights, Lady Sophia was pale and haggard. "Shall I sit with her now, my lady? You need some rest—"

"No!" Sophia's whispered, her voice low but fierce. She would not leave the child's side. After all her hours of nursing, Sophia would not leave her.

Lizzie persisted. "My lady, the doctor is here. He says you will become ill yourself if you do not rest—"

"Time enough for rest when this child's fever breaks. Do you have the herbal tea your mother prepared?" Sophia would not be moved.

Lizzie nodded. "She brewed it with feverfew and rosehips. Can you get the wee one to take it?" She looked down at the still child. "Her lips be so dry—"

"Sponge her face and chest, and I will try to spoon some tea down her throat." Sophia reached up for the cup of hot liquid.

Heavy footsteps sounded on the stairs. Sophia winced. The doctor was a big man; his heavy feet announced his approach. "Tell that idiot not to make so much noise!" she ordered her servant.

Lizzie gulped. "Me, my lady?"

Sophia sighed in exasperation. "Just wring out that cloth with cold water and wipe the child's body." Sophia rose and went to the door.

"Mr. Alcott!" She spoke in a loud whisper. "Do be quiet!"

Lewis stood at the head of the stairs. He looked worn out, his broad face stubbled with two days' growth of beard. "Lady Rowley, why are you still here? I sent Lizzie to relieve you. You must sleep! The Browns are convalescing and should be up and about in a day or two, but you—"

"I am not at all tired, sir," Sophia lied, her ravaged face telling the truth her words would not.

The surgeon rolled his eyes heavenward. "Where in Hades is that bloody vicar when he is needed?" he wondered aloud.

"What has Mr. Heywood to do with this?" Sophia bristled, annoyed at the profanities.

"He seems to be able to speak some sense to you occasionally," Lewis retorted, annoyed.

"You need not shout, sir," Sophia glared at him.

Lewis adjusted his spectacles, pushed the hair back from his face, and reached for Lady Sophia.

"How dare you!" she whispered harshly, ineffectually beating her fists against him as he forcefully dragged her downstairs.

★ ★ ★ ★ ★

It was the worst week Charles had experienced since the death of Baron Rowley.

Three people in the village and its environs had died swiftly from the contagion. One was an elderly man in his ninth decade of life, another the child of wealthy land-owners, the last a young farmer's wife. At times like these, his own comforting platitudes made no sense to him, sounding hollow and false. He prayed for the souls of the departed and hoped there would be no more deaths.

Lewis was a tower of strength, marshalling help from all around, exhorting neighbor to help neighbor. Servants from Rowley Hall had taken the lead, following the example of their mistress. Mrs. Mathew and Mrs. Chipcheese had kept everyone—invalids and caregivers—fortified with calf's foot jelly, broths of chicken and beef, and other strengthening foods, the nourishing fare delivered by maidservants in baskets and footmen on horseback throughout each day.

Charles intended to check on the Browns, who'd been among the first to fall ill. He was worried about their child, Chloe. He wondered where Sophia was; all he knew was that she had left with Lewis. He prayed that she was all right; putrid sore throat was deadly.

As he drew up to the Browns' farmhouse, he heard voices raised in anger. Puzzled, he tied his horse's reins to a post and went inside, where he found Lady Sophia pointing her finger at the embattled surgeon, her wrath terrible to behold. Both looked exhausted and unkempt: clothes rumpled, hair tangled, faces drawn.

"My lady!" Charles called out. "What is amiss?"

Sophia turned toward the vicar. He thought she had never looked more beautiful. His breath caught in his throat.

"Tell your friend," she said through clenched teeth, "that I am going back upstairs to be with that child! He has no right to order me from her bedside."

Lewis seemed beaten-down. He threw up his hands in disgust. "You deal with her, Charles. I have had enough!" He turned and again ascended the staircase to the sickroom.

Charles caught Sophia's flailing hands. She was beside herself. "Charles, oh, Charles."

"Easy now, my lady. Let Lewis see to the child," he soothed her, his voice low and gentle.

"Charles, you look dreadful." Sophia brushed his cheek, feeling the rough stubble.

"I am fine," he caught her hand and kissed it on the palm. She closed her eyes and shivered.

"Sophia? Are you unwell?" Charles was suddenly concerned. Her body swayed against his.

Bloodshot eyes blinked open. "I am just tired—" she began to explain.

"We all are, my dear. You must try to sleep a little." He led her to a low bench by the unlit fireplace.

"But . . . Chloe . . . I must see to her," she protested.

"Lie down, love, I will go upstairs and see how she fares, I promise. Now rest, please."

Lewis Alcott raced down the stairs, taking them two and three at a time and looking fair to break his neck. *The child!*" he shouted.

Sophia roused quickly. "*No!*" she screamed, running to the surgeon in terror.

"Nay, my lady, do not despair! The child's fever is broken, thanks be to God. She will recover. Lizzie is with her and will not leave her bedside. It is you yourself who must rest now." He looked meaningfully at the vicar. "Charles, will you not take Lady Rowley home?"

"I don't want to leave," Sophia stated flatly. From behind her, Charles shrugged his shoulders.

"My lady, as your physician, I would prescribe bed rest for several hours at least." He winked at Charles, out of her sight. "Can you see to my lady's bed rest, Vicar?" he asked.

If it were not such a joyful moment, due to the miraculous recovery of the young girl, Charles would have planted a facer on the grinning face of Lewis Alcott. The man went too far! But he decided to ignore the surgeon's insulting double entendre and took Sophia's arm.

"Come, my lady, I will stay here with you while you rest." He indicated the comfortable-looking bench, padded with blankets and pillow. Exhausted, but now relieved of worry for the child, Sophia nodded and allowed herself to be led to the resting place.

As he settled her, Charles glared at his friend, muttering sotto voce, "When this is all over, Lewis, I swear to you that we shall have it out!"

"I look forward to dancing at your wedding," Lewis grinned, as Charles snorted. "And now, forgive me, but I still have patients to attend." He fetched his bag and took his leave, whistling a jaunty tune.

Dancing at his wedding, indeed! Lewis Alcott never ceased to tease, even during these perilous times. Perhaps it was the only defense the man had in the face of death and disease. Perhaps Charles should cultivate more understanding and not be so quick to judge, though the surgeon's comments were often unwelcome.

He looked down at Sophia, now asleep, the lines of worry erased from her brow. Charles smoothed the lank tendrils from Sophia's face and sighed wearily. His heart ached with love for her, a love that was perhaps also unwelcome, if not thoroughly ill advised.

A sworded man, whose trade is blood . . .
— "Separation," Samuel Taylor Coleridge, 1805

CHAPTER FOURTEEN

The dilapidated, unused barn was in a desolate area not far from Roslyn Town. The highwaymen had ridden hard and arrived before nightfall, carrying the two boys. John was still comatose from the hard blow to the side of his head, and William had grown weary of struggling. Trussed with rope, they were tossed onto a pile of rotting hay and left alone while the two men went to eat and drink at the Cock and Bull and await the nobleman who'd engaged their services.

Arthur Coats, the younger and smaller of the men, addressed his companion in crime. "Bert, be we holdin' the lads fer ransom, then?" he asked.

Bert Coats, his cousin, guffawed. "Ransom! Be ye out o' yer mind?"

Arthur's worst fear surfaced. "Ye would not *kill* 'em?"

Bert turned to him in disgust. "Yer too soft. That was what I agreed with the toff."

"Bert! Did ye not see the crest on that carriage? They be Baron Rowley's lads!"

"So?" Bert was not impressed.

Arthur was beside himself. "The baron was good to us, Bert. Have ye forgotten, man? He was good to all his folk."

"The baron's gone to God, as we all will, as his sons will, shortly." Bert responded, laughing in appreciation of his cruel remark.

No, Arthur thought, *no.* He would not be a part of this. He took the heavy pistol from his belt and clipped his older, stronger cousin on the back of the head. With a strangled oath, Bert fell to the ground. Arthur dismounted and hit him again, then tied Bert's hands behind his back. After relieving him of his pistols, boots and horse, Arthur Coats rode back to the rundown barn.

The earl sensed that something was very wrong. The highwaymen had not returned to the tavern with proof that the boys were dead, as planned. No one seemed to know where they were, and the innkeeper averted his gaze when questioned. Frustrated, Dunhaven left the premises, swearing to have the villains' gizzards on a spit. What was he to do now? It was entirely possible that the gallows rats had taken his blunt and fled the county. His threat to them was idle; he had no idea where they were. How could he run them to ground? Or perhaps the plan had gone awry. That younger man had seemed unwilling.

Maybe it was time to switch to his alternative plan. He had a bad feeling about the situation and he had learned over the years to trust his instincts. Perhaps he should flee, but he vowed not to leave empty-handed. If the truth were revealed, 'twas a dead surety Rowley's penny-pinching lawyer would turn off his annual allowance. He needed to replace it somehow . . .

Lord Brent was inexpertly milking cows at the Harlow farm, much to the amusement of Joan. She admitted, though, that he was trying hard to accomplish the task. The cows were cooperating; they even seemed to enjoy it. Well, she thought, they were female, after all, and Brent was a handsome fellow! She noted, too, that the hens never

150

pecked him when he collected their eggs. Neither would she, if she were a hen, that was!

Charles had persuaded Sophia to return to Rowley Hall for a bath and a change of clothing. She acquiesced only after seeing with her own eyes that little Chloe was improving. She sat by the child's bed and spoke to her softly, assuring her that she would return to tell stories of princesses and fairy gold.

She insisted on entering through the servants' entrance, so she could ascertain the well-being of her staff. "I am concerned that they are driving themselves too hard."

Charles countered, "No harder than you have worked yourself, my lady."

Sophia raised tired eyes to meet his. "How can I ask them to do what I will not do myself?"

For a moment, it seemed that he heard the voice of the late baron. It was something that man would have said himself! Recovering his aplomb, he agreed, "Of course, my lady, you are right."

Mrs. Mathew's arms were covered from fingertips to elbows with flour, and her mobcap was hanging askew over one ear. Bromley, aproned from chin to knees, was scrubbing pots like the lowliest scullery maid, while Mrs. Chipcheese filled baskets for the ailing. They all looked up as Charles and Lady Sophia entered the kitchen.

"My lady! What can we do for you?" Mrs. Mathew asked, wiping a grey lock of hair from her eye and thereby dusting the side of her ruddy face with flour.

"You have all been doing more than enough!" Sophia exclaimed, gesturing with arms wide, taking in all the early morning activity. "I wanted to tell you how much your efforts are appreciated. The doctor seems to think that the worst is over." She hesitated briefly, then continued, "There have been some losses, alas, but people are on the mend and there are no new cases today. So, thank you, thank you very much."

Bromley stepped forward, wiping his hands on the capacious apron. "My lady, we merely followed your example." The two cooks nodded their agreement.

"Thank you, Bromley. You honor me, as I honor you."

Charles lifted his eyes heavenward. Somewhere in that celestial sphere, he knew for a certainty, the baron was pleased.

After a hot bath—the vicar had brought up the water so as not to burden Bromley with the task—Sophia was almost herself again. She dressed in a simple muslin frock and plaited her long, blond hair. Reappearing downstairs, she looked like a schoolgirl or an extraordinarily pretty young serving maid.

"I will take the dogcart to the Brown farm, Charles, and stop at the Harlows' on my way, to see how Joan and Brent are faring. I told Mrs. Mathew I would carry provisions for both farms."

Brent . . . Charles had wondered where that gentleman had disappeared. The earl had made himself scarce during the medical emergency, and Charles had assumed that Brent was in Dunhaven's company. So he was at the Harlow farm with Lady Sophia's pretty abigail! Lewis had told Charles about the incident involving Dunhaven and the maid, Sarah; could Brent be trusted with Joan? The vicar was still not certain about the character of the man he considered a rival for Sophia Rowley's affections.

"Brent is at the Harlows', then?" he commented.

Sophia nodded, settling herself in the dogcart and securing the baskets for the short drive. "Lizzie tells me he is an expert at cow milking." She giggled at the thought of that fashionable buck in shirtsleeves, squeezing bovine udders. What a picture for the *ton!* If Rowlandson himself drew the caricature, they'd not easily believe it of this nobleman.

"He and Joan are managing well?" Charles lifted himself into his saddle. Lancashire Lad, his grey, stood steady.

"Very well, according to Lizzie," Sophia remarked. "She says they are clucking after the Harlows like hens with chicks, and bickering cheerfully."

"The Harlows are hardly chicks, my lady. They've farmed that land for nearly fifty years," Charles replied.

Sophia chuckled. "I know! That is what is so amusing. Those two young people treating that aged pair as if they were sick children. Brent has shown his mettle, has he not, sir?"

"As you have proved yours, my lady," Charles said with feeling.

Sophia blushed. "Do not make too much of my contribution, Charles. You . . . Lewis Alcott . . . my household staff . . . we have all done the same." She continued, "And though Lewis is most exasperating at times, he is a good man and an excellent surgeon. We are lucky to have him."

Charles nodded. "Your late husband thought well of him, my lady."

Sophia raised her dazzling blue eyes to his. "George was an excellent judge of character. He wanted me to rely on you, and, though I resisted, he was correct. You have been a rock to me; I am glad, now, that he appointed you guardian for the boys."

Now it was Charles's turn to blush. "When did the baron speak of me, my lady?"

Sophia wrapped the reins about her wrist. "Lawyer Norton gave me a letter George had written a few weeks before he died. I read it with a good deal of annoyance when I first arrived here, and again a few days ago, with a much different attitude."

Charles's response was drowned out by the arrival of Fred, a very dusty, road-weary Fred, on horseback.

"Oh, my lady," he cried, "the boys are gone! They were taken!"

From his outlook in Sophia's bedroom, the Earl of Dunhaven saw the arrival of Sophia's trusted footman. Damn and blast! he muttered, gathering up the rest of his daughter's jewels in a leather bag that also held select items of silverware. It was time to depart, with not a moment to lose! His horse was saddled and ready at the stable, his pistols clean and primed.

To the north was Scotland, and from that coast ships sailed to the continent. The baubles should ensure a pleasant sojourn, and perhaps 'twas also time he looked for a wealthy continental lady to wed. Much as he despised married life, the blunt from the jewels would not last forever. Not if he were to continue to follow his favorite pastime, those elusive games of chance. If nothing else, life had taught Tom Eliot to be a realist.

Lady Sophia had fainted. Charles had carried her into the Hall, while a frantic Fred had poured out the rest of his story. Bromley had hurried to fetch the vinaigrette from her dressing room, only to return in a matter of minutes with more news of an unsettling nature for the vicar. Lady Rowley's boudoir was a shambles, clothing and effects strewn everywhere. Her jewelry case was missing.

"Where is the Earl of Dunhaven?" Charles asked the butler.

"Lady Rowley requested that we keep a watch on him, sir, but with all that has been happening—" Bromley was distraught. Too many unspeakably vile things were happening at once. It had not been so in the baron's time.

The vicar clapped Bromley's shoulder. "I know, man, I know. Do not blame yourself. Right now, we must decide what's to be done to find the boys. That is the most important task."

On the sofa, Lady Rowley was stirring. "What happened? Fred? Charles? Bromley? Please! You *must* tell me what has happened!"

Charles sat down beside her. "My lady, Fred has told us that the carriage was set upon by brigands, highwaymen, two days' drive from here. It overturned, injuring the coachman and Horatio; Fred and Horatio were also shot and wounded. The boys—"

Sophia began to wail, tearing her hair from its smooth plait. But he stayed her hands. "No, my lady, do not despair! The boys were taken, yes, but I expect they were kidnapped for ransom, as they were not injured." Charles was aware of his lie; Fred had said that John had received a blistering blow to his head during the scuffle that had ensued.

Sophia was sobbing hysterically. "This is because of me, is it not? 'Tis because I am a dreadful person, a bad mother, I know it! My boys! Why them? Why not me?"

Charles fixed her with a steady look. "We will find those boys, trust me! Trust in God, my lady. We *will* find them; I pledge my life and my honor on this. And you must never hold yourself responsible. You are not ever to think that."

Sophia hiccupped as Bromley handed her a large square of white linen to dry her tears. Charles passed the piece of cloth to her, keeping hold of one of her hands.

"God has not abandoned you, my lady," Charles reassured her, hoping that the boys were safe, wherever they were.

Fred said, "We can round up the male staff and the villagers and find the young masters!"

Charles shook his head. "There are few men to send, Fred. There has been sickness in the village. All the great houses and the farms have been affected, too. People are still weak and unwell. We must see who is fit to join a search party, and report this to the magistrate. Where are Horatio and John Coachman now?"

But Fred's face was ashen at hearing this news. "Sarah? Is she well?"

Sophia nodded, wiping the last of the tears from her face with the linen. "Sarah has been helping here with Mrs. Mathew, Fred. She has been fine."

Fred let out a deep breath.

Gently, Charles reminded him. "Horatio, Fred? And the coachman? Where are they?"

"Oh, beg pardon, sir. They are in a tavern; the innkeeper's wife said she would attend them. Horatio was shot and the coachman was hurt when the carriage turned over, but the doctor said they will be well enough to travel shortly. They will look about for folk who might have seen men on horseback riding off with the young masters."

"Good," Charles commented. "Good! We can make a small search party here. I can go, and perhaps Lord Brent and Bromley, for a start." He turned to Sophia. "My lady, I will take those baskets to the Harlow farm and return with Brent. I will also take the basket for the Browns."

Sophia shook her head. "No, I will take them the basket. I promised Chloe, Mr. Heywood, that I would tell her stories about princesses and fairies." She shuddered, then made a decision to carry on. There was nothing more she could do. She was in despair; weeping and wailing and tearing her hair was what she wanted to do, but she could not, not in front of everyone.

Sophia knew she must regain control of her emotions and carry on, for her sake and for the sake of her distraught staff. Telling stories to Chloe, keeping her promise to the child, would erase this horror from her mind for a short time while she waited for Charles to summon men for the search. Then she would return to do what she could at home. There was not much she could do, she realized. It was up to the men, to the search party. She accepted the fact of her helplessness, but she must be strong. "Then I will return to do whatever has to be done," she vowed.

She took a deep breath and continued, suddenly recalling her discussion with Brent on the day of her sons' departure. "Where is my father?" She looked at the men, her brow furrowing as suspicion began to grow into certainty. "Where is the Earl of Dunhaven?"

She could not know that the earl was hell-bent for Scotland, even as the reluctant highwayman Arthur Coats was releasing the boys from their bonds and setting them free.

To me the past presents
No object for regret;
To me the present gives
All cause for sweet content,
The future? . . . it is now the cheerful noon,
And on the sunny-smiling fields I gaze
With eyes alive to joy . . .
  —"To a friend inquiring if I would
    live over my youth again," Robert Southey,
    early 19th-century Romantic poet

CHAPTER FIFTEEN

St. Stamia's Fair was a typical three-day festival—the vigil, the feast, and the morrow, so it was termed—when it began in late Saxon times. By the time of the Virgin Queen Elizabeth, it had extended to a fortnight. Its saint was a contemporary and rival of Rowley Village's St. Mortrud, the relict of a wealthy landowner who'd converted to Christianity late in life. She made up for those lost pagan years with fervor and zeal to the very end.

Lady Stamia founded a nunnery that fortuitously escaped the depredations of King Henry VIII and also those of Cromwell's Roundheads a century later. It had flourished so deep in the hills above the sleepy town of Shepton, some miles from Rowley Village, that it was easily overlooked. Fittingly, good St. Stamia had evolved into the patron saint of things lost and not easily found.

Two such lost items were the brothers Rowley, John and

William. Deposited rather hurriedly outside of Shepton one night by a repentant Arthur Coats, they'd crawled onto the side of a ferny hillock and slept. When they awoke at dawn—John with the remnants of a splitting headache—the lads found themselves not far from a double row of stalls, temporary affairs of wood and canvas for hawking buns and other sweet pastries, rolls of woven cloth, bags of raw wool, beer and wines, all manner of beasts (four-footed, two-footed, winged), and trinkets galore. Mouths agape in wonder, John and William saw the fair come to life as they gazed at Gypsies reading palms and the requisite Punch and Judy show, as well as a traveling troupe of actors reciting from the works of Shakespeare.

A monkey shared a booth with a squawking green parrot, both watched over by an old tar claiming to have seen service with the king's navy in exotic Far Eastern ports of call. If the promised bear appeared, there might be bear-baiting. A shifty-eyed conjuror pulled rabbits from a hat while another dodgy fellow performed card tricks, and a sheriff arrived to watch suspiciously over both sleight-of-hand masters. There was no bearded lady, but a family of midgets, little manikins smaller than William, strutted and tumbled.

John was beginning to feel better. Though his head ached and he had no idea where he was, the sights of the country fair were cheering him considerably. William jumped up and down in glee. Drinking in the myriad wonders before them, the boys temporarily forgot their mother and the hosts who were expecting them. They listened to tunes played by fiddlers and hurdy-gurdy men, enjoyed the colorful costumes of the mummers and puppets, and were transported to a world of fantasy beyond their dreams.

The boys had never heard of Stamia, that good but ob-

scure saint, and did not realize this was the fair they'd anticipated visiting all summer. They simply knew that their
dream of attending a fair had come true. Aches, bruises, the
horrifying ordeal and hardship of being waylaid and kidnapped, receded into the distance as they melted into the
crowd of merrymakers. They were transported into another
realm.

Sophia was determined to stay calm. She trusted that
Charles and Lord Brent would find her sons. She had also
sent word to the baron's lawyer, Stokes Norton, asking for
help, perhaps a Bow Street investigator from London. As
teams of searchers rode through the countryside, she remained at Rowley Hall, coordinating their efforts, taking
notes, and consulting maps. A letter was dispatched to the
Mainwarings, explaining the circumstances. And she had
brought little Chloe Brown to the Hall to recuperate, giving
her parents a chance to convalesce at their own speed
without the worry of nursing their child. Chloe was
cosseted to within an inch of her young life, as Sophia
dreamed of sweet little daughters of her own some day, sisters for John and William.

She was remarkably calm, considering that nearly a
whole day of concentrated effort had brought no results and
that her father—whose role in this event was increasingly
suspect—had disappeared. She cared not at all that the jewelry she'd brought with her from London—including many
valuable gifts from her last paramour—was all gone. The
Rowley family jewels were locked safely in George's bedroom. Bromley had noted that several good pieces of silver
were also missing. All these were replaceable, but Sophia
could not replace her boys.

She had been reunited with them so briefly . . . To lose

them now in this horrible manner, as she was on the road to a new, better life, would be excruciating. She was, however, determined to remain hopeful. Charles had pledged that he would bring the boys home safely, and she believed him. Lord Brent was aiding Charles's effort and they were both intelligent, caring, trustworthy men. She was also praying; it never hurt to pray. She asked that God would punish her, if she deserved it (as she probably did, she thought), but not John or William. The sins of the mother should not be visited upon the sons; Charles had assured her that the Lord was not vindictive.

She would soon find out if that was indeed true, would she not?

Charles and Lord Brent had scoured the countryside all day. It was almost nightfall of the second day when they happened upon the village of Shepton.

"The fair!" Charles exclaimed. "I'd forgotten all about it."

Brent looked thoughtful. "The one that the boys were so eager to attend?"

The vicar nodded. "The same. Let us have a look." They dismounted and walked their horses towards the center of the activities.

The fair was about to shut down for the night. Canvas flaps were flipped over booths and fairgoers were wandering homeward, but Charles saw a small crowd at a stall midway down the row. A placard at the right proclaimed the feats of a mental calculator.

Charles began to laugh in relief. Brent gave him a perplexed look, a look that seemed to ask if the vicar was losing his mind. "Sir? What is so amusing?" It had been a long day of fruitless searching and questioning of witnesses who'd seen nothing out of the ordinary.

Charles pointed to the crude, hand-lettered sign:

Match Wits With The
Midget Mental Calculator!

Brent peered at the sign, then grinned, slapping Charles on the back. He, too, had witnessed William's amazing facility with numbers. They ran toward the stall and took up positions at the rear of the small group of villagers. William stood on a small platform, frowning in concentration as John posed a question.

"In a library of ten thousand, three hundred and forty-seven volumes, if the average number of pages in each be three hundred and fifty-nine, how many pages are there altogether?" William closed his eyes.

The crowd held its breath as Charles counted thirty seconds. Then the boy opened his eyes and stated in a firm voice, "Three million, seven hundred and fourteen thousand, five hundred and seventy-three."

Behind him, two men were furiously computing the sums. "More time!" they called out. John nodded, waiting before posing another mathematical problem. When the previous answer had been verified after some minutes, a country lad in the audience stepped forward.

"Can you take my question?" Both boys nodded as the audience grew still. "I am now fourteen years old, and suppose . . . suppose I spend two shillings and six farthings every day of my life, and I live . . . oh, say fifty years more. How many farthings shall I spend during my life?" He stepped back.

Charles had barely begun to count out the seconds when the answer came: "Two million, eight hundred and five thousand, one hundred twenty farthings."

Behind the platform, the adults computing the answer called, "He's correct again, the little bugger!" The crowd cheered at the amazing swiftness and accuracy of William's calculations.

The "midget mental calculator" blushed, and the crowd began to disperse. Charles and Brent moved forward.

"Mr. Heywood!" John cried out. "You have found us!"

A wrinkle-faced farmwife paused, hearing John's exclamation. "Thanks be to our good St. Stamia, lad! She sees to it that the lost are found!"

"Indeed, madam, indeed," Charles agreed. "She has led us to these boys."

William ran up to Lord Brent. "We meant to ride home with a farmer in a hay wagon who was to be bound for Rowley Village, sir, but he left before we could ask him. You see, Arthur deposited us here, and we had no money, and no way to get home."

Lord Brent squatted in the grass. "Whoa, boy, whoa! Take a breath, now! Who is Arthur? And what happened after your carriage was stopped by the highwaymen?"

John, holding tightly to the vicar's hand, answered for his excited younger brother. "There were two highwaymen, sir, two scurvy rogues! They tied us up with rope and left us in a barn, but one of them, the less scurvy, I reckon, returned to release us. His name was Arthur, he said. He dropped us here during the night and we didn't know where we were until morning."

Lord Brent looked up. "You are all right, then? No physical harm? You have been fed?" The boys' clothes looked a bit ragged and dusty, but they were alert and cheerful, for all that.

William nodded. "We are fine, sir. We have been having

a grand time. Joseph and Jacob," he pointed towards the two men who had been computing the answers to the problems posed by John, "gave us half of the money the crowd threw and food to eat."

Brent rose and opened his purse. "How much do we owe you, sirs, for taking care of these two young men?"

Joseph pulled his forelock. "It were our pleasure, sir, to keep the lads safe." He grinned. "Brought good business to our little booth, they did." Jacob, behind him, nodded in assent. Then Joseph turned to John. "Why did ye not tell us who ye were?"

"We were afraid that if you knew . . ." John began, then hung his head, ashamed to admit his lack of faith in the men who'd been so kind to them, but Joseph nodded kindly.

"Take this as a reward, please," Brent insisted, passing a shiny gold guinea to the duo.

"Thankee, sir," they cried in delighted unison.

"Now, boys," Brent turned to the Rowley brothers, "I think your mama is looking forward to your return!"

Rowley Hall was full of strangers. They continued arriving, much to the consternation of Bromley and the serving staff, who had just begun to return to their normal schedule after the upheaval caused by the outbreak of putrid sore throat and the mysterious flight of Lady Sophia's father. A Ramsbotham retainer brought the news that the Earl of Dunhaven had been seen consorting with two unsavory characters at the Cock and Bull Inn some days previously. The landlord of that establishment, when questioned and threatened by the magistrate, had supplied their names. Unfortunately, Bert and Arthur Coats could not be found; they, too, had left for parts unknown.

For aught that I could ever read,
Could ever hear by tale or history,
The course of true love never did run smooth . . .
        —William Shakespeare,
            A Mid-Summer's Night Dream,
            Act I, Scene 1

CHAPTER SIXTEEN

Lady Sophia hosted a joyful open house to celebrate the safe return of her sons and to thank those who had searched for them and had sought news of the earl. She had been overwhelmed by the generosity of her neighbors and the outpouring of genuine affection for John and William. Her guests included a party from the Lake Country. After receiving her letter concerning the children's kidnapping, Sir James Mainwaring and his grown son Percy had traveled posthaste to Rowley Hall. They were accompanied by Viscount Ashley—Charles Heywood's father—and Harry, the vicar's elder brother, all come to lend their aid and support.

Sophia cornered Charles on the lawn, where tables groaned under the weight of the food and drink that had been laid out. "Charles, I can never thank you enough for your great kindness. All of this generosity . . . Well, I am quite overwhelmed." She could barely speak, her heart was so full.

"My lady," the vicar replied, "George was respected by all who knew him as a fine man and neighbor, ready to assist whenever he was called upon, and you have shown yourself to be a good neighbor as well. The boys are highly thought of by your tenants, the villagers, and the local gentry. And I . . . I pledged to George that I would do all in my power for you and his sons."

Sophia shook her head. "You do not realize, Charles, how little kindness I have known in my life." She squeezed his hand. "No one in London cared if I lived or died. And I, alas, could also have shown more concern for others. Now . . . now I am affected by Sarah's broken wrist, by the gunshot wounds suffered by my footmen, by the deaths of those poor folk from the putrid sore throat."

She gave a wry laugh. "It was as if all of their misfortunes were my own. I have never felt this way before. It is unsettling, I must say. It is . . . it is quite startling to me."

"Sophia—" Alone at the edge of the great lawn, they were openly calling each other by their Christian names. "Sophia, you have been accepted by the people of this community, and, more important, *you* have accepted *them*."

She nodded. "I shall have to become accustomed to this. It is all so very new to me." She turned the full force of her brilliant blue eyes on him. "Charles, about us—"

William approached running, careening into the vicar and almost bowling him over. Sophia reached out a hand to steady him. "William! Take care, my dear," she quietly admonished her son.

"Sorry, Mama! Sir James wanted to know if we still intend to visit Hal and Thaddeus. He says we can return with him in their carriage, as ours has been damaged. May we, Mama, may we?" William turned imploring eyes up at her. Sophia smiled, ruffling his hair. She moved her hand to the side of his face, feeling his warm cheek. He was alive, safe. *Hers.*

"I see no reason why not, William, but allow me to consult with your guardian." She turned in mock-serious fashion toward the Reverend Mr. Heywood. "Sir, what do you think of this proposition?"

Following her lead, Charles frowned, hand on chin, as if seriously considering the request. "Well . . . I suppose . . ."

"Say yes, Mr. Heywood, sir, please, say yes!" William begged.

Charles laughed. "Of course, you imp! Did your brother put you up to this?"

The boy lowered his head. "Well—"

"Off with you!" Charles chuckled, and Sophia saw him nearly knock John over as he ran to him with the good news.

"The trouble with children so near in age, my lady, is that they often plot together against their parents," he informed her.

"I am beginning to see that, sir." She smiled. "I was my parents' only offspring, and had few playmates, so I had no one with whom to conspire."

She added, "I find your brother Harry quite charming, Charles. Your father, also. The family resemblance is very marked; I knew them at once." They were handsome men, Sophia thought, though Charles was perhaps the most well-favored. At least in her eyes . . .

"Everyone says we are much alike, my lady, but not so much as John and William, who could be twins except for the difference in their sizes."

Sophia's eyes flickered to where little Chloe Brown was amusing both John and William with her antics. She was blindfolded and attempting to catch hold of them with her pudgy arms, in a game of blindman's bluff. John had just pushed William right up to her, so she could grab her quarry. She laughed as she took hold of his coat, and he groaned in mock dismay as she pulled him toward her.

Joan, who was talented with her needle, had fashioned a frock for the child from an old sprigged muslin of Sophia's, with enough remaining for two more dresses. Chloe was now, without doubt, the best garbed little girl in all of Rowley Village. The wide green riband trim at the neckline brought out her leaf-green eyes. "I will hate having to return that sweet child to her parents," she averred. "I long for a little girl of my own."

Charles Heywood's cravat felt very tight, of a sudden. "You are thinking of marrying again, my lady?"

Lady Sophia closed her eyes demurely, the long golden lashes fanning her cheeks. "Only if I find the right man, Charles," she whispered.

"Wh . . . what kind of man . . . would this fellow be?" he stammered.

"Not a man who would marry me only for my fortune, sir," she replied. "Nor a man who could not love my boys. Also, we should have to suit in temperament and in beliefs, I think. We should be of like minds, though not necessarily holding the same opinion on all things. For, if so," she smiled prettily, "I might as well marry myself."

"And . . . have you found this man yet, my lady?" Charles stared into her lovely face.

So engrossed were they in conversation, they had not heard Lord Brent's approach; the nobleman cleared his throat loudly to make the two aware of his presence. Sophia smiled at him now as he joined them.

Was Brent her ideal man, her putative husband? Charles wondered, glowering at his rival and excusing himself with the comment that he must have a word with his father.

"Ah, yes," Brent chuckled, "the match-making is underway."

Sophia was perplexed. "The match-making, sir? I'm

afraid I do not understand . . ."

Brent elaborated on his comment. "I was speaking with Percy Mainwaring, Sir James's son. He told me that it has long been understood that your vicar and the youngest Mainwaring daughter, Charlotte Anne, would someday wed."

Sophia recoiled as though suddenly doused with cold water. "What are you saying, Brent?"

"That it is all but done, my lady. Mr. Heywood was reluctant to agree to the marriage this past year, using the excuse of your late husband's declining health, but now it seems he has no further excuse for delay. The Mainwarings are hoping for late fall nuptials, if not before."

Sophia felt as if she had taken root where she stood. She could not move any of her limbs. It was an effort to force words through her lips. "I . . . I have not been led to believe that . . . that Char . . . that Mr. Heywood's affections were otherwise engaged, my lord."

Sympathy reflected from Lord Brent's warm brown eyes. "Otherwise, my lady? Does that mean, then, that they are engaged at this moment?"

Sophia could not meet his direct, questioning gaze. "You ask too much, sir."

Gently taking her hands in his, he asked, "You *are* in love with him, are you not?"

She would not answer and attempted to turn away, but Brent held her hands. "My lady, he is a fine young man. If you and he—"

Now Sophia did turn, fixing Brent with a stare. "He is younger than I, and the rector of this parish." Unflinching, she enumerated the list of obstacles that, of late, had been much in her thoughts. "I am a woman of somewhat dubious reputation. I have been married and widowed thrice. My father plotted to kidnap—and likely to kill—my sons. My mother died under mysterious circumstances. Could any greater scandal be connected with my name?" She laughed ruefully.

Brent's voice was soft. "What, my lady, does any of this have to do with the love you and Mr. Heywood may have for each other?"

"His father would never agree to such a match, Brent, and he is a good and obedient son. As you have just described, they favor another for his future wife and are even now in the midst of solidifying a marriage contract. And though I tell you, my friend, that my notorious reputation is somewhat exaggerated, it still clings to me and damages me."

Sophia shook her head. "I am no fool. If Charles Heywood has any ambitions in the church, any inclination to rise further in that hierarchy, they would be better served by marrying a pure young woman like the Mainwaring daughter, a girl untainted by the slightest breath, the merest whisper, of scandal." She raised her head. "I am considered damaged goods, Brent, certainly in the eyes of a young man of the church."

"Nonsense!" Brent's voice was firm. "You are an exemplary female, my lady, intelligent, brave, loving . . . No one would dare—"

Sophia released her hands from the nobleman's grasp and placed two fingers over his mouth. "Shush, my lord, shush. I appreciate your words more than you can know, but my reputation would compromise Mr. Heywood's future. *That* is the plain truth."

"And, yet," Brent teased her, "you have kissed him in your rose garden, my dear lady."

Sophia smiled. "More than once, my lord! Yes, I have

kissed him, with great enjoyment. And though I blush to tell it, even to such a good friend as yourself, I would bed him with greater enjoyment. I would not lie to you about that! But, *marry* him? That is out of the question." She looked to where her sons were still playing with Chloe Brown, imagining another child, a little girl, hers and the vicar's. A fairy tale! She was too old for such stories.

She hooked her arm in Brent's. "I was engaging in some fantasies earlier, my lord, pretending it would be possible for someone such as I to marry Mr. Heywood, but such perfect endings are for little girls like Chloe, there." She indicated the child, turning her head. "It is past time that I grew up and accepted my fate. I shall never marry again, sir."

"You do not give that gentleman enough credit, Sophia Rowley. He is, I believe, enamored of you. I have often been the recipient of his murderous looks, proving that he thinks me a potential rival!" Brent laughed. "He may not accept so easily his family's wedding plans, and you must have faith in your rector. He has shown me that he is a man with his own mind."

Brent leaned over and pressed a feathery kiss on Sophia's temple. "I never thought you faint of heart, my lady," he whispered. "Now, as never before, you should be bold and dare much."

"You are a wretch, my lord, to say these things," Sophia complained, slapping his forearm.

"Perhaps, but a truthful wretch, for all that." They shared a comradely laugh as they made their way to the tables.

"I have never said no to you, Father, but in this particular instance, I am adamant." Charles ran a hand through his hair. "I will not marry Charlotte Anne Mainwaring."

Benedict Heywood, Viscount Ashley, fixed a puzzled look on his son. "You have known Charlotte Anne all your life. It was always assumed . . ."

"By you and Sir James, perhaps, but not by me," Charles interrupted.

"What objection could you make to marrying that demure, pretty, devout young miss? She would make an ideal vicar's wife. 'Tis the consensus of our families . . ."

Charles shook his head. "Charlotte Anne is sweet and lovely, I agree, but she is also the veriest simpleton. Father, the girl is hen-witted."

Lord Ashley was visibly perplexed. "What difference does that make in a wife? She will manage your household, bear your children, be steadfast and loyal . . ."

"No, Father. I prefer someone with whom I can hold intelligent discourse, someone whose wit challenges me. I could not abide a sweet peagoose, no matter how pretty."

The viscount fixed his youngest son with a frown. "Let me understand what you are saying. You would prefer a bluestocking, then? Is that the sort of wife you seek?"

Charles was not looking at his father. He had just caught a glimpse of Sophia and Brent, arm in arm, walking across the lush green grass. A look of dawning comprehension replaced the frown on his father's face.

"Or is it, my son, that you are more intimately involved with the widow of your late, good friend? I understood that you were carrying out the baron's wishes in looking after his wife, and that he named you guardian of his sons, but is there something more?"

When Charles replied, his voice was flat, devoid of emotion. "And if there was?"

Viscount Ashley shook his head. "Then I would say you

were a fool, my son, a great fool. Taking up with this lady would be most inappropriate. If you are contemplating marriage to such a woman, my boy, you must think of the consequences for your future in the church!"

Charles raised his chin, defiant. "You misjudge the lady, sir." He lowered his voice. "As does everyone, I fear. She has been more sinned against than sinning, I assure you."

Ashley ran his hand through his thick brown hair, the gesture reminiscent of his son's nervous habit. "She is a glorious creature, I grant you that, and any man would . . . But, my dear boy, she is older than you are, and infinitely more experienced in ways that you—" He bit his lower lip, unwilling to be more explicit.

Simply, quietly, with great restraint, the vicar replied, "I love her."

"This will not do!" Ashley's frustration with his son was clear. He took Charles's arm and shook it, hard. The gesture barely registered with Charles; he was oblivious, his attention riveted on Sophia, who now laughed aloud with Lord Brent. Brent, a more appropriate suitor for the beautiful widow than he, a poor cleric, would ever be.

He sighed. "It matters little, as Lady Sophia is not interested in wedding me. But I tell you, sir, with respect"—his tone was adamant—"I will not marry anyone simply in order to be wed. Charlotte Anne Mainwaring and I do not suit, and that is the end of it. I am truly sorry if I have disappointed you, and Mother, and the Mainwarings, but Charlotte Anne would be happier with another man."

"I beg you to think upon this, Charles. You should marry soon and set up your nursery. It is expected of you. And your rise in the church—" Ashley left the last unsaid, but implied. A proper wife would aid a young man desiring higher office in his chosen calling.

Charles shook his head. "I doubt that I shall ever wed, Father."

Still the older man persisted, shaking his head. "This is but a temporary infatuation! You will soon forget her, my son. Trust me on this! Women such as Lady Rowley—"

Charles's face twisted in pain. "I beg you, Father, not to further disparage the lady in my hearing. I hold her dear, whatever the future may bring to either of us."

Both men knew that the conversation was at an end. Viscount Ashley had run out of arguments. There was nothing that he could say to sway his stubborn son.

The Rowley family lawyer, Stokes Norton, had been waiting for a chance to speak to Charles. Now he approached the vicar of St. Mortrud's.

Charles hid his distress over the unhappy conversation with his father and greeted the bluff, jolly lawyer in kind. "Mr. Norton, how do you do, sir. I am happy to see you here."

Norton indicated the gentleman at his side. "Mr. Jarley, here, is a Bow Street investigator. He was visiting me on other business when I learned of the kidnapping and called on Lady Rowley to see if we could be of assistance. We are indeed fortunate that you and Lord Brent came upon the lads." The lawyer shook his head. "At a fair! Was it true those rascals were performing at a country fair?"

Charles grinned. "They are rare children, indeed."

Norton sighed. "Ah, youth!"

"Indeed," Charles agreed. "But young John was somewhat logical in thinking it best not to reveal their identities to any stranger, in light of their recent experience. He hoped to find a local farmer to bring them home."

A passing footman served champagne from a silver tray.

Refreshed, the trio walked to a bench set under a spreading oak tree and continued their conversation. Jarley, it seemed, was the investigator Norton had hired to look into the background of the Earl of Dunhaven at the baron's request, before his marriage to Sophia.

"A bad 'un, that one, sir," Jarley commented. "Bad to the bone."

Norton nodded. "This latest escapade! What could the heartless man have been thinking? His own grandsons! And absconding with Lady Rowley's jewelry! But the sad truth may be that he has done even worse—"

Charles's ears perked up. "Worse?"

Jarley elaborated. "The death of his young wife, sir, Lady Rowley's mother . . . it were suspicious from the first. The earl was the last person to see her, and he left the house afore her body was found tangled in the weeds at the far side of that lake." He shook his head, as if soured by the evil in the world, adding, "And he did not return for the good lady's funeral. When he did come back, several years later, he was a right devil to the staff."

Charles frowned. "What did he do?"

"He had his way with the maids. There's more than one bastard in Kent with those distinctive blue eyes and light blond hair like the Eliots," Lawyer Norton replied, his disgust clear. "And the governess, Miss Bane—" He spread his hands wide. "She disappeared, vanished into the air. That was just before the earl took his daughter to London for the season, before he married her off to that vile cur, Rushton."

"Did she meet the same fate as the Countess of Dunhaven?" Charles asked. "Lady Rowley remembers her very fondly, and I am certain that she would like to know."

"Ah, Mr. Heywood," Norton turned to the investigator,

the Bow Street Runner Jarley. "That is where this man comes in."

The trail had grown cold by the time Jarley was set upon it by Stokes Norton, acting on the orders of Baron Rowley. The pretty young governess had last been seen just after luncheon on the day of her disappearance. Young Sophia was in the library all afternoon working on her lessons. Her father, the earl, had been drinking heavily since the noon meal. The servants all remembered his particularly foul humor, and that a loud argument had erupted between him and the governess in the upper hallway, some distance from the library.

Miss Bane and her employer had clashed several times, but the earl's frequent absences from the estate enabled her to remain in her post, as he'd taken little interest in his daughter's education except to rail against the teaching of Greek and other subjects he deemed unsuitable for a woman. On that fateful day, however, the earl had been heard to shout that the governess was no longer in his employ and that she would not be accompanying her charge to London for the Season. He told her that he intended to marry the girl to the highest bidder. Sophia's youth and beauty would command a very high price.

Miss Bane objected vociferously to his plans for her charge, and the earl had backed her into a corner, shoving her hard. She slapped his face. This scene was witnessed by a timid serving girl who'd slipped hastily down the back stairs, fearing for her own safety if the master should notice her cowering nearby. The servant had been the unwilling object of the earl's brutish attentions herself and knew what he was capable of doing to anyone who thwarted his wishes. Years later, the girl tearfully remembered what had occurred in those minutes in the hallway in detail, telling all to Jarley, but she had not lingered to see more of what had transpired.

The staff did not know what followed next, as they dared not venture upstairs until hours later when the earl reappeared, demanding his dinner. The governess was never seen again; she had vanished. Her clothing and personal effects, including her Bible (a gift from her vicar father), remained in her bedchamber. When young Sophia questioned the earl, he would only say that Miss Bane had been discharged and had left straightaway. Sophia could not believe that the governess would leave without saying goodbye, but she was powerless to do anything else but accept her father's version of the events.

Though the suspicious menservants, fearing foul play, quietly searched the grounds near the lake, and even dragged the lake itself, remembering what had happened to their late mistress, no trace of Miss Bane was ever found on the Dunhaven estate.

Lady Sophia later told her husband, Baron Rowley, that preoccupied as she was with her own unhappy circumstances, trapped in marriage to the brute her father had chosen, she never had the opportunity to pursue the case of the missing governess. If Miss Bane were alive, she would have sent for her belongings, but Jarley learned that no instructions had ever arrived at the earl's home concerning their disposition. They were eventually packed away by the servants and stored in an attic.

At about this time, coincidentally, the governess's father passed away. Word was sent to Miss Bane at the estate, her last known address, but she had already been absent some weeks. The staff thought it a blessing that the old vicar did not know his daughter was missing. As the deceased clergyman had no family save his missing daughter, all his possessions were donated to the poor of his parish, while her belongings continued to be stored in the attic.

Jarley's dogged perseverance produced no new evidence. Eerily like the case of the earl's late wife, Dunhaven was the last person to have seen Miss Bane alive. Suspicion ran deep that he had something to do with the matter or knew more than he was telling everyone, but, as the years passed, the cold trail grew even colder. If the governess was still alive, where was she? Why had she never sent for her belongings? Why had she never contacted Sophia? They had been so close!

The baron kept Jarley on retainer for years, desperate to find an answer to the mystery. Though he himself began to lose hope that Miss Bane was alive, he encouraged the Bow Street investigator to keep the search active. George Rowley had wanted to put his young wife's mind at ease, to give her the gift of knowing her governess was alive and well, but he was never able to accomplish this.

Now, Norton wanted to know, should Jarley continue his so far failed, futile quest? What, he wondered, was Charles Heywood's opinion? Should the Bow Street Runner continue to search for Miss Bane? It was now over fifteen years since she had disappeared.

Journeys end in lovers meeting,
Every wise man's son doth know . . .
—William Shakespeare, Twelfth Night
Act II, Scene 3

CHAPTER SEVENTEEN

"In what parish did the Reverend Bane serve as vicar?" Charles asked Jarley.

"For many years, sir, he had a living on the Duke of Weymouth's estate in Shropshire," the investigator replied.

Charles nodded. He saw an avenue that Jarley had not explored. "A vicar's daughter would likely have become acquainted with other clerical families. There is a network, as it were, of people with whom she would be at ease. If she were in danger, fleeing for her life, perhaps she would seek these people out."

Jarley stroked his chin whiskers. "I made a circle, sir, around the Dunhaven estate, and I went to the nearby villages and asked questions. No one remembered a young lady in distress, seeking aid, but I did not particularly question clerics when I made my investigations in Kent and Shropshire; I spoke to whoever would speak to me. I did make a trip to see the Reverend Bane's successor, but he didn't know Miss Bane, he said."

He looked thoughtful. "Do you think a clergyman would have hidden her, at her request and would have kept it secret when I was making my rounds?"

"If Miss Bane were fleeing from a man who, it now

seems clear, had no compunctions concerning the committing of murder, a ruthless man who assaulted young women at will, it would seem natural that she would seek a man of the cloth, tell him all, and ask for his help," Charles replied.

"You, sir, could have easily been hired by the Earl of Dunhaven as by anyone else. The person or persons in whom Miss Bane had confided would not have taken any chances on your character. If she had asked for pledges from these people that her whereabouts never be disclosed . . . Those confidences would never have been betrayed to a stranger," Charles averred.

"So I could have been lied to, then, by those men of God to whom I spoke?" Jarley wondered.

"The circumstances—a matter of life or death, perhaps, for Miss Bane—would have warranted such lies, sir, in my opinion."

"Then, Mr. Heywood, what can we do? They would not answer me honestly at that time, so why would they answer me now, after a lapse of several years?" Jarley asked.

"Because this time, Jarley, I will accompany you. We will go to Kent and to Shropshire. The clergy will talk to me. Especially when I inform them of what has just occurred here, and when I assure them that the earl has permanently left these shores, never to return, and no longer a threat to any honest Englishman—or woman."

It was decided, Charles thought. This was the last matter he had to tie up for George, and it would be his parting gift to Sophia. For it was clear to him now that he could not linger in the lady's vicinity, a lovelorn suitor. Better to make a clean break before Sophia and Brent married and his heart was torn to shreds. Lady Sophia had flirted with him, kissed him, teased him, much as she teased and flirted with Brent. Whether she had kissed Brent or exchanged any

other gestures of mutual affection with him, Charles preferred not to consider, for the sake of his sanity.

He and Sophia would not suit; his father was correct.
Brent was the kind of man she should marry, a man of the
beau monde. They would be happy together, and the boys
liked him. He, Charles, was the odd man out. But this
matter of Miss Bane was unfinished business, and he had
promised George he would do all in his power for Sophia
and the boys. He would discover what happened to the
missing governess. Then, he could get on with his life.

Marriage to Charlotte Anne Mainwaring, however, was not
part of the equation. If he could not marry Sophia Rowley, he
would never marry. That was a vow he intended to keep.

"Charles! What is this nonsense?" Much to the amusement of Mrs. Chipcheese (who was watching from the
kitchen window), Lady Sophia accosted the vicar as he was
loading his saddlebag onto his horse shortly after daybreak.
Lancashire Lad snorted at her sudden intrusion, his hooves
beating an impatient tattoo on the hard-packed earth.

"My lady," Charles said in greeting, noting her high
color. She had arrived on her mare, Jezebel; both were lath-
ered with the haste of their ride.

"Where are you going? Lawyer Norton said that you and
Jarley would be journeying together today. What business
do you have with a Bow Street investigator?" She leaned
down toward him. Tendrils of pale blond hair had escaped
from her coiffure and her riding hat was askew. She had
dressed in a hurry.

Charles stood on his tiptoes and reached up to straighten
Lady Sophia's Hussar-style hat. It was most attractive, the
black fur trim contrasting with her light locks. Her face was
a perfect oval, forehead, cheeks, chin—

Sophia slapped his hand with her riding crop. "Stop that!" she shouted, causing Lancashire Lad to step nervously to the side. "I want you to answer me, sir, now!"

He smiled, loving her passionate nature, wanting to take that flushed, beautiful face between his hands, and—

"Mr. Heywood!" The lady would not be put off.

Charles sighed, unwillingly coming out of his reverie. The time was past for fantasies about Sophia; he would have to adjust to that fact. "My lady, the boys are off to the Mainwarings, Mr. Duncan is in charge of St. Mortrud's, and I have church business to conduct elsewhere."

A look of irritation crossed Sophia Rowley's exquisite face. She scowled. "I had looked forward to your company, sir. With all the excitement of these past weeks over, I was hoping—"

"My lady, I am honored that you desire my company, but I have church matters to attend in York. Mr. Jarley is also riding that way, and I am simply riding with him for company." Charles did not need to mention that there was safety in numbers on the highway; this was well known. As for his lie about this traveling on church business, in a manner of speaking, it was exactly that. He was planning to interview fellow churchmen to see if he could get their help in solving the fifteen-year-old mystery of Miss Bane's disappearance.

Sophia's face fell. "Oh." She twisted the crop in her gloved hands, pouting.

The pouting lips and disappointed expression almost undid Charles. His knees buckled. No, he would be single-minded now. He had a quest to perform for his lady.

In a small voice, Sophia pleaded, "Please take care of your business . . . and come back as soon as possible,

Charles. I shall miss you, and we must talk of serious matters when you return."

Charles nodded. She wanted to tell him that she was marrying Brent. If, by staying away, he could delay hearing that unwelcome news, he would stay away as long as possible.

Sophia bent from the saddle, swaying gracefully, and kissed him on the cheek. "Godspeed, then, my dear," she whispered, and, turning Jezebel back toward the lane, left for home.

Lancashire Lad butted him between his shoulder blades, reminding him sharply that 'twas time for his own departure.

Sophia was suspicious, and restless. With the boys and Charles away, she had too much time to think. She had returned Chloe to the Browns and had no child over whom to fuss. Brent was still at the Hall, and good for occasional conversation, but he was curiously absent at times. He was a bruising rider and she knew he enjoyed racing over the moors with his large, powerful horse. Was that how he was spending his days? No, there was something else, some other matter, occupying his time. What was it?

Ever since he'd returned from aiding the farmers, she'd sensed a new caution in Brent, unlike his previous candor. There was something afoot with him. Her abigail Joan also seemed secretive of late. Sophia knew the girl well; Joan was hiding something. Should she confront her? Joan could not keep a secret from her mistress for long, that Sophia knew.

A thought had taken root in Sophia's brain, and she hoped she was wrong, but the looks she had intercepted between Joan and the handsome nobleman set off warning signals that could not be ignored. Had Brent and Joan, unlikely as it seemed, developed a *tendre* for each other in those few days of close contact on the farm? Was it possible?

"Joan," Sophia called to the young woman, who was brushing Sophia's riding habit in the dressing room.

"Yes, my lady?" Joan paused, clothesbrush in hand.

"Lord Brent is a handsome gentleman, is he not?" Sophia remarked, watching the girl's face closely. The red-haired abigail's white complexion always betrayed any uneasiness in flaming blushes.

Joan averted her face, absently picking long blond hairs from the dark blue wool of the riding habit. "Yes, my lady," she responded in a low voice, "he is that."

"La," Sophia continued, "but handsome is as handsome does or so the old saying would have it. I myself think Mr. Heywood is the better looking of the two gentlemen."

Joan shook her head, the bright red curls bouncing about her heart-shaped face. "You may find him so, my lady, but I think Lord Brent is by far the handsomer." She began to brush down the skirt of the habit vigorously.

"Do you, indeed?" Sophia drawled. "My boys admire him immensely. He might do very well as a father for them, if I were to consider marrying again."

The heavy clothesbrush fell with a loud thump on the polished wooden floor. "Beg pardon, my lady," Joan murmured, as she bent to pick up the brush. Her back had been turned to Sophia during their conversation. Sophia strode to the dressing room and looked Joan in the face.

The answer was plain to see in the girl's flushed face. Sophia frowned; she must speak to Brent before this nonsense between him and her maid went any further.

"My lord," Sophia hailed Brent as he dismounted from his steed in the stable yard. "A word, if you please."

184

"Certainly, my lady." He handed the reins to a groom lurking close by, then removed his gloves and inclined his head in a slight bow to Lady Sophia, taking her hand and brushing his lips over her knuckles. "Your word is my command," he smiled.

Sophia frowned. He was a consummate flatterer and just the sort of handsome gentleman wont to bed silly, lovesick serving girls. Sophia was fond of Joan and did not intend to allow Lord Brent to trifle with her affections.

"This concerns my abigail, Joan," Sophia said, looking directly into Brent's eyes.

His expression shifted from affable to guarded. "Yes? What of Joan? She is an admirable young woman."

Sophia nodded. "That she is, my lord, and I will not have her good heart and affections trifled with, not by you or any other gentleman skilled in the art of flattery. I will not allow you to turn that girl's head and lead her into mischief."

The muscles in Brent's face stiffened. "What makes you think I would do so, my lady? I am not the Earl of Dunhaven, a fact of which you are well aware."

Sophia waved away the testy remark. "I do not wish to insult you, sir. I know that you are endeavoring to become an honorable man and to forswear your profligate ways. As we have discussed, I am delighted to be your hostess while you make important decisions concerning your future, but why trifle with that girl? I vow she is half in love with you."

She knit her brows together. "Where will that lead, I ask you? At worst, you may get her with child; at the least, you will break her very good heart. I want neither to happen to her while she is my responsibility, under my care in this house."

She waggled her index finger at him. "Nor would my late

185

husband have allowed such mischief under his roof. I care no less than he for the welfare of the servants, and Joan is particularly dear to me. I want you to understand that clearly."

"That is admirable, my lady, but I assure you, I have no intention of trifling with the girl's affections. We rubbed along tolerably well playing the farmer and his wife, collecting eggs from the henhouse and milking the dairy cows, but that is now over. I never touched Joan in an improper fashion. Never!"

Outraged at the suggestion that he might have behaved improperly, Brent's color was high. He slapped his riding gloves against one thigh, emphasizing his indignation.

Sophia's tone was severe. "I do hope that is true, for Joan's sake, and for yours."

Brent seemed flustered now. "My intentions toward your abigail are nothing but honorable, I assure you."

Sophia nodded, but his last comment left her unsettled. He had said more than he wanted to, she thought. Much more, from the flush arcing once again along his strong cheekbones. He protested too much.

Sophia slept past dawn, an odd occurrence these days. Joan usually brought her mistress a cup of hot chocolate and roused her soon after sunrise, the appointed hour having grown earlier since their removal to Yorkshire. Now Sophia squinted at the late morning sun streaming through the windows. Something was amiss.

"Joan!" Sophia scrambled from her bed and ran to the dressing room, where Joan slept. Sophia had asked the girl to sleep there temporarily when they moved to Rowley Hall, for company; she had felt so alone in Yorkshire. The maid's bed was undisturbed, its covers neatly drawn. No one had

slept there last night. In her heart, Sophia knew instantly what had happened. *She would murder Brent!*

Hastily donning a wrapper, Sophia strode into the hallway and called for a footman to bring Bromley to her immediately. When the butler appeared moments later, she learned that the household was in an uproar and no one had thought to awaken Sophia and apprise her of the events.

Joan and Brent had eloped to Gretna Green! The maids Sarah and Lizzie had stars in their eyes at the romance of it all. A mere lady's maid and a nobleman! Perhaps it could happen to any of them!

Sophia was furious. "How could this happen, Bromley?" she accused the butler. "Did none of you see what was happening under our very noses?"

"My lady," Bromley attempted to explain, "I had no idea—"

Lady Sophia threw up her arms. She was still in her wrap, her long hair in a plait down her back, pacing back and forth in the morning room. "Pah!" *She* had known, that was the rub, *she* had known that something was afoot. Brent had lied to her.

Or had he? She paused. Had he lied to her? He'd insisted he was not trifling with Joan's affections and he had now proved that his intentions were honorable—he was marrying her! Could anything on God's earth be more unlikely than this? Sophia sat down weakly at the table and Bromley made haste to pour her a cup of freshly brewed tea, placing the sugar bowl within easy reach. Hot, heavily sugared tea was good in any emergency.

Sophia began to laugh. Head in her hands, she shook with mirth. "Bromley, we have all been blind," she chortled.

"Yes, my lady," Bromley agreed, pushing the sugar closer. He ventured an opinion. "So much has occurred here of late. It has not been easy to follow comings and goings of those in the Hall or to be certain what is transpiring, even among the servants."

She nodded in agreement and took a sip of tea, gesturing for the butler to be seated. When he hesitated, she took his arm and forced him to sit. "Pour yourself a cup of tea, Bromley. We both need it."

Bromley, shocked by this breach of etiquette, nevertheless did his mistress's bidding. Life had become too exciting since Lady Rowley had returned to the Hall. Yet, for all that, it was strangely pleasant. He was learning to expect the unexpected. The old master would be chuckling with them now, he thought. The baron was ever one for taking delight in human foibles. There had certainly been plenty of those at Rowley Hall in the last several weeks, to be sure!

He sipped his tea; it tasted good.

Absence diminishes weak passions and increases great ones, as the wind blows out candles and fans fires.
—Francois de La Rochfoucauld, Maxims, 1665

(HAPTER EIGHTEEN

She missed him.

She missed him every moment of the too-long day, so used was she to seeing him at the Hall, fresh from a lively Greek lesson in the nursery, returning from a morning of fishing with a creel full of fat trout, or exuberant and rosy-cheeked from a brisk ride on the moors with the boys. He had become a part of her new life here, and she expected to see him at the Hall and answering her summons when she sent servants to the vicarage. He had never failed her when she had needed him. During the outbreak of the putrid sore throat, he'd been everywhere at once, yet had found time to see how she was faring, also. He'd located her boys when they were kidnapped. That alone was enough to make her treasure him forever.

Her intent had been to seduce him, but unexpected events had gotten in the way. His diffident manner, sweet good looks and long-limbed body; his passionate kisses, even his hesitant stammer . . . she had grown accustomed to all of these and so very fond of each. He had seduced her, instead, just by being himself.

If he stayed away much longer, she would be witless with despair; she would lose her mind. When would he return to her? Where was he?

* * * * *

Jarley had gone west; Charles Heywood had traveled east, and they would meet when the circuit was completed. Each had a copy of the list of churches in the area surrounding the Dunhaven estate where they would interview clergy. It was a long list. If either discovered an answer to the puzzle of what happened to Clarissa Bane fifteen years ago, he would immediately ride to find the other. That was the plan. The woman could not have disappeared into thin air. Someone must know what happened to her, and, pray God, could be persuaded to share that information.

Charles was weary, and he missed Sophia. He felt her absence like a burning ache that grew larger and more painful every day. Pushing ahead, at the end of a week he had made no progress but remained hopeful that the next town, the next village, the next pointed spire indicating a modest church and parsonage would be the place that supplied the answer he sought.

The hop-picking season in the Weald of Kent was underway when the vicar of St. Mortrud's passed through on his quest. Golden hop blossoms—prized for clarifying, preserving, and flavoring beer—had been harvested in this southeastern area of England since the sixteenth century. Thousands of pickers convened from all over the country, even the teeming slums of London, to aid in the massive effort. The quiet roads and byways soon gave way to hectic activity as Charles neared the outskirts of Maidstone.

Men, women, and children walked up and down the hop rows, cloth bags of hops slung over their shoulders. Dotting the lush green acres were the curious contraptions called ventilators, or cowls, that dried the blossoms right in the fields. Timing was crucial, for the hop-picking season was short. As

he rode past, Charles saw the golden ripe, papery heads of
Humulus lupulus, set on twisting, woody stems that grew to a
height of some twenty feet. The day was sunny yet cool, perfect picking weather. Charles imagined Kent-born Sophia as a
young girl witnessing the same scenes that met his eyes.

He sighed, urging Lancashire Lad by the milling, sun-
burned pickers, looking for signposts indicating the village
of Bickley and the church of St. Mary Croy, his next stop
on the search for Clarissa Bane. From the dismal lack of information gleaned previously, he was fast losing hope of uncovering a single clue that might lead to her whereabouts.

The Reverend Asa Cantwell regarded Charles suspiciously, looking him over as he explained his errand.

"Sir, I am looking for a Miss Clarissa Bane, the daughter
of the late Reverend Zibah Bane, of St. Mary the Virgin in
north Shropshire. She disappeared some fifteen years ago
from the estate of the Earl of Dunhaven, where she was
governess to his daughter, Sophia Eliot—"

Mr. Cantwell interrupted him. "Why should I be
thought to possess information concerning her disappearance, sir?"

"Lady Sophia Rowley—who was Sophia Eliot—believes
that an action of her father, the earl, may have led to the
disappearance of her governess. She and Miss Bane were
very close, and she has felt her loss deeply all these years.
She wants to know what became of Miss Bane, and if she is
still alive." Charles fixed his fellow clergyman with a look
that could not be interpreted as anything but sincere. "It
means a great deal to Lady Rowley, sir."

"It was a long time ago," the Reverend Mr. Cantwell
murmured. "What good would be served by uncovering
events that are better left buried? Perhaps the lady does not

wish to be found. Surely, if she did, she would have contacted her former charge long ago."

Charles's heart leaped in his chest. Cantwell knew! From the way the man was speaking, he was certain of it. He had to press on.

"She may have tried to contact Lady Sophia and been thwarted, for Lady Sophia has been thrice-married and thrice-widowed in the long interim. With all those changes in surname and residence, and lack of mutual social connections, Miss Bane may not have been able to locate Lady Sophia." He held his breath, waiting.

Asa Cantwell clasped his hands behind his back and walked to the small window in his study. For a moment, he stood contemplating the green and gold hop fields in the near distance and shaking his head. Charles's heart sank.

Then the priest turned, fixing the younger man with a hard stare. "Can I trust you, sir? Are you truly an emissary of Lady Rowley?"

Charles stood tall, nodding. "You have my word upon it, sir, and I am prepared to swear upon the Good Book."

Cantwell nodded slowly. "I like the look of you and cannot help but trust a fellow priest; there is no need to take an oath, sir. I will tell you of that evening fifteen years ago when Clarissa Bane knocked upon my door." His eyes hardened. "She was a sad sight." He motioned for Charles to take a seat. "It is a long story, so please make yourself comfortable. I will ask my wife to make tea and to join us."

Miss Bane had been beaten and raped by her employer, the earl. Nearly witless from shock and fear, she had wandered in a daze, accepting rides from farmers in her frantic flight from the Dunhaven estate. She had appeared at the vicarage of St. Mary Croy at twilight, her hair disheveled, her dress dirty and torn. There was a wild look in her eyes, and her face was badly bruised, her mouth swollen and split. She could barely speak.

Like the good Christians they were, the Cantwells took her in and fed her, asking no questions. They put her to bed in their spare bedchamber, where she slept most of the next day. When she awoke, she asked for water to bathe. Susan Cantwell lent her a frock and laundered and mended her dress.

Another day passed before she recovered from the worst of her shock and was able to speak coherently. She had refused the attentions of the local surgeon, and though her battered face had healed tolerably well, a long, deep cut near her eye looked as though it would scar. The Cantwells learned that it had been inflicted by a heavy signet ring worn by the Earl of Dunhaven.

Miss Bane feared for her life. She had long suspected, from servants' gossip, that her employer had murdered his wife, the Countess of Dunhaven. She knew he was a callous, violent man and she had stayed on solely for the sake of his motherless young daughter, whom she loved dearly. The incident leading to his savage attack on her had started with a quarrel. The earl was taking Sophia to London to arrange a profitable marriage without delay; he had added that his daughter no longer had need of her services. Miss Bane had the temerity to argue.

"He assaulted her because she would not abandon her charge?" Charles asked, unable to believe that any man could so mistreat a woman guilty only of loving his own child.

The Reverend Cantwell nodded. His wife now sat beside him, holding his hand. She was a pretty woman whom age had treated well. Her grey eyes were kind.

"She did love that girl, Mr. Heywood, and she feared no good would come of the trip to London's Marriage Mart," Mrs. Cantwell murmured.

Charles nodded, his lips set in a grim line. "She was correct, ma'am. The earl arranged the marriage of his innocent young daughter to a depraved brute. God be thanked, Lord Rushton, Lady Sophia's first husband, died in a fall from his horse a scant year after they were wed, and she was released from his cruelties."

Susan Cantwell's eyes filled with tears. "That poor child—" She grasped her husband's hand, hard. "What happened then?"

"Her father sold her into marriage again. This time, her husband died from the ague. She was once more a widow. But, as luck would have it, she caught the eye of the kindest gentleman in the world, Baron Rowley. He was the first of her husbands to treat her as she deserved to be treated."

Charles ran a hand through his hair. "The baron sent an investigator named Jarley to find out what had happened to Miss Bane, but he ran into a brick wall of silence; his inquiries were useless. He found no one who knew where she had gone."

Cantwell nodded. "It came to my ears that someone was seeking information about Miss Bane, some years after she had escaped from Dunhaven. We thought it best to volunteer no information. Clarissa had been badly hurt. We feared this man might have been sent by the earl; he had a rough look about him, we were told. We had to protect her, you see."

Charles did see. "You did what you thought best, sir. No one, least of all our Lord, could fault you for that."

"Yet—" Susan Cantwell's features were troubled. "Yet, if we had contacted Clarissa ourselves—" She did not finish her statement.

"You know where she is, then?" Charles hoped.

The Cantwells looked at each other, and the cleric nodded at his wife, who said, "She is in York, sir, married to the Reverend Jesse Walters, secretary to the archbishop. You have come all the way to Kent while Clarissa was near the beginning of your journey, unbeknownst to you. She and her husband live in York Close, on the grounds of York Minster."

Charles breathed a deep sigh of relief. His long journey was over. Miss Bane was alive and in York.

Two letters sat on the silver tray brought in by Horatio that morning. The few missives Sophia received these days were of more interest to her than those dozens she'd discarded daily as an active participant in the *beau monde*. She fingered the first one, savoring the feel of the thick, cream-colored stationery, then broke the red wax seal and opened it. It was from the Mainwarings and included notes from John and William.

The boys had arrived safely and were busily exploring the Lake District. They had never sailed before and greatly enjoyed that experience. Greetings from the Mainwaring children to her and Charles were also passed on. A Charlotte Anne, Miss Mainwaring, particularly wanted to be remembered to Charles. A twinge of jealousy struck Sophia.

The other letter looked, from the hastily scrawled address, to have been written rather in a hurry. Puzzled, she cracked the seal and scanned the few lines of text. It was from Robert Winton, Lord Brent!

Brent had married Joan over the anvil in Gretna Green. He tendered apologies from himself as well as Joan for not being honest with Sophia, but they had thought it better to do what they must do, and then explain. Brent said that they were in love, and added that Joan was the sweetest, most honest, and true female he had ever encountered, as well as being decidedly pretty. He hadn't known that he'd been looking for a redheaded woman all his life!

They were on their way to Nottingham, where he had a small estate. His family would be furious, but he'd deal with them at a later time. Right now, he had other things to think about. He wanted Sophia to know he was happy, and he urged her, too, to follow her heart. He sent his regards and Joan's to the vicar and to the Rowley Hall staff.

What an *on-dit!* Sophia mused. The *ton* would savor it with their morning newspapers and Charles's housekeeper would soon spread it all over the county, giving hope to maidservants everywhere. Sophia wished the newlyweds well, though she remained exasperated with them and vowed she would ring a loud peal over both their heads when next she saw them!

And where would she ever find as good an abigail as Joan? She sighed and wondered briefly about a suitable wedding present for the couple. The poor dears would be shunned by the *ton*—until, of course, the next scandal erupted.

Her thoughts returned to Charles, as they so often did these days. She wanted to marry him, that was the truth of it, but she did not expect him to propose. Must she, then, do the proposing herself? She tapped Brent's letter against her front teeth slowly, pondering the situation.

It took the better part of a day for Charles to catch up with Jarley. Then Lancashire Lad needed a rest and so did his master. They would wait until the next day and ride at a leisurely pace, not *ventre a terre,* arriving at York prepared to seek out and speak with Mrs. Jesse Walters, *nee* Clarissa Bane. What irony—she'd been in Yorkshire the entire time! Charles thought of George Rowley, who had wanted so much to interview that lady and reunite her with Sophia. The vicar felt the presence of his late mentor's spirit and believed he was pleased.

Charles was elated, yet a bit blue-deviled, also. He had fulfilled his self-given quest but had probably lost his fair lady forever. The image of Brent and Sophia at the recent festivities at Rowley Hall was etched in his mind. They seemed to belong together. They were part of the same world, a world in which Charles, despite his lineage, would never quite fit. The *beau monde* was a far cry from St. Mortrud's modest church where he shepherded his flock amongst the rustic environs of Rowley Village.

If you are able to say how much you love, you love little.

—Petrarch, circa 1350

(HAPTER NINETEEN

The cathedral city of York had an ancient history. Named Eboracum by the Romans, it had been home to the distinguished Sixth Legion. In more recent times, Christianity had spread to the far reaches of northern England and Scotland from this city. The Archbishop of York bore the title Primate of England, and the cathedral was one of the largest and grandest in the British isles.

A far cry from modest St. Mortrud's, Charles mused, a far cry indeed. When his father asked Charles if he had ambitions to succeed in the Church of England, he implied that his son could aspire to the mitre of a bishop or the grand robes of an archbishop, and all the splendor, honor, and prestige such offices could confer upon an ambitious man.

The two weary travelers regarded the massive cathedral from the vantage point of the city walls, walls that dated from the fourteenth century and were probably built on the circuit laid down by the Romans. From here they had a magnificent view of the river Ouse, the church of St. Mary, the Roman Catholic St. Wilfrid's, and numerous other small churches that surrounded York Minster, the Castle, and Clifford's Tower. That thirteenth century structure, built on a Norman keep from the time of William the Conqueror, had been the site of an infamous massacre of five hundred Jews during the reign of King Richard I.

Charles preferred quiet, benign St. Mortrud's. If he had any calling at all, it was to serve God in that backwater village. The pomp of the established Church, the majesty of its primates, were anathema to him. His father might want such for his son, but he did not. His stammer, not the problem now that it was used to be, would erupt in full force were he to attempt to launch a sermon from mighty York's imposing pulpit. The very thought made him shudder! He was not an ambitious man.

York Close was a hidden enclave only a few hundred yards from the massive cathedral, a three-sided rectangle of simple two-story terraced houses, each with its long front garden and enclosed back garden. The open side of the rectangle fronted a gravel drive. Here lived the canons, the choirmasters, the vergers, the sextons, the bell-ringers—all those nameless folk who toiled at York Minster and their families. It was a small, tight community of like-minded church folk. Number Five was the home of the Reverend Jesse Walters, Secretary to the Archbishop.

As Jarley unlatched the wrought-iron gate, Charles closed his eyes and prayed fervently that Mrs. Walters would receive them and hear him out. What she must have suffered at the hands of the earl was beyond imagining. He hoped she had put it behind her and that he would bring her no nightmares, no bad memories. He sighed, signaled Jarley that he was ready, and together they approached the door, where he rapped firmly on a brightly painted oak panel.

A petite young maidservant greeted them with a smile and asked them to step inside. "I will see if Mrs. Walters is receiving visitors today," she informed them smartly as

Charles handed her his calling card, one edge folded neatly to show that he was indeed calling in person.

Jarley and he exchanged nervous glances. They could barely speak, tense as they both were with anticipation. Would the lady receive them? They were, after all, strangers to her.

The little maid came back to ask the nature of their visit, if they would not mind?

Charles's throat was dry; he cleared it. "It concerns an old acquaintance of Mrs. Walters, Lady Sophia Rowley—"

Mrs. Walters now emerged from behind the drawing room doors, where she'd been eavesdropping, hidden from sight. They saw a small brown-haired woman with a gentle face marred by a white, ridged scar below her right temple, close by her eye. *Miss Bane!* It must be the governess; Charles remembered Susan Cantwell's vivid description of that facial scar.

He bowed his head and introduced himself and his companion. "I am the Reverend Charles Heywood, ma'am, and this is Mr. Jarley. We bring you greetings from the Cantwells of Bickley. They were so kind as to furnish us with your direction."

Mrs. Walters frowned. "Susan and Asa? It has been ages since I have seen them. Marigold, please bring us tea. Gentlemen, please do come and sit down, rather than stand about chatting in the hallway."

Charles smiled at the woman's commanding presence, despite her diminutive size. He could imagine her as the governess who'd so thoroughly taught Sophia her Greek and Latin and mathematics. She swept through the drawing room doors and motioned them to a sofa and side chairs.

"Now, gentlemen, pray continue," she demanded.

"I am the vicar of St. Mortrud's, ma'am, in Rowley Village—"

"Yes, yes, St. Mortrud's," Clarissa Walters interrupted again. "My husband was acquainted with Mr. Fairbourne of that parish. He has retired to Brighton, I believe."

Charles nodded. "Indeed, ma'am, he was the gentleman whom I succeeded three years ago." He paused for breath, expecting another interruption from the formidable little woman, but there was none. He continued. "Baron Rowley, who appointed me to that living, passed away earlier this year—"

"God rest his soul," the lady interrupted.

"Ah, yes . . . He was a good man, an exemplary husband and father, also. He was married to Sophia Eliot, your former charge." Charles waited for an exclamation of surprise, but Clarissa Walters merely clutched her hands tightly together.

"Sophia? *My* Sophia?" she whispered, then asked, "Is she well?"

"She is quite well, ma'am, quite well indeed. And she wants to see you again, very much. She speaks of you lovingly." Charles's heart was thumping loudly and happily in his chest, curious to see Mrs. Walters' next reaction. So far, she'd seemed amazingly calm.

Now Clarissa Walters brought her hands to her face; her shoulders heaved. She began to weep quietly. Alarmed, Charles rose and offered his handkerchief. Taking it gratefully, she blew her nose, sinking back onto the sofa as if the wind had been sucked out of her small frame. She wiped her tears daintily with the edge of the cloth.

"My dear child, my angel," she murmured. "Ah, it has been so long . . . I feared . . . You said her husband had died? How old was the gentleman?"

"He was sixty-six years old and had been ill for several years," Charles replied.

"Her father married her at fifteen to a gentleman over three times her age?" Mrs. Walters asked.

"No, ma'am, it is a very long story." And, over tea and cakes, Charles related that tale. Clarissa Walters heard it through, from beginning to end, and wept silently from time to time into the vicar's handkerchief as she listened.

Jarley, a hefty reward from Lawyer Norton bulging in his pocket for his long, ultimately successful pursuit of Clarissa Bane, set off for London even as Charles headed west to Rowley Village. Charles was contemplating the best way to break the news to Sophia that her old governess was alive and well and would be arriving within the week, accompanied by her husband, to be reunited with her charge after fifteen years.

He would, however, leave it to the ex-governess to explain what had happened to her. Charles had little desire to recount how ill used the woman had been at the hands of the despicable Tom Eliot, Earl of Dunhaven. Whatever Clarissa Walters chose to tell Sophia or to omit was up to her alone.

As he rode his horse into the stableyard of the Hall, Charles was relieved to see that the atmosphere seemed to be relaxed and calm. Rowley Hall had had enough crises and emergencies, he thought, to last him through his dotage and beyond. The grooms went sedately about their work, mending harness, currying horses, raking straw, and mucking out stables. One was whistling a jaunty country air. Peace fairly thrummed in the air. The vicar sighed happily as he dismounted and Lancashire Lad was taken away for a rubdown.

"How have things been, Smithers?" Charles asked the head groom, a man of the late baron's generation.

"Ah, sir, more excitement!" Smithers responded, a twinkle in his rheumy eyes.

Charles's heart plummeted in his chest, resting near his knees. Complacency had taken flight with Smithers' words and Charles' fantasy of life returning to normal at the Hall had flown away with it. "What has occurred, then, since I have been away?" He was almost afraid to ask.

"Lord Brent and his lady eloped to Gretna Green, and were wed o'er the anvil, they were! Took us all by surprise, they did, e'en Bromley—"

Charles felt faint; he had not expected Sophia and Brent to marry so quickly! While he was haring up and down the Kentish countryside looking for lost governesses and agonizing over losing her, they had wed.

Stammering slightly, he asked, "Ha . . . have they returned?"

Smithers gave the vicar a strange look. "Returned? Now sir, why would they?"

Surely Sophia would not go off and leave her boys! "Where are they, then?" Charles queried.

"Why, at Lord Brent's estate, near Nottingham, we heard. We'll not see them again for a while!" The old groom snickered.

"But why . . . how . . . why would Lady Sophia abandon her boys like this, even for Lord Brent?" Charles was confused.

"Lady Rowley? But, sir, what does she have to do with this?" Smithers replied. "Sure, and she has lost her maid, but—" The groom scratched his bald pate.

"Her *maid*, Smithers?"

Smithers nodded, eying him somewhat askance. "Joan, sir, milady's abigail that eloped with Lord Brent a fortnight ago. The mistress is looking for a new girl, but—"

Charles resisted the impulse to gather the old man into his arms and kiss him. Her abigail! Joan, eloping with Lord Brent? Who would have thought it? The Lord truly worked in mysterious ways. His heart singing, Charles ran to the Hall, eager to see Sophia and to impart his great news.

Sophia was reading a new letter from her boys. It was smeared with inkblots, its lines so crossed as to almost be unreadable, but no less dear to her. She wore a simple long-sleeved dress with a roller printed design of alternating yellow and black flowers over white, the first dress made to her specifications by Mrs. Clover, Rowley village's premier seamstress. A far cry from the fashionable frocks cut for her by Madame Gruyon in London, it was nevertheless cool and comfortable and easy to don.

With no personal maid, Sophia had to make do. The fewer buttons and hard-to-reach fastenings, the better she could dress herself. She sighed and stretched her arms high, her full bosom rising with the movement. She must see about replacing Joan. No one on her present staff was right for the position. Perhaps she should consult her new friend, Katherine Ramsbotham. It was past time that she paid that lady a visit, at any rate, to see how the baby was faring. Sophia was feeling maternal tugs that only being in the presence of young children like the Ramsbotham infant and Chloe Brown could alleviate.

She wanted more babies of her own but could not achieve that goal with no husband. She did not even have a lover! Never had she been so long without a man. It was a unique experience and not entirely unwelcome, except when she thought of Charles Heywood. For the first time, not just any man would do.

Bromley scratched at the open door. "My lady," he intoned, "the Reverend Mr. Heywood has returned."

Sophia shot out of her chair like a bolt of lightning electrifying the midsummer sky. "Charles! Oh, do show him in, Bromley, please!"

If Bromley was shocked by the use of the vicar's first name, he hid it admirably. A good deal of stiffness had gone out of the butler's rump, Sophia thought, and all for the better. There were fewer formalities at the Hall these days, and she felt more relaxed and the better for it.

His clothes wrinkled from the long ride, his hair in its usual tousled state, his face fresh as all outdoors, Charles exuded health, youth and vigor as he strode into the morning room. Sophia went to him with arms extended and hugged him to her bosom. There was no denying it; she now knew that she loved this man.

Overwhelmed by her greeting, Charles held her close, savoring the smell of almond blossoms in her hair, exhilarating in the warmth of her lush body. "My lady," he began.

Impulsively, Sophia raised her face and kissed him on the mouth. Charles closed his eyes and deepened the kiss of welcome, losing himself in her delicious mouth, her soft, yielding lips. Her tongue traced the seam of his lips and gently intruded, tested, probed, tasted. Charles allowed her egress and crushed her body closer to his. He was dizzy with her, his mind reeling.

Then she pushed him away, breathless, almost shy. "Charles, I have missed you so."

He came back to earth, though the heaven of the last few seconds was a far better place to be. "Sophia." He could barely get her name past his lips. "Sophia, I have missed you, too."

They looked at each other, hands clasped, drinking the other in as they could never have enough. Charles swallowed. "I bring you news, my dear, news that I hope will make you happy."

Sophia blinked. "Your mysterious journey." She scrutinized him more closely, her eyes narrowing. "What *were* you up to, Charles, you and that Bow Street Runner?" She waggled her index finger at him. "For you two were up to something! I could have placed a wager on it—"

Charles grinned. "The spirit of good St. Stamia was with us; we found what had been lost. Right under our noses, that was the irony of it." His smile was rueful.

Sophia shook her head. "I do not understand. Please, begin at the beginning."

"Perhaps we should sit down," he suggested.

"Should I be worried, Charles?" Sophia asked, quirking an eyebrow at him.

"No, my lady, no, this is good news."

She turned to the bellpull. "Let me ring for fresh tea. I have a feeling that this is a long story."

"Well," Charles agreed, "it did begin some fifteen years ago."

Fifteen years ago! Sophia's hand flew to her throat. That was the year of her first marriage, that dreadful, dreadful time. She looked up at Charles, her eyes wary, but he was smiles and happiness. What had he found? And was it truly good news?

"Please, Charles, do not keep me in suspense any longer, I beg you," Lady Sophia pleaded.

Charles took her hand, turned it over, and kissed her palm. "Jarley and I found Miss Bane, my lady."

There was a loud roar in Sophia's ears. It was the last thing she heard before an icy hand gripped her and the world went black as she fainted away.

Down on your knees,
And thank heaven . . .
For a good man's love . . .
—William Shakespeare,
As You Like It, Act III, Scene 5

CHAPTER TWENTY

Miss Bane was alive!

Sophia felt the fool, falling into a faint! She never fainted! But this was the second time, the first occurring when she heard the news that her boys had been taken by the highwaymen. It looked to becoming a habit.

But, such news! It hardly seemed true, even now, with Charles sitting at her side, chafing her cold hands and reassuring her. Bromley stood to one side, vinaigrette in hand and a worried look on his face.

Sophia gave a wobbly smile. "I am fine, Bromley. Thank you for fetching the vinaigrette, but I do not need it now. I became lightheaded for a moment, that was all."

The butler, a relieved look passing over his stern features, nodded slightly. "Very good, my lady." He shut the morning room door behind him.

Sophia could feel the color coming back into her cheeks. She rose from her semi-recumbent position on the small sofa, exuberant and full of questions.

Charles had found Miss Bane! Was there ever such a man for finding things and putting them right? He had certainly cut through the underbrush and brambles and

207

found the long-lost pathway to her heart.

A few days later, Sophia was preoccupied with preparations for the arrival of her former governess (whom she persisted in calling Miss Bane instead of her proper married name of Mrs. Walters). So busy was she that the issue of her relationship with Charles was temporarily shelved.

For his part, the vicar had resolved to talk about marriage, but the time was not appropriate now, with the imminent arrival of Mrs. Walters. Instead, he unburdened himself to his friend Lewis Alcott as they walked across the moors early one morning.

In the distance, the endless tumbling songs of skylarks infiltrated the summer skies, and every so often one of the brown creatures would swoop by, so close that the tuft of its crest could be seen clearly. Other birds also made their presence known, and a steady continuo of birdsong accompanied them on their walk.

Lewis stooped and plucked a blade of grass, flushing a startled meadow pipit. He chewed on the stalk, his mood contemplative. "You missed the great elopement, Charles, with your mysterious journey to Kent and York."

Charles nodded. "Lady Sophia remarked that no one saw it coming, but she, of course, was probably the unlikely cupid, throwing Lord Brent and her abigail together during the outbreak of contagion."

Lewis nodded. His eyes narrowed, and he pointed to a number of pale grey birds clustered on a hummock of turf in the near distance. "Wheatears," he identified them. "They are here very late, no? It is now midsummer." A birdwatcher like his friend, Charles nodded in agreement. Wheatears were among the earliest harbingers of spring, making their nests in crevices on the ground or in abandoned rabbit burrows.

"They are culinary delicacies in France, are they not, Lewis?" Charles remarked, idly chucking stones as he walked.

Lewis snorted, correcting him. "Those are ortolans, Charles, not wheatears."

"Close enough," Charles remarked, not especially interested in the avian discussion. He had other things on his mind.

The birds clicked in alarm as the two friends drew closer, flying away in a flutter of white tails and rumps. Charles picked up a handful of rocks and aimed them at a jutting boulder, aim precise and on the mark.

Lewis regarded him. "You are in a peculiar state of mind this morning, if you do not mind my saying so."

"Only this morning?" Charles quipped.

"No, you are right." Lewis chuckled. "You have been in a peculiar state of mind for many weeks now, since, I believe, the arrival of the Widow Rowley to this rustic paradise we call home."

"Pray, do not jest, Lewis, though I know it is against your nature to be serious."

The doctor sighed and sat down on a hummock, his face grim, as if resigned to what was to come. "You are going to ask for my advice again, are you not?"

Charles stiffened. "If it inconveniences you so much—"

"Cut line, Charles. I am accustomed to being the confessor's confessor. What are friends for, after all?" His eyes winked behind his spectacles.

"I am going to ask Lady Sophia to marry me, Lewis," he proclaimed.

"Why do you make it sound as though you are planning your own funeral?" Lewis wondered.

"Does it sound that way?" Charles shook his head. "No,

not a funeral. It's simply that I am unsure of myself in this situation."

"How much kissing has been going on since you returned from your journey?" Lewis guessed.

A slight flush crept from the edge of Charles's neatly tied white cravat. "Some," he acknowledged.

Lewis snickered. He began to speak, stopped, and cleared his throat loudly, uttering his next words with difficulty. "Charles, Charles, you amaze me!"

Charles made a movement to rise. "If you are going to laugh at me, Lewis—" he began.

The other man's big hand stayed him. "Sit, sit. Allow me to indulge myself, Vicar." Lewis sighed, turning his face to the blue, cloudless sky and addressing the meadow pipits, the wheatears, and the hovering skylarks. "He kisses the most beautiful woman in all of England. She allows him these liberties, mind you, and, in point of fact, would not at all mind if he took even more liberties with her delicious person—"

"*Lewis!*" Charles's voice was tinged with warning.

The surgeon put up his hand. "All right, all right. Do not get yourself into such a lather." Lewis turned to him. "You know I mean nothing by this banter. But, Charles, I still do not understand the nature of this problem you see concerning Lady Rowley. Allow nature to take its course, man!"

"If nature took its course, I would be less than a sterling example of a man of the cloth, and unfit to serve the church." Charles's tone was grim.

Lewis regarded his friend gravely. "If you will not bed her outside the holy bonds of matrimony, have done with it and propose to the lady. She finds you attractive enough to kiss you on every available occasion or so you say. Perhaps she would not find it too awful to have you at hand whenever she needs . . . ahem . . . your services!"

"And if she rejects my proposal? What then? How humiliating that would be!" Charles threw a rock with great force at the boulder; it split exactly in half.

"I think you are more worried that she might *accept*, Mr. Heywood." Lewis's eyes gleamed. "My Lord, but that is it, is it not? You are concerned that she *might* accept you?"

Charles rose, brushing the dust and grass from his trousers. "I grow weary of confiding in you, I vow. You are no help at all! First, my father tells me not to even think of marrying Lady Sophia, then you tell me I fear she might accept me—"

"Your father?" Lewis was interested. "You have discussed the matter with him?"

Charles grimaced. "He guessed. I told him I had no interest in his neighbor's daughter, Charlotte Anne Mainwaring, and he was disgusted with me—"

"Well, Charles, I do not mind admitting that, in truth, I do not envy your marriage to a lady of such volatile temperament. But what was his reasoning?"

Charles shrugged. "He implied that she was much too—" He blushed fully now. "He said that she is too experienced for someone like me. She is worldly. I am not."

Lewis adjusted his spectacles, pushing them up the bridge of his nose. "He is probably right, but, ah, what joy there would be in gaining the benefit of that lady's intimate knowledge, Charles. No, do not hit me!" He feinted as Charles turned toward him with an evil glare, then clapped the vicar's shoulder.

"In seriousness, I believe that you and the widow have a good deal to offer each other. Methinks she craves a stable presence in her life, and the boys—who adore you, my friend—certainly need a father. She could do much worse. For God's sake, man, you should be relieved that Lord Brent eloped with her maid!"

Charles ran a hand through his hair. "I did believe him to be my rival, Lewis. I truly believed that. It made me crazed."

"Your *greatest* rival, Charles, one not so easily overcome," Lewis commented shrewdly, "may be yourself."

The Reverend and Clarissa Walters arrived at mid-day early in the week, accompanied by Charles Heywood. The clergymen stood aside as the women greeted each other, at first tentatively, and then with such force and emotion that Charles was moved almost to tears. He turned to the Reverend Walters and indicated that they should, perhaps, leave the two women alone.

The archbishop's secretary nodded, following Charles out the front door. Bromley, who had been standing nearby, gave Charles a speaking look as they passed.

"See that tea is served, Bromley, then make yourself scarce. Inform the others that the ladies are to be left in privacy. They have a good deal to discuss," Charles whispered.

The butler nodded, stepping back and closing the door behind them.

"Do you like horses, Mr. Walters?" Charles inquired, walking toward the Rowley stables.

"I do, sir." Jesse Walters nodded his head. "And, please, call me Jesse."

There were tears in Clarissa's eyes as she stroked Sophia's cheek. "You have grown even more beautiful, my dearest," she whispered.

"I would have recognized you anywhere, Miss Bane," Sophia replied, her voice quavering with like emotion. "I cannot believe you were so nearby all of this time."

Bromley had silently brought a tea tray into the drawing room and then closed the doors behind him. Sophia brought Mrs. Walters to the long, green-and-white striped divan in front of the fireplace and they sat drinking in each other's faces, their fingers entwined.

It was time for the question that must be answered first, after fifteen long, puzzling years.

"Why did you leave me?" Sophia asked, her lips quivering.

Clarissa placed her fingers over the younger woman's lips, to stop their trembling. "Oh, my dear, my dear, I never wanted to leave you. Your father—"

A hard look flattened Sophia's blue eyes. "What did that blackguard do?"

The former governess had decided she would never tell her beloved girl the true story of the events that had led to her departure from the Dunhaven estate. She had debated the matter with her own conscience, at length, and had concluded that she would only tell Sophia part of the truth. The whole truth of the awful matter would serve no purpose now. It had happened a long time ago, and at times, Clarissa thought it must have happened to someone else. She had removed herself from the injury and distress with a great effort of will; if she had not done so, she knew she would have gone mad.

"Dearest Sophia, my child," she began, stroking her arm, "your father would not allow me to accompany you to London. He dismissed me. I was so distraught that I argued with him." Her voice was firm as she recounted her expurgated version of that last encounter with the Earl of Dunhaven. "I argued with him too forcibly, it seems, and he . . . well, he struck me, my dear."

Sophia cried out in dismay at the outrage. Her eyes brimmed with tears.

"No, my dear, do not weep. It was a very long time ago and I am fine, now, but—" Clarissa moistened her dry lips and continued. "In his great anger at my defiance of him, your father shoved me. I hit my head against the mantelpiece. It caused a kind of forgetfulness, a jar to my memory. When I saw a surgeon, much later, he called it amnesia."

Clarissa endeavored to explain, "By the time I had regained my senses, I had wandered far off. I came to not knowing who I was nor where I had been. It was a nightmare, my dear, but gradually, I regained my memory." Now she blinked back tears.

"It was too late, though, to help you. Your father had married you off, three times by then, or so your nice Mr. Heywood told me. You must understand that I did not know to whom you were wed, or whence you'd gone. I did not have the connexions among the *ton* to find out. Nor did I know of such things as Bow Street investigators. I was not a sophisticated Londoner."

"Amnesia . . ." Sophia rolled the strange word on her tongue. "How long did this strange ailment, this amnesia, last?"

"Over two years," Clarissa Walters lied. In discussions with doctors, she'd discovered that the loss of one's memory —amnesia—was a rare occurrence. She had fashioned her version of the circumstances leading to her removal from Dunhaven around this unusual medical state. As there was no one expert in the condition, she felt she could fabricate at will. She hoped Sophia would believe her, although she deplored the necessity of having to lie to her dear girl. But the truth, Clarissa thought, would be so much more hurtful.

"Oh, Miss Bane!" Sophia wrapped her arms around her former governess, holding her tight. "I thought you dead, just like my mother!" She shook uncontrollably, then recovered, looking Clarissa in the eye. "I thought my father had killed you, too!"

The Reverend Jesse Walters seemed very interested in him, Charles thought, as they rode the horses borrowed from the Hall's stables. Why would an eminent churchman take such an interest in a lowly rural vicar, he wondered idly.

"Do you plan to spend the rest of your career here, sir, in Rowley village?" Walters asked Charles.

"This is a pleasant corner of the world," the vicar responded. "Unless circumstances mandate a change, yes, I would like to remain here. I am guardian to the late Baron Rowley's two sons, and I take that responsibility seriously. They are fine lads and need a male figure to—"

Walters interrupted him. "But surely Lady Rowley will remarry. She seems to have a penchant for the wedded state." He laughed.

Bristling at the unkind statement and the priest's laugh at his own little jest, Charles attempted to calm himself. He was growing too thin-skinned, perhaps, concerning remarks about Sophia.

"You, sir, are a young, single man," Walters continued, unaware that Charles had taken umbrage over his last remark, "surely you are considering taking a wife? The proper kind of wife is an asset to a young man seeking advancement in the Church; she helps him to step up the ladder, as it were. My own wife, Clarissa, was a priest's daughter and fully understood her role in my career. She was eminently suited to the task of helping me achieve my goal."

The older man's comments were beginning to annoy Charles. The wonderful Miss Bane, the woman who had educated Sophia Eliot so well, now seemed relegated to an ancillary position, merely the useful helpmate of an ambitious churchman. There was, surely, more to Mrs. Walters than that! She seemed a gifted, intelligent woman, fit to be a man's true mate, not merely a glorified servant.

"I do have a lady in mind, sir," Charles responded, his lips stiff.

"Ah, I thought so! Mr. Heywood, I will be retiring in the next five years. I have as yet found no one I would consider worthy to fill my post as secretary to the archbishop. What say you to transferring to York Minster, as my assistant? In time, with the right woman behind you, you might ascend to my position. Would you consider it?"

"Sir, I m-m-mean, Jesse—" It was not easy to address the older man by his Christian name, as he had asked. "You know nothing about me."

"Ah, there you are wrong, Charles! I have made inquiries. You come from a distinguished family, Baron Rowley thought very highly of you, and the other priests in this region have noted your devotion to your congregation. Your record at Cambridge was above those of the majority of young men who take orders. You are personable and popular. In addition, you have a fine mind. I have spoken with you long enough to ascertain that fact."

The archbishop's secretary beamed. "We must simply be sure that you marry an appropriate helpmeet before too long, and you will be on your way. St. Mortrud's is a delightful small parish, and fine for undistinguished men like the previous vicar, who was not good for much else, but you are a candidate for a much larger position in the Church."

Walters reached over and clapped Charles on the back, not noting the resulting wince. "I would be very glad to see you achieve these goals."

"Thank you, sir, but I . . . I don't know if—" Charles protested.

"Nonsense, nonsense! You are too modest." The clergyman's knowing smile seemed to imply that modesty was a fine virtue, in its place. "Now, you did say that you have a young lady in mind?"

"Yes, sir, I do." Not exactly a young lady, Charles thought, knowing that Sophia was possibly two or three years his senior.

The priest's smile grew broader. "Well, lad, do not keep me in suspense! Who is the lucky young woman?"

"I . . . I . . . I have not yet asked for her hand, sir," Charles stammered.

"As if she would refuse a fine young man with such a career ahead of him, sir! Come now, who is she?"

"Lady Rowley, sir. She is the woman to whom I plan to propose," Charles averred, sitting straight in his saddle.

The other man's face fell. He began to speak, then cleared his throat. "Surely you are jesting, my son? That lady would not suit, not at all! She is the last woman an ambitious young churchman should consider!"

Charles looked the archbishop's secretary in the eye. How could Miss Clarissa Bane have ever married such an uncharitable man? He had noted, too, the disparity in their ages; Jesse Walters was at least twenty years older than his wife. His heart ached for that good woman.

"I do not jest, sir, especially not when a lady is involved."

"You need to think this through, Charles. It would be a shame to throw away a promising career for mere . . . well, I think you know what I mean, sir."

Charles's lips thinned. The man was insulting! "No, sir, I cannot imagine what you mean."

"You are not a man of the world, my son. Lady Rowley is not what one looks for to fit the role of a clergyman's wife! Your career would be irrevocably damaged." Walters shook his head.

"I tried to persuade Clarissa not to come here, but she insisted. I informed her that perhaps it was not a good idea to renew her acquaintance with such a notorious woman as Lady Rowley, that it might reflect badly upon me—"

Charles felt the tips of his ears redden. Out of respect for the man's office, he would not say what he thought, but the temptation was strong. "Sir, Lady Rowley loves your wife as a daughter loves her mother. She—"

Walters waved away the remark with an impatient gesture. "The woman is no better than a courtesan! Her reputation is exceedingly infamous."

"Let he who is without sin cast the first stone," Charles responded, turning his borrowed horse toward Rowley Hall. Christ in his infinite mercy had defended a woman taken in adultery, shielding her from the angry crowd that would have stoned her to death. One of the most faithful of His little flock was Mary Magdalene. Sophia was hardly the Magdalene, but Charles felt that he would be damned forever if he continued to listen to the vile words issuing from this prominent churchman's mouth.

Sophia Rowley was well on her way to becoming the woman God meant her to be—he was sure of it—a decent, loving woman and mother, a good neighbor and friend. And he, Charles Heywood, humble man of the cloth, loved her. He would not sell his soul or his heart for worldly success. The prospect of advancement in the church, with the backing of a man like the Reverend Walters, did not tempt him. And it was well past time that he proposed to Sophia, whatever the consequences.

She was all that mattered to him now.

. . . love, bittersweet, irrepressible,
Loosens my limbs and I tremble . . .
—Sappho of Lesbos, circa 7th-6th century BC,
poem fragment

CHAPTER TWENTY-ONE

As an adult, Sophia had never had a confidante, a true and sympathetic female friend in whom she could place her trust. Now, pouring out her heart once more to her former governess, she was overjoyed. She had told Mrs. Walters all about her darling sons, rapscallion John, the improbable new Baron Rowley, and mathematical prodigy William, so small and yet so bright. Now the conversation had turned to another dear to her, the vicar of St. Mortrud's.

"I do believe I am in love with him," she confessed.

Clarissa Walters laid her hand on top of Sophia's and patted it. "He is a lovely young man, Sophia. You could not do better than Mr. Heywood. And I suspect that he is very fond of you, too."

Sophia's eyes flew to Clarissa's face. "You think so?"

"I do, child," she smiled.

Sophia's cheeks flamed. "I fear I have been very—" She cleared her throat, then continued. "I fear I have been very forward with the vicar."

Clarissa frowned. "What have you done, my dear?"

"I . . . I have been bent on seducing him for several months now. I have spoken to him shamelessly," she replied, hanging her head.

Mrs. Walters patted her former charge's hands and dispensed kindly advice. "You were in London too long, Sophia, amongst worldly and fashionable people who scorn modesty and laugh at high moral principles."

Sophia raised her head. "That is true; I know it now. It would have been far better if I had stayed with George. He gave me my freedom, thinking it was what I desired most in the world, but it was my undoing." She shook her head vigorously, blond tendrils flailing, "And I have doubtless given Mr. Heywood a disgust of me."

"How could you do that, child?"

Sophia's whisper was so faint that Clarissa bent close to hear her. "I told him that I desired to bed him. And other things."

The older woman smiled. "He appears to me to have only respect, and, I would say, love for you, my dear. He is a man of God, like my own good husband, and has heard many confessions. I do not think that anything you might have said would shock such a fine man as he." She paused. "Do you truly love him, then, Sophia?"

"I do! I do! I never thought to marry again, but now—"

"Encourage him to propose, then, my dear," was the prompt reply.

A rueful smile curled Sophia Rowley's full lips. "Charles, propose to me?" She chuckled. "I believe that I would have to be the one to ask!"

"Well, then, do so!" Clarissa stroked Sophia's soft cheek with the back of one hand. "If you truly want the man to be your husband, it is no disgrace to do so!" Her eyes twinkled. "Faint heart, my dear, ne'er won fair gentleman."

John and William arrived home from their sojourn in the Lake Country at the end of that week. The summer had passed quickly, and so much had happened. Even now, Sophia could not believe it. Country life was not as boring as she had first thought. Kidnappings, contagions, elopements, and the promise of love . . .

She had taken to heart Mrs. Walters's suggestion concerning a proposal of marriage from her to the vicar, and she was summoning up her courage. It would take all that she had. The loss of her last lover had dealt a great blow to her self-assurance; more so, she realized now, than to her heart.

The love she felt for Sir Isaac was a shadow compared to the fierce passion engendered by Charles. When with the vicar, she could not keep her hands to herself. She struggled to keep him at arm's length. It was almost embarrassing. Never, never, had sophisticated, worldly Lady Sophia Rowley so loved a man.

With the boys home, she was temporarily distracted from her mission. Their tales of hiking the massive fells, fishing in the icy tarns, sailing on Lake Windemere, and getting to know their host's neighbors whetted Sophia's appetite to follow in their footsteps.

"You would like Mr. Heywood's family, Mama," William told her solemnly.

"And they are very curious about you," John added. Both boys were sitting at her knees in the rose garden. John swatted a fly as he spoke.

"They are?" Sophia had her arms around William's neck, hugging him close.

John swiveled to face his mother. "Lady Rosina, Mr. Heywood's mother, asked us many questions about you."

Sophia's face flushed slightly. She would wager that lady had many questions she would not venture to ask a ten-year-old boy about his notorious mother! "Such as?"

William piped up. "She wanted to know if you talk of marrying again."

John poked his brother in the chest. *"Gudgeon!"* Sophia gave him a stern look. "Beg pardon, Mama," he mumbled in apology.

"She wants to know!" William defended himself. He turned to Sophia. "Miss Mainwaring asked if you are pretty," he continued. John rolled his eyes.

Sophia smiled. "What did you tell Miss Mainwaring?" She ruffled William's baby-fine hair.

"What could we say her but the truth!" John exclaimed. "We told her that you are the most beautiful woman in the world, and the best mother, too." His eyes, so like Sophia's, gleamed with pride.

William pursed his lips. "That did not make Miss Mainwaring very happy," he stated.

Sophia bent down to kiss the crown of John's head. "Am I truly the best mother?" she teased her sons.

Both boys jumped to their feet and threw their arms around her, nuzzling her neck, tickling her, and making her laugh. Their whoops of laughter reached inside the Hall, where Bromley was discussing the dinner menu with Mrs. Mathew.

"I wish the old master could see this," Bromley said, a catch in his throat.

The cook nodded, wiping a tear from the corner of her eye with her apron. "Who would ever have believed it, Mr. Bromley? That she—that Lady Rowley—those boys—" Overcome, she could not go on.

Bromley patted her shoulder. "It is nothing short of a miracle, indeed. We must all thank God, truly."

"And dear Mr. Heywood, too," she added in a firm voice.

"Mr. Heywood, too," Bromley agreed, his eyes moist.

★ ★ ★ ★ ★

Lady Sophia was an infrequent attendee at church services. Over the past months, however, she realized that her position as mistress of Rowley Hall demanded that she make an appearance at St. Mortrud's on the Sabbath. That, and the urging of her boys, found her in the first pew at the old church every Sunday, setting a good example for the villagers and tenant farmers.

Today, Lizzie was helping her dress, as a replacement for Joan had yet to be found, and the question of what to wear was of utmost importance. "What do you think, Lizzie?" She turned to the servant girl. "The printed muslin?" She furrowed her brow and debated the cut of the neckline with herself: it was high, but was it high enough?

"This spencer would complement the costume," she thought aloud. "The blue of the dress pattern is the same hue as the spencer." She held the long-sleeved, waist-length jacket with the high standing collar against the dress; it was an item she'd rarely worn, but it did suit the simple, high-necked frock.

"What a pretty print it is, my lady, all the little crosses. Good for church-going." Lizzie dimpled at her joke.

The "little crosses" were fleur-de-lis. The deep gold dress sported an all-over pattern of fleur-de-lis, an indication of its smuggled origins across the Channel. It had traveled from a smuggler's boat overland to Mme. Gruyon's dressmaking establishment. To Lizzie, the French heraldic symbol of the lily flower looked like a cross, and Sophia would not disabuse her of the notion. Fitting for church, Lizzie said; well, then, so be it!

"Yes, you are right. Most fitting." Lizzie helped her don it, and Sophia surveyed the result in the looking glass. She liked the effect. "Can you do my hair, Lizzie?" As the girl nodded, Sophia instructed her. "The bonnet will hide my hair, so a simple bun low at the back of my neck, with some curls to the side of my face, will do."

It would not do to be flamboyantly dressed or coiffed at St. Mortrud's. Sophia's goal was to be unobtrusive, to blend in with the woodwork and the congregation. She had grown fonder of the little country church. Charles and she had discussed a memorial for George on two occasions, but they'd made little progress owing to recent events. It was important, however, and they must endeavor to firm their plans to honor the late baron's memory.

Lizzie set the plain silk bonnet, in a shade of blue that matched the jacket and the field of fleur-de-lis marching across the dress, on Sophia's head, then adjusted it. The girl stood back, as if admiring her creation and Sophia smiled.

"That will do, Lizzie, yes, that will do very well."

Mrs. Walters and her disapproving husband would share the Rowley pew on this day. The Reverend Walters's dislike was apparent to Sophia; she was sensitive to such from long experience with notoriety. It was an amazing contrast, the unconditional love that flowed to her from her former governess and the dislike on her husband's face whenever Sophia caught his eye.

Clarissa and Jesse Walters were childless. Sophia, always Miss Bane's child, still was, so it seemed, but Walters would never acknowledge her as a kind of foster daughter. Sophia felt unclean when he looked at her. As a whole, she was not keen on men of the cloth. In her experience, they tended to be far too judgmental. Except, of course, for Charles, who would not presume to judge another, and who was love and caring.

Sophia flushed. It would not do, she thought, catching

her suddenly pink cheeks in the looking glass, to have im-
pure thoughts about the vicar in his church. As always, she
must restrain herself. She giggled, hoping once again that
the stout stone walls of St. Mortrud's would not fall down
when she walked inside. Reverend Walters would never forgive her. She giggled again, picturing that austere face in a
hail of broken stones.

She covered her mirth before she made a goose of herself
in front of her servant, whose puzzled look was reflected in
the glass. It would not do. She hurriedly pulled a handkerchief from her reticule and dabbed at her eyes, which were
beginning to stream.

Lizzie, alarmed, asked if anything was the matter.

Sophia shook her head. Regaining a modicum of composure, she rose to join her sons and her guests for the service
at St. Mortrud's.

God help me! she prayed. *If I giggle during Charles's
sermon, he will never forgive me.* The Rowley family seating
was in the first row, directly in front of the pulpit. She was
more accustomed to having his curate deliver the service, as
Charles had been away so much of late, but when he was
there, it was difficult for them both. She had learned to look
down, away, anywhere but into his beautiful grey eyes. To
do otherwise would be both their undoing. They were a rare
pair, she and the vicar, were they not? The notorious widow
and the stammering priest.

"Mama!" Sophia saw William, his hair slicked back,
dressed in his Sunday best, John behind him, the nursemaid
Harriett hovering nearby. "You look beautiful!"

"She always looks beautiful, you nodcock," John hissed,
so low that Sophia barely heard him. She smiled. At least
her older son was not pushing or pummeling his brother, as
was his custom. Was it because it was the Lord's day? Well,

if John could force himself into his best behavior, than so must she.

No giggles, no making faces at Charles and discombobulating him. She was Lady Sophia Rowley, after all, mother of the late baron's sons and heirs, was she not? She would behave herself in church. She owed it to dear George as much as to the congregation and to the vicar.

Sophia looked forward to seeing Charles in full clerical regalia today; the rich robes suited him. She was impressed and awed. He seemed to have an aura that was not present when he wore his everyday garb. He seemed taller, more distinguished, older: God's representative on earth.

The church service was full to its ancient rafters this morning. Even Lewis Alcott was present, grinning broadly from the last pew. Well, Charles would not focus on Lewis's grin, or on Lady Sophia's lovely presence. The addition of the Walterses was unnerving, given his recent exchange with the archbishop's austere secretary, but he had prepared himself as well as he could, though his knees were knocking under his grand ecclesiastical robes.

Charles focused on his sermon and on the fact that the Reverend Jesse Walters had no choice but to hear what he was going to say. And the vicar of St. Mortrud's had a good deal to say this morning, he reflected as he mounted the old stone pulpit.

The congregation sang the first hymn in lusty, full-bodied voice. As the people shuffled back into their seats, Charles gripped the lectern, resisting the impulse to run both hands through his hair. He fixed his gaze on the baptismal font at the rear of the church; he would be undone if he looked into anyone's eyes. Totally undone if he looked into Sophia's beautiful eyes.

He began with a prayer for the souls of all the living and dead of his parish, noting the deaths from the contagion and the loss to them all of Baron Rowley earlier in the year. He told them that in a short time a simple marble memorial to the baron would be affixed to the wall of the church.

"George, Baron Rowley, would think even this simple remembrance was excessive, but we know better. He was a good man, humble, always, before God, and his goodness and humility must be acknowledged. The Rowleys have been part of this land since the time of King Henry I, and they made their mark here. Baron Rowley was part of a long line, a line that is continued with John and William. We will honor him with this plaque as he deserves to be honored."

There were muffled "amens" from the congregation. Charles resisted the temptation to steal a glance at Sophia. The big old Bible lay closed before him; he opened it to the Book of Amos. Mindful of the many sermons that had been launched from that worn pulpit, he cleared his throat and began yet another one.

"These are 'The words of Amos, who was among the shepherds of Tekoa, which he saw concerning Israel in the days of Uzziah, king of Judah and in the days of Jeroboam, the son of Joash.' "

Charles read selected passages from the prophet's words concerning the dark fate of the indolent and the unrepentant and of the glowing future to come for the people of Israel, when the Lord had promised that "the plowman shall overtake the reaper, and the treader of grapes him who sows the seed," and when "the mountains shall drip sweet wine, and all the hills shall flow with it . . ."

Charles shut the Bible and regarded the congregation. This time he focused on dark-haired Chloe Brown, who sat between her parents a few rows from the front. He smiled at the child and she smiled back sweetly. He saw her raise a little hand and flash a half-wave at him.

"Why have I come to read the words of Amos this morning? Why this fiery prophet who brought the wrath of the Lord down upon sinners, punishing them for their transgressions? Why this dark, solemn book and this solitary prophet from the poor kingdom of Judea, this simple farmer dressed in wild animal skins? How can this ancient prophet speak to us, a people so many years removed from his time?"

His glance swept the congregation, then focused on the wooden timbers that supported the roof of the church. He gazed at the purlin, that heavy, horizontal beam set along the roof's slope to conduct and distribute the weight of the old rafters. This fine, time-weathered old church, he mused briefly, standing tall so many years. St. Mortrud would be pleased that it still stood whole. He brought himself back sharply to the thrust of his homily.

"Our present-day church is the spiritual descendant of the solitary Amos and the disciples, the apostles of Christ, who went two by two into the cities and into the wilderness to convert souls yearning for God. Yet spirituality is an individual pursuit," Charles stated, his voice firm and mellow, echoing in the silent church.

"All of us are alone before God. Yes, now we are all here together, worshiping in unison, but, ultimately our belief in God is a personal matter, between each man and the Creator of us all." He paused, shut his eyes, and took a shallow breath.

"All human unhappiness, I do believe, comes from not being able to sit quietly, alone, to ask what sort of person we are, and what sort of person we want to be. No one can do this for another. But God can help each of us accomplish the task. With the grace of God, many things that seem impossible can be made possible."

Now he looked at John and William, who were attentive, not squirming; at Mrs. Walters, who listened raptly, her lips parted; at the Reverend Walters, whose eyes were shut, arms crossed against his chest. And at Lady Sophia, whose white brow was furrowed, her mouth almost grim, her solemn gaze fixed on his face.

For that moment, only Sophia existed for him in the full-to-bursting congregation. It was as if a bright white light surrounded the two of them, blocking out everyone else. He caught his breath quickly and continued.

"The p-p-prophets of old," he stammered, "p-p-prayed on the mountaintops or in the desert, both lonely places, yet God heard them. He spoke to them. We seek God here, in this humble church, we endeavor to speak to Him and hope He hears our feeble cries." Charles's voice, overcoming his attack of stutters, was anything but feeble now, as it filled the high, wide ceiling of St. Mortrud's.

"The Book of Amos is about redemption for sinners. The Lord punishes, yes, that is true, but He also forgives. Cast not the first stone at another, but look to your own heart. Seek your own redemption, with the love and help of God. As the Lord promised redemption after great suffering to the Israelites, so it is no less for any of us."

Charles returned his attention to Sophia, who was now smiling at him. Her lips mouthed something he could not catch. It would not do to look at those lips, ripe with promises of . . . He hurried to finish the sermon.

"Do not be quick to condemn your neighbors. Realize that we all have a spiritual quest to fulfill, and that all men need help in attaining that goal. Redeem yourselves in the love of God and in the love of your fellow man."

Sophia's eyes glistened with unshed tears. Charles looked quickly toward Chloe Brown, who had fallen asleep against her mother's side. Behind them, old Smithers, the Rowleys' head groom, dozed silently, to the patent embarrassment of his son and daughter. The vicar smiled, ever mindful of sermons that went on far too long and sent the congregation to sleep. He must finish now.

"It is entirely up to us. With the help of God, we can change for the better; we can become the people God intended us to be. We are none of us without sin, but we have the means at hand to redeem ourselves. Each of you, look to his own spiritual state. We can all become better people; it is in all of us."

Having completed the homily, Charles glanced at the back of the church, at Lewis. With his forefinger and thumb, Lewis fashioned the circular gesture of approval that had become a ritual between them. The physician could be just as quick to give him a thumbs-down or a vigorous shake of his leonine head, but not this time.

Charles smiled, relieved at his critical friend's approval, and continued with the liturgy.

Sophia was dazed. Charles was a magnificent, good-hearted man. That sermon had burrowed its way deep into her heart. Had he meant it for her alone, she wondered? Was he giving her hope, hope for her own redemption, hope that she could indeed change her life for the better? Was it a message primarily for her, Sophia Rowley? But, no, how selfish she was!

That sermon was not for her alone. She looked into the faces of her fellow congregants, their eyes shining with the hope Charles had given them all, not simply her. This was not the usual church sermonizing, the harsh, undiluted fare of fire and brimstone rained down upon the poor heads of worshipers by zealous evangelical ministers, spreading despair. This was a message of hope and love.

William pushed his prayerbook toward her, whispering, "Here, Mama, we are reciting the Creed now."

Sophia hugged him close. The boys were her redemption. They, and Charles . . . She had never believed in miracles until now, not after what she had endured in her life. But, lately, there had been so many miracles! Whence had they all come? She looked at her children, at her beloved Miss Bane, and then at Charles standing tall in the stone pulpit, leading his congregation. The high voices of her sons filled her ears and she hurriedly joined them, raising her voice with the others in the affirmation of their faith in God.

At last love has come . . .
—*Sulpica, Roman poetess, 1ˢᵗ century BC*

CHAPTER TWENTY-TWO

The time had come.

It was now or it was never. Lady Sophia had graciously accepted his invitation to Sunday luncheon at the vicarage with the boys, Reverend and Mrs. Walters, and Lewis Alcott. After dinner, Charles would walk with his guests down the short, winding path through the woods that led from St. Mortrud's to the Hall. He would ask, on that walk, if he could have a private audience when they reached her home. Then he would propose to her.

The time had come. There was no putting it off any longer.

The time had come. It was now or it was never. Sophia's thoughts were similar to those going through Charles's mind. After luncheon at the vicarage, Sophia would ask him if they could walk back to the Hall along that path through the woods, the short, winding path that led from the church to her home. She would ask him, on that walk, to come into the Hall and stay awhile. Then, once they were alone in the library, morning room, drawing room, or even the rose garden, she would propose to him.

The time had come. There was no putting it off any longer.

★ ★ ★ ★ ★

Mrs. Chipcheese was beaming with delight at all the compliments for her cooking. With the help of two serving girls from the Hall, and after cooking for the better part of two days, she had presented an admirable menu. She knew that Mrs. Mathew would hear of the successful repast, and that the sweet melon soup, salmon pie, pigeons fricando, epigram of beef, celery with cream, stuffed artichokes, and asparagus in French rolls, topped off by not one but three grand desserts, lemon pudding pie, Duke of Buckingham's pudding and a Florendine of oranges and apples, would sour her rival's milk.

Thanks to her several bibles of good English cookery, the compendia of Hannah Glasse, Charles Carter, and John Farley, she had presented a meal fit for the Baroness, if not the grand Secretary to the Archbishop of York! Mrs. C. had bankrupted the food budget of the vicarage, searching throughout the county to secure choice, fresh ingredients. It would be hardly more than simple bread and ale for the Reverend Mr. Heywood for the next several weeks, but, all in all, she thought, it was in a good cause: getting the better of her counterpart at the Hall and, yes, spreading her reputation as far east as the cathedral city.

If she were a bird, Mrs. Chipcheese would be crowing.

Everyone, even Lewis Alcott, decided to walk off his large and tasty meal by accompanying Lady Rowley, her boys, and her guests back to the Hall by way of the little-used path from St. Mortrud's cemetery. The boys had paused to pick flowers from the vicarage garden—lily of the valley, yellow iris, and sweet-scented pink roses—and lay them at their father's tombstone. Mrs. C. had provided a plain white crockery jug filled with water in which to set the blossoms.

Charles, Lewis, and the Walterses stood apart from Lady Sophia and her children to give them privacy as they prayed over the baron's last resting place. The sight of those three pale golden heads bowed in stillness filled the vicar's heart with a bittersweet combination of joy and sadness.

As the group later trod along the dusty, rocky path, the boys skipping ahead jubilantly and playing an impromptu game of hide-and-seek among the trees and bushes, Lewis engaged Clarissa and Jesse Walters in a lengthy conversation, leaving Charles and Sophia lagging behind.

"Charles, when we arrive at the house, I want to—" Sophia began, at the precise moment that Charles was saying, "Sophia, I need to speak to you in private when—"

They laughed at their simultaneous, garbled attempt at discourse. Charles put a hand to his starched linen cravat, pulling on it nervously. "After you, my lady, please."

"I—" Sophia took a quick breath, swallowed, then began again. "I would like to speak to you privately when we reach the Hall, Charles." She looked directly into his eyes, cerulean blue drilling into stormy grey.

"We must latch the doors firmly behind us, my lady, and pray that no emergencies—such as those that have arisen frequently this summer—occur," he replied.

Sophia looked ahead at the groupings of people. "Perhaps I should ask Miss Bane to let the boys recite for her, and you can encourage your friend Lewis to engage the Reverend Walters in arcane esoteric argument. What say you?" She smiled.

"A good plan, my lady. Excellent!"

They walked arm in arm back to the Hall, seemingly content, but their emotions roiling inside them. Charles's brain was abuzz—much as if he had taken snuff, save for the sneezing—and a large colony of exuberant butterflies were sporting in Sophia's stomach, to her great consternation.

It was time.

Charles took pains to latch the drawing room doors securely. He would brook no interruption now, whether juvenile, adult, or servile. Taking a deep breath, he turned to face Lady Sophia, who sat demurely on the divan facing the fireplace. Charles looked down at his polished boots, and checked the oriental rug beneath his feet. The rug was flat against the richly shining wooden floors, smooth and flat. He would not disgrace himself this time by tripping and falling.

"May I pour you a glass of sherry, my lady?" he inquired, even as he made preparations to unburden his heart.

Sophia nodded. "A tiny amount, Charles, would be welcome." If she imbibed any more than that, she would drown the butterflies, leaving them no choice but to flutter from her mouth, impeding the speech still being formulated in her mind. A tiny bit of liquid would but wet their wildly flapping wings and perchance slow the little demons down.

As Charles did her bidding and also poured a large sherry amount for himself—to settle the buzzing in his brain box—Sophia rose and went to the French doors leading out to the rose garden. She opened them, letting in the heady scent of full-blown blooms. *Blanca Gloriosa* was still blooming; it was a prodigious rose, indeed. A good sign, mayhap, for what was to come.

The sweet, heavy fragrance hit Charles's nostrils as he turned with the filled glasses, unsettling him slightly. His sense of smell had always been acute. "My lady?" He set down the drinks and went to the garden doors, latching them securely. Reclaiming the refreshments, he offered one to Sophia.

She took the delicately etched sherry glass from his hands. "Thank you, Charles, but please refrain from 'my-ladying' me. You are aware my name is Sophia, I believe?" She winked at him.

Sophia was in a playful mood, Charles saw, and his was a serious speech. He had given one such already today; was he good for another? As he began to sort out his thoughts, Sophia took the reins from his hands.

Dashing down the small amount of sherry, she began. The butterflies, dampened by the wine, were temporarily stilled. "Charles, it is time to discuss a most important matter with you."

"Yes, Sophia, it is certainly time."

She held up her hand. "No, you must listen, and not in-terrupt. I shall not be able to say this otherwise, my dear." She laughed. "My courage is at the sticking point, and I must say my piece. So do bear with me."

Charles frowned. Whatever was she nattering on about? He nodded, hoping this trifle would soon be over and he could get on with his proposal. He took a gulp of his drink.

"I know that I am older than you, and perhaps more ex-perienced in the ways of the world. I have been married three times; you are a bachelor. I have two children, and you have none." She took a quick breath. "And the life that I lived in London—" With a sharp, decisive gesture of her head, she indicated that her former life was past, never to be resumed.

He nodded. She was confusing him. What did he care what others thought of her? Had the woman not understood his sermon? He took another quick gulp of sherry.

"I thought . . . I thought that I would never marry again,

that marriage and I did not suit."

Charles's ears perked up. He finished his glass of sherry and went to pour himself another, filling it to the brim.

"But now I find that I do want to wed once more, this time, with God's help, for a much longer time than my three previous marriages, to someone of my own free choosing, for that, I feel, will make all the difference—"

Lord Brent had eloped; he was wed! She could not be speaking of him. So who was the lady planning to marry now? *Lewis?* Who else was there in Rowley Village? By all that was holy, he would kill Alcott with his bare hands if he had dared to—Charles took two gulps of wine this time.

Sophia frowned. "Charles, why are you gulping down that sherry? Are you so thirsty? 'Twill go to your head, if you are not careful."

Still standing, he placed the half-full glass on the marble mantelpiece. "Sophia, I cannot bear to listen to any more of this."

A look of confusion crossed her face. "Listen to any more of what? Charles, I am nowhere near finished."

"Yes, you are, Sophia. Now, hear this." He took hold of her hands and sat beside her on the divan. His face was slightly flushed from the wine, but he seemed to be in control.

"Sophia, I love you! I love you to distraction, my dear, and I must know now if you will marry me. I cannot bear the thought of losing you to anyone else. I am half-crazy already." He placed his hands over her lips as she attempted to speak.

"I know that I am only a poor vicar, but my father has a home and land he has been saving for me when I married, and I can borrow money from him to buy more land to put to farming and raising sheep, and, yes, I know this is not the high standard of living that you have been used to, but—"

"Charles, we don't have to leave the Hall yet." Sophia

interrupted. "Not until John comes into his majority. We can stay here until then, and with my money we could purchase all the land we want. Dearest, I have more money than either of us could possibly need."

Charles cocked his head and regarded her quizzically. "Sophia, are you proposing to me, or I to you?"

Sophia was about to give him her opinion when a raucous chorus of voices erupted from behind the locked drawing-room doors.

"Who *cares* who proposes to whom!" came one shout suspiciously Lewis Alcott-like. "Say yes, my lady!" said a number of others, male and female, together. "We want Mr. Heywood to be our father!" shouted a loud, imperious voice that could only belong to John Rowley. "Mama, please, say yes!" William's high pipes implored. "Mr. Heywood, this is Mrs. Walters," came a voice that could only belong to a former governess, its tones firm and brooking no nonsense. "Say yes to her, please, and quickly! None of us can stand the suspense any longer!"

There came a loud rapping at the doors and more exhortations to say yes, please, yes! Charles and Sophia looked at each other and smiled broadly. *"YES!"* they both screamed in unison.

Sophia held on to Charles as he embraced her; they were both quaking in gales of infectious joy. "Whatever made us think we could do this alone, my dearest?" Sophia asked him. "Latched doors, unlatched doors, privacy, the lack thereof . . . These dear and gentle people are merciless!"

Charles was kissing her all over, not paying one whit of attention to the rapping on the doors or the shouts of affirmation. His hands cupped her face, his lips brushing her eyes, her cheeks, her temples, her shell-like ears, her mouth.

Sophia savored the sweet pressure of his dear, soft

mouth on hers, licking and nibbling at his lower lip as he groaned in ecstasy. "Charles," she whispered, "the doors are latched very tightly, are they not?"

"Yes, I made certain of that," he whispered huskily, nibbling her neck, feathering kisses on her breasts as he opened the impossibly small buttons that held the bodice of her dress together. He unpinned her hair and ran his fingers through the silken strands, nuzzling its softness, inhaling the almond blossom perfume that was his lady's unique and special scent.

"I suggest that we ignore all of them. They surely have much better things to do than intrude upon this too-rare private moment. They will eventually give up." Charles was losing himself in their private moment, and Sophia saw no reason to stop him.

"Shall we ask them to go away, Charles? I do not want to be rude." Sophia was nipping at his ear now, and pulling apart his cravat.

Charles looked up, his eyes locking onto hers. "Oh, all right, allow me." He walked to the drawing room doors and rapped smartly. The Greek chorus quieted down immediately. "Now, hear this, all of you," he ordered them, "Lady Sophia and I have a great deal to . . . to discuss . . . yes . . . and we need some privacy."

A familiar snicker sounded on the other side of the doors. Lewis! He addressed his friend. "Lewis, I promise that you will dance at my wedding, but, for now, please take yourself home. Likewise, John, recite your Homer. William, perform some calculations for Mrs. Walters. I will see you all tomorrow."

That should be clear enough, Charles thought, even for this rowdy crew of well wishers. He added, "Oh . . . er . . . Bromley, you can tell the staff that no one needs to remain on duty for Lady Sophia tonight. We shall see to our own needs. Thank you!"

"Hear, hear!" A clapping of hands—large ones, no doubt belonging to the surgeon—and a whistle erupted, along with a new chorus of congratulations. The Reverend Walters spoke up, "Mr. Heywood, I would be honored to perform the wedding ceremony. I will post the banns for you upon my return to York Minster."

Charles was dumbstruck at the generous offer. Jesse Walters was waving an olive branch, an apology of sorts, for his earlier remarks about Charles's intended bride. The vicar accepted it. "Why, thank you, sir. We shall have need of your good services very soon, I think." Sophia giggled in confirmation. "Very, very soon," she whispered naughtily.

Then a scuffle was heard at the keyhole, and a small voice whispered, "We love you, Mama, and we are so glad that you and Mr. Heywood love each other, also."

Sophia ran to the door, bent down and blew a kiss through the keyhole to her sons. "I love you, too, my darlings, I love you very much. We are going to be one big, happy family, I promise."

"Amen," added the vicar, squatting at the side of his wife-to-be and wishing his boys good night through the crack in the doors.

And then there was silence. Sophia and Charles, hunkered at the keyhole, turned to each other and smiled. "We are halfway to the floor again, my darling," Sophia whispered in a lusty, husky voice.

"So we are, my love, so we are," said Charles, lowering his lady to that self-same expanse. He experienced a heady rush of *déjà vu* from the last time they were both flat upon the rich oriental carpet, the occasion of their fateful first encounter, and smiled at the memory. But now, methodically, purposefully, he concentrated on the vastly more important matter at hand, both hands, as he took care of the few buttons that were securing Lady Sophia's bodice, but not for long.

As Charles undid the last button, Sophia nipped at his earlobe like a mischievous little kitten and purred into his ear, her voice low and husky, "Methinks you would make a fine abigail, Charles, and I do have need of one."

"I would be honored, my dearest Sophia, to undress you at any time," Charles responded, "but you will have to find someone else to *dress* you, I fear." His long, warm fingers spread apart the cloth of her bodice and gently pushed down the top of her silk chemise.

Sophia pretended to be shocked. "Why, vicar! You do surprise me with these brazen words!"

"Ah, Sophia, never forget that though I am a man of God, I am, first and foremost, merely a man, like any other."

As his mouth moved slowly over her breasts, Sophia thought, *No, Charles, you are not at all like any other man.* She gasped as his tongue slowly licked a particularly sensitive part of her anatomy, and moaned softly. *And I, of all women,* she mused, as her heightened senses took over and she melted under his touch, *should know.*

"I do love you so very much, Charles," she sighed.

Suddenly she sat bolt upright. "Mr. Heywood!" she blurted out, surprised, amazed, and thoroughly delighted.

"Yes, my lady?" Charles's voice, languid, honeyed, floated up from the region of her gently splayed lower limbs.

"*Where* did you ever learn to—" Sophia's face flushed, and she could feel the heat traveling south in a great, flooding pool of warmth. In a calmer tone, she said, "You have deceived me, sir. I thought you an innocent in the ways of physical love between man and woman!"

"Do I displease you, my lady?" Charles raised his head, his hair tumbling over his forehead, his lips quirking with pent-up smiles. His grey eyes shone with mirth.

"Hardly, sir, but that is not the point!" She waggled her finger at him and he—*the wretch!* Sophia thought—playfully bit the tender pink tip. She winced in mock pain. "I fear that there is more to you, sir, than meets the eye."

"Yes, I think you will soon discover that."

"You rogue! Where *did* you go on your Grand Tour?"

"Italy, Greece . . . Turkey," Charles answered.

"And what did you there, in Turkey, sir?"

"I had many interesting adventures, my lady, among them the opportunity to speak with an elderly man, a eunuch, if I recall, who served many years in the caliph's harem. But surely we have more important things to do now than to discuss my scholarly interviews in the mysterious east?"

"It is a good thing we are to be wed very, very soon, Charles, for I fear you will ruin me tonight, ruin me utterly and entirely." Sophia sweetly chastised her lover as her eyes devoured his face, her fingers tracing his soft mouth.

"Ah, my lady," Charles laughed, "from your sweet lips to God's own ears!"

Sophia's voice was muffled as Charles laid her gently back upon the carpet. "And do stop 'my-ladying' me, you . . . you . . ."

She never finished her sentence.

We are all so framed, that our understandings are generally the dupes of our hearts, that is, of our passions . . .
—Lord Chesterfield, Letters to His Son, 1774

London, The Little Season, 1811–12

EPILOGUE

Lady Stanhope's large drawing room favored the archaeologically inspired décor of Thomas Hope, a style drawn from classical discoveries in furniture, sculpture, and painting during the many excavations of the last two decades. The Etruscans, Romans, Greeks, Turks, Egyptians—all these served to influence Hope's eccentric ideas of decoration. Sir Isaac Rebow winced at one of the more atrocious of the man's designs, a candelabrum composed of a lotus flower emerging from an enormous bouquet of ostrich feathers.

Equally hideous was a wine cooler shaped like a lavacrum, an antique Roman bath, which stood on a triangular pedestal of green bronze. Overhead, a massive chandelier of gilt bronze sported large-winged sphinxes and fanciful, exotic plant forms spewing wild, feathery fronds. Rebow shuddered at the excess; he was a conservative gentleman in all things.

"Isaac! I never thought I would see you here. What a lovely surprise!" Lady Sophia Rowley was garbed in a stunning blue, high-waisted, low-cut gown that displayed her charms, its color almost matching the warm blue of her eyes. She beamed happily at her former paramour.

Sir Isaac Rebow blinked. The very last person he had expected to see in Town during this season was his one-time lover, Sophia Rowley. No, he remembered, she was now Mrs. Charles Heywood. She had recently remarried, according to the *on-dits*. Number four! The woman, he vowed, would set a record rivaling that of the Wife of Bath for the greatest number of husbands, before she departed this blessed earth. He took her hand and brushed his lips over her soft fingers.

"My dear, you are looking more beautiful than ever. Marriage seems—" his dark eyes twinkled, "to become you." Always a beauty, with features of classical perfection, there was now something new that emanated from her. She was stunning, bright, her hair, the color of burnished moonlight, a veritable halo shining around her oval face.

"*This* marriage does, Isaac," she replied, her voice low. She blushed, the color staining her cheeks pink, emphasizing the perfectly angled bones.

Now Isaac's eyes were wide open. Never during their long liaison had he seen Sophia blush! He observed her more carefully. She had changed from the inside out, he decided. The brittleness that had always been part of her persona had disappeared. She was warmth and happiness. This Sophia was truly mellowed, softened. . . .

Had the new husband been the miracle worker? Lord, she seemed at peace! Isaac had regretted the abruptness of the break-up of their relationship. He knew he'd been cruel, uncharacteristically so. In the ensuing few months of his great happiness with his new bride Mary, he had not thought of Sophia often, but when he had . . . Ah, but he had behaved badly toward her, and he regretted it. She had not deserved such treatment from him.

"Sophia," he began, trying to make amends, "I regret our last meeting. I was harsh and cruel. You did not deserve that, not any of it. I beg your forgiveness."

She seemed taken aback. "Isaac . . . that was so long ago, my dear . . ."

Isaac frowned. " 'Twas scarce five months, Sophia!"

Sophia smiled benevolently, patting his shoulder affectionately. "A lifetime, my dear."

"You have changed," Isaac Rebow told her, assessing her even more frankly. "You are a different person, I vow."

"Isaac—" she hesitated. She had never been honest with her former lover. The old Sophia rarely told anyone the truth, rarely expressed her deepest feelings. "Isaac, I am in love for the first time. And I never knew before what that could be." She wet her lips and looked into Isaac's eyes. "I thought I loved you, my dear, but I did not. I had no idea what true love was."

She looked across the room, fixing her gaze upon a slim, handsome gentleman with curling brown hair that he was even now running a hand through, tousling it. Sophia smiled, and Isaac further noted that the look in her eyes was one he had never seen fixed on him. Sophia, in love! Remarkable. He gazed at her in wonderment.

The young man caught her look across the wide room and returned a smile of great sweetness. Isaac took a deep breath. *A love match!* All was possible, he realized, all things were possible in this world.

Sophia turned back to Isaac, the smile softening the contours of her serenely beautiful face. "That gentleman with Charles sent him a tract on atheism written by a Mr. Percy Shelley, who was ejected from Cambridge rather summarily for writing it. The fellow is asking Charles his opinion on the subject, I believe, and Charles will tell him!" She laughed.

Isaac looked her up and down, his gaze lingering on her

abdomen. Did he see there a slight, soft swelling?

"My dear, are you increasing?" he asked, with the familiarity of a past lover.

Sophia blushed again. "Does it show, Isaac?" she teased, looking down at herself and the contours revealed by the sheer silk gown. "And early days, too! I shall be a behemoth before long!"

Now it was Isaac's turn to blush, but it barely showed under his tanned skin. He shook his head. "Nay, not at all, my lady, not at all! I noted it first in your features, where I saw a look I have also seen recently on the sweet face of my lady wife."

"Oh, Isaac!" Sophia's answering smile was wide and genuine. "Never say! Oh, I wish you and Mary happy." It was the first time, Sophia realized, that she'd said the name of her former rival in the game of hearts aloud, acknowledging her. She truly wished her well, her and Isaac both. He deserved to be happy, and she was glad the girl had made him so.

Isaac took Sophia's hands in his. "I am so happy for you, my dear, so very happy." His eyes reflected the sincerity of his words. "Your husband is indeed a lucky man." He looked over at Charles, who was still engaged in animated debate with the other gentleman.

"No, Isaac," Sophia Heywood disagreed, her voice soft and low, "it is I who am the lucky one."

Music swelled behind her as Lady Stanhope's German chamber group picked up their instruments and began to play Mozart's *Eine Kleine Nachtmusik* with exuberance, if not skill. The charming strains flowed about and around the former lovers, who had found the true mates of their hearts and minds and had each made their separate peace with the past.

Jo Manning was born in New York City and received all of her schooling through undergraduate level there. In 1961, she applied to the Peace Corps where she met her husband who makes documentaries and independent feature films. Manning has degrees in English and Library Science, and was the founder and Director of the Reader's Digest General Books Library for over twenty years.

Manning has published fiction in a number of magazines. In 1996, her short story "By the Rivers of Babylon" was included in the *Herotica 4* anthology published by Plume. She also wrote an audio book entitled *The Prairie Princess and the Sanskritologist*, a contemporary romance set in Kashmir.

Manning's short story "Belvedere" was published by Regency Press in 1999, in *A Regency Sampler*. Her first Regency novel, *The Reluctant Guardian*, was published by Regency Press in 2000, to enthusiastic reviews.

Currently, Manning mans the Reference Desk and also teaches online computer searching techniques at Barry University, part-time, as she continues to write.